STARTING OVER

Tony Parsons is the author of *Man and Boy*, winner of the Book of the Year prize. His subsequent novels – *One for My Baby*, *Man and Wife*, *The Family Way*, *Stories We Could Tell* and *My Favourite Wife* – were all bestsellers. He lives in London.

Praise for Tony Parsons

'A touching novel . . . full of quiet tenderness and written from the heart'   *Independent*

'Memorable and poignant – nobody squeezes more genuine emotion from a scene than Tony Parsons'   *Spectator*

'His stories show all too well how we muddle along in search of love and fulfilment, and when we fluff it . . . sometimes that's just because it's easier'   *Observer*

'Parsons poses some interesting questions about love and life in the modern world, proving once again that he's a writer with his finger firmly on the pulse'   *Glamour*

'Bursting at the seams with romantic dilemmas, sex and second wives, this is another triumph for Parsons'   *Heat*

'Tony Parsons is the master of the bittersweet love story'
Red

'Because he so successfully links personal with public, and people with place in a way he hasn't quite done before, Parsons has created a much bigger and more compelling book . . . a major achievement'   *Mirror*

'His evocation of modern China – "a medieval country with broadband" – is vivid and unsparing'   *The Times*

D1016743

TONY PARSONS

Starting Over

HARPER

Harper
An imprint of
HarperCollins*Publishers*
77–85 Fulham Palace Road, London W6 8JB

www.harpercollins.co.uk

A paperback original 2009
1

Extract from *Zen and the Art of Motorcycle Maintenance*
by Robert Pirsig, published by The Bodley Head/Vintage
Reprinted by permission of The Random House Group Ltd.

A catalogue record for this book
is available from the British Library

ISBN 978-0-00-722651-1

Typeset in Sabon by Palimpsest Book Production Limited,
Grangemouth, Stirlingshire

Printed and bound in Great Britain by
Clays Limited, St Ives plc

For Yuriko

That was the last time the girl Wendy ever saw him. For a little longer she tried for his sake not to have growing pains; and she felt she was untrue to him when she got a prize for general knowledge. But the years came and went without bringing the careless boy; and when they met again Wendy was a married woman, and Peter was no more to her than a little dust in the box in which she had kept her toys. Wendy was grown up. You need not be sorry for her. She was one of the kind that likes to grow up.

J.M. Barrie, *Peter Pan and Wendy*

part one
the canteen cowboy v the careless boy

the shape of a heart

She doesn't feel comfortable driving this car. It is too big, too unfamiliar, too much her husband's car. And the woman on the sat nav just will not shut up.

'If possible, try to make a U-turn . . . try to make a U-turn.'

It is late now. She doesn't know this neighbourhood. The big BMW X5 rolls past strips of worn-out shops, ugly superstores, unlit yards protected by razor wire. And everywhere, there are the children. In groups of three or four or more, standing by their bikes, the light from their phones glowing in their fists, their faces hidden inside their hooded tops.

'Try to make a U-turn . . .'

'I'm trying!' she shouts, suddenly aware that she has had perhaps one glass of wine too many.

Eyes follow her. At least that is how it feels. She is too well dressed for this area, the car too conspicuously expensive. She should have taken her own beat-up little runaround. But her husband had pressed the BMW X5 on her, telling her she would feel safer.

Yeah, right.

The terrain changes. Suddenly the exhausted shops and the superstores and the herds of sullen youth have gone. There are no signs of life here. These are streets full of – what are they? – warehouses. Old warehouses. Big, black buildings with long skylights that have been smashed. They look as though they were deserted years ago, as though they are rotting, as though they are waiting to be swept away and built upon. The big car barrels through the dead streets. She is perhaps a few miles from home but this no longer feels like her town.

'Try to make a U-turn . . .'

'Oh, try to put a bloody sock in it!' she cries.

And then she sees him.

The boy lying in the middle of the road. He is curled up in a foetal position, but one arm is stretched out, supporting his head. Her foot touches the brakes, but only for a moment. It is the arm stretched out, making a pillow for his head, that makes her feel that this is wrong, all wrong, that this is trouble waiting to happen.

So she does not stop.

She puts her foot on the throttle and yanks at the steering wheel, swerving around the boy at the last moment. In the rear-view mirror she sees that he has not stirred. The car almost hit him and yet he did not move a muscle. And all at once she believes that she is mistaken.

This is someone who is really hurt, she thinks. This is someone who needs her help.

The car comes to a halt.

She pulls out her phone.

No signal.

Then she finally obeys the woman on the sat nav and makes a U-turn, abruptly pulling off the road and into an abandoned petrol station where the pumps are gone but the roof still bears the fading name of an oil company. There is a low wall running around the petrol station and beyond it the place has been turned into a rubbish dump. Debris everywhere. She registers black bags that have been ripped open by sharp teeth, a burned-out car, a grease-blackened oven, and some old computers with their screens stoved in. Suddenly it is like driving on the surface of the moon. The BMW X5 bounces over God knows what and now she is glad to be driving this thing.

She pulls up next to a pothole where a petrol pump once stood and she leans forward, the engine idling, staring at the boy in the middle of the road lit by her headlights.

And she still doesn't know.

She still doesn't know if he is really hurt. She can't just leave him lying there. But she can't get out of the car.

So she puts her foot down and drives through the ruined petrol station, the big car lurching and bumping, and all the while she watches the boy, illuminated by her lights, and then receding in the rear-view mirror.

And he never moves.

But she knows she is not getting out of this car and so she swings it on to the road and heads back the way she came with the woman on the sat nav silent now, as if happy at last.

They could not be more understanding at the police station. They tell her she did the right thing. You don't get out of your car in that neighbourhood. A young red-haired cop in a suit and tie drives her back to where she saw the boy in the road.

And he has gone.

The cop and the woman get out of the unmarked car.

Perhaps this wasn't the place? No, this was definitely the place. She recognises the petrol station with the disappearing name. This is it, she insists.

And that is when they see the body.

He must have been hiding behind the low wall that skirts the petrol station. Waiting for her to stop. Waiting for her to get out of the car to help his friend. Waiting for her to do the right thing, which would have been exactly the wrong thing.

And when the woman had turned her car round, when she had finally made that U-turn, she had driven right across him.

The one who was hiding, the one who was waiting. She looks away quickly but not fast enough to avoid seeing the tyre marks on his face. Too young, she thinks. Still in his teens. Too young for this to happen.

And then he makes a noise and both the woman and the cop cry out.

Somehow he is alive.

Somehow he is still alive.

But not for long.

And at the hospital, after the young unknown male has been pronounced dead in the A&E, the red-haired cop stands with the duty nurse and signs a form acknowledging receipt of the sad contents of the dead boy's pockets. One by one, the policeman drops them into a small plastic bag.

Some keys. An Oyster card. A wallet with a picture of a small child, somewhere between a baby and a toddler. A little boy, thinks the cop, but only because the Babygro is blue. A woman is holding the child. You can see her hands, her arms, and a part of her smile.

There are a handful of credit cards, each bearing a different name. *Hiroshi Yamamoto. Deirdre Smith. Elisabeth Kubler-Ross. A few crumpled notes. And a cheap mobile phone, still switched on. It suddenly lights up and begins to ring. Some popular tune or other. The cop places it to one side, staring at it, as if trying to place the melody.*

And finally there is the blue plastic card. The cop looks at the card.

It's not much.

It is just a blue plastic card with a few white words and a splash of red, in the shape of a heart.

And the woman is at home, safe and sound but still shaking, with her husband and a stiff drink, and he says thank God she did the right thing by staying in the car.

And she sips her drink and she thanks God too.

Once upon a time she would have got out of the car. She would have reached out a helping hand to her fellow man.

But you grow out of all that.

one

I waited for my son to come home.

I watched the late news and turned it off. I flicked through the paper and tossed it aside. I went to the back door and smoked a cigarette with one foot in the kitchen and the other in the garden, watching the smoke disappear into the night sky, waving it on its way, destroying the evidence.

But all the while I was waiting.

My head ached with all the things that can go wrong at seventeen. The wrecked car. The knife pulled. The powder cut with poison. Beyond my window there were children killing children, and my boy was out there among them.

And all I could do was wait.

Rufus was a smart kid but he was raw. That was his problem. Not his recklessness, or his stupidity, but his youth. I trusted him but I didn't trust the world. You need a bit of luck at that age, I thought, and I waited at the window, and still he did not come home.

My son at seventeen. Most nights he went out in a

clapped-out old Beetle bought with his own money from a summer job. We didn't know where he went. We didn't have a clue. You lose them after a certain age and they never come back. They start out as a part of you, indistinguishable from yourself for years and years, and they end up as people that you hardly recognise. I could see it coming.

My son and I were not quite strangers yet – I could still glimpse the same father and son who went to the park on a bike that had stabilisers. But it was a big thing between us, this not knowing, this unknown other life, the Grand Canyon of ignorance, and it felt like it was growing bigger every time he went out the front door.

And when midnight came and went I suddenly knew that I would never see him again. I knew it with a total certainty that choked my throat and tightened my chest. And I knew exactly how it would be when I told his mother and sister, and I could see the look on the faces of his grandparents, and I could imagine his dumbstruck friends and schoolmates, attending their first funeral, far too young to be wearing all that black. And I knew exactly what it would be like. It would be like the end of the world.

Then I heard his car coming up the drive.

There were lights in the window, the engine dying, a door slamming – boys do not have a light touch at seventeen – and suddenly there he was, towering above me, eye contact not easy, and as always I was both relieved and uneasy at his physical presence. Glad to have him back in one piece, yet baffled by this oversized man-child.

Who was he? Where did he come from? What was his connection to the little boy with the blond Beatle-cut? On tiptoes – and I am six foot nothing – I kissed him on the fuzzy cheek he shaved once a week, and when he gave me a sort of half-hearted sideways squeeze in response, I felt the sharp bones of my only son.

We had always kissed each other, but for a while now there had been self-consciousness and shyness in our embrace. Somehow I knew that Rufus would prefer it if the ritual, long since drained of all real meaning, would stop. But stopping it would feel like we were making too big a thing of it. So we continued with our manly kisses, even though they made both of us uncomfortable.

I felt him pull away.

'So,' I said, as lightly as I could manage, 'what have you been up to?'

'Just driving around,' he said in his deep, booming voice – that big man's voice coming out of my little boy! – and I felt myself flinch at the voice, at the words, at the blatant and obvious lie.

Whatever my son did at night, I knew it was not just driving around.

'Okay,' I said evenly, and I reached for the AlcoHawk Pro that was waiting on the coffee table.

It was a rectangular piece of plastic, gun-metal grey, about the size of one of those palm-held devices that the world and its brother seem to spend their entire lives staring into these days, when they could be looking at each other, or the stars. There was a stubby mouthpiece on one side, about the size of the cigarette butt that I had booted into the rose bushes.

'I didn't drink anything,' Rufus said in his defensive baritone, although I could smell the contents of a small brewery on him.

'Good,' I said flatly. 'Then it will be clear.'

I pressed the power switch and on the AlcoHawk Pro's

circular screen the red digits quickly counted down from 200 to zero. Then I handed it to Rufus. He took a breath, and blew into the mouthpiece until there was a sharp beep. He gave it back to me and we waited, saying nothing, not looking at each other, just the ambient noise of the city between us. Then there was a series of little beeps and the reading was displayed.

Three zeroes, it said; 000 – like the winning line on a fruit machine. Strange, I thought. I knew I smelled booze. I shook the AlcoHawk Pro and looked at it again. But it still said 000, and that meant there was no alcohol in the bloodstream of my son. At least he was telling me the truth about one thing in his life.

I showed the reading to Rufus and when he nodded politely, I felt like hugging him. It was such a gracious gesture, that polite little nod. There was a real sweetness about my boy, even now, a sweetness that had everything to do with his mother and nothing to do with me. I felt like hugging the kid. But I didn't hug him. And the moment passed.

We said goodnight without risking any more embraces, and as I climbed the stairs I could hear him clumping noisily around the kitchen, foraging for food. My wife was sleeping. But when I slid into my side of the bed, I felt her stir.

'Is he back?' she murmured, her voice foggy with sleep, her face pointing away from me.

'He's back,' I said. I listened to her breathing for a bit. That was enough for her. The fact that he was back. That was all Lara cared about.

'But where does he go?' I said, all despairing.

She exhaled in the darkness, a sound that was half-yawn, half-sigh. 'He's a good boy, George,' she said, already sliding back into sleep. 'And he's fine. And he's home. And he's safe.

Does it matter where he goes?' Then she thought of something and half sat up. 'You didn't breathalyse him again, did you?'

'I just wonder where he goes,' I said.

I turned on to my side and we lay there, back to back, the position of animals who had found their home a long time ago. I felt Lara's small feet on the back of my calves, the swell of her buttocks, the angle of a shoulder blade under brushed cotton pyjamas.

'And I just don't want him to get hurt,' I said, very quietly, although she was sleeping by then.

I had a feeling that I would not sleep much tonight. But then I felt Lara's body making itself comfortable against mine, and I knew that sleep would eventually come if I didn't think about it too much.

And I knew that there was something more that I wanted for our son, something more than good sense and safety first, and cool heads to prevail, and the bit of the luck you need at seventeen, and perhaps less lies once in a while, just for a change.

And it was this – what every parent wants for the gawky teenage boy who they suddenly see accelerating towards the grown-up world without a crash helmet or a safety belt, imagining that everything is completely under control.

The silent prayer of the terrified parent.

I wanted to stop the clock.

We rarely saw Rufus at breakfast. In the morning he was an almost mythical figure, elusive yet lumbering, his enormous form sometimes glimpsed banging out the door, rucksack stuffed with books slung over one shoulder like the Yeti of Year 13, or whatever they call the sixth form these days.

The kitchen was full of clues that he had already come and gone. His chair pushed roughly back. A lone Coco Pop on the floor. The cereal bowl dumped in the sink for someone else to wash up.

I felt a ripple of irritation. I knew what this was about. He just wanted to avoid my porridge.

I made one meal a day for my family, and it was breakfast – tasty, nutritious Scott's Porage Oats. I figured a healthy start balanced out the unhealthy remainder of my day – the cigarettes I secretly puffed, the junk food I noshed at work, the spikes of blood pressure. Every morning I built a barrier against early death. A wall of porridge. But my son never stuck around for it.

Lara appeared as I was drying his bowl. 'He makes me so angry,' I said.

She kissed my cheek and patted my ribs. 'Everything makes you angry, darling.' She looked up at the ceiling. 'Ruby!' No response. She took the bowl from me and put it away, shaking her head. 'She'll be late again. Go and get her, will you?'

I checked that the porridge was simmering nicely and went back upstairs. The door to our daughter's room was open. She was sitting at her computer, in her school uniform, pulling her hair back and knotting it in a ponytail. I smiled at the seriousness of the expression on what was a fifteen-year-old version of her mother's perfect face.

It wasn't true that everything made me angry.

My daughter never made me angry.

I could hardly look at her without smiling.

And it had always been that way.

Apocalyptic images moved across her computer screen. Factories belching industrial filth. Dead fish floating in polluted rivers. Highways jammed with unmoving cars.

'Anyone in here like porridge?' I said, knocking on the open door.

'Just let me . . .' Her voice trailed away as she stared at ice caps melting, the earth's crust boiling, the sky ripped asunder by plague and pestilence. 'I just have to see . . .'

'Ruby,' I said, 'don't worry about all that stuff. It's not the end of the world.'

She looked at me and grimaced. 'That's not funny, Daddy.'

But it made me laugh.

When we came downstairs the porridge had gently bubbled to that perfect consistency of creamy thickness that I liked.

Lara came in from the garden, holding something in her right hand. A cigarette butt. She threw it at me. It hit me in the middle of the chest, just where I always felt the tightness. *A spitfire,* my dad would say. *She's a little spitfire.*

'Do you know what that is, George?' she said, her eyes shining. 'That's another nail in your coffin.' She sat down at the breakfast table and covered her face with her hands. Ruby and I looked at each other and then back at Lara. 'Thanks a lot, George,' my wife said, her voice muffled by her hands. 'Thanks a bloody million.'

Then we ate our porridge.

Rufus was still at the bus stop.

I stopped the car on the other side of the road and opened the window. He looked across at the car containing his father, his mother and his sister, and seemed to cringe, and looked away. There were a few other kids from his school at the bus stop, but he didn't seem to be with any of them.

'Do you want a lift?' I shouted, the rush-hour traffic roaring between us.

He tore his eyes from the pavement and screwed up his

15

face. 'What?' he said. 'Can't hear.' Other kids stared across at us.

I looked at Lara in the passenger's seat. 'What could I possibly be asking him? What else could I conceivably be asking the kid?'

Ruby leaned forward. 'What's the capital of Peru? If God really exists then why is there so much suffering in the world?' She sat back with a chuckle, smiling wearily at her big brother scanning the street for a sign of his bus. 'He wants to get the bus, Daddy.'

She was right.

So we left him at the bus stop, and took Ruby to school – right up to the gates. We were still allowed to do that. She even gave us both a peck on the face, without first checking who might see.

She really did make me smile all the time.

And the smile only faded when she fell into step with one of her classmates, and I saw her moving her skinny hips from side to side as she hiked up her grey skirt. She had started wearing her white school socks above her knee and it was not a good look.

'Young lady,' I called.

She turned, raised her plucked eyebrows, and gave us a little wave of the hand that could have meant anything. *Okay. Goodbye. Bugger off.* But the hemline on that grey school skirt did not go any higher, and that felt like the most I could ask for.

Lara touched her watch as we eased back into the slow morning traffic. 'I'm going to be late,' she said.

I hit a switch on the dashboard.

'No, you're not,' I said.

I swung the car to the wrong side of the road as the siren

began to wail, watching the oncoming traffic pulling over at the sight of the two blue lights that were flashing inside my grille, and everyone hearing me long before they saw me, and all of them getting out of the way.

Life the way it should be.

'You know you shouldn't do this,' Lara said, sinking into her seat with embarrassment, but laughing at the same time.

I smiled, happy to make my wife happy, proud that I could get her to work on time, and looking forward to the moment when I was alone at last, and lighting up the first one of the day.

two

Just as Eskimos have fifty different words for snow, so the police have endless terms for the copper who never leaves the station.

Station cat. Canteen cowboy. Shiny arse. Clothes hanger. Uniform carrier. Bongo (Books On, Never Goes Out). Flub (Fat Lazy Useless Bastard). And an Olympic torch (yet another thing that never goes out).

And despite the light show that I had put on for Lara, that was me. A shiny-arsed canteen cowboy. Or at least, that is what I had become.

I was third generation. My father and grandfather were both coppers. Unfortunately, policing wasn't the only thing that ran in the family. So did heart disease. Health issues, a man with glasses called it, not an expression that my grandfather or my father ever had to hear. So despite the dodgy tickers that ran in the family, the old boys never suffered the humiliation of being a shiny-arsed station cat.

But that was another time.

When I got to the station, I went straight to the parade.

This is the part of the day that the cop shows get right – a room full of men and a few women, most of them in uniform, all of them drinking the first caffeine of the day while listening to an Onion – onion bhaji, sargie, sergeant – also known as the skipper – talk them through the shift ahead. At the back of the room I saw someone watching me. A heavy man in his forties wearing a cheap suit, grubby white shirt and a tie as lifeless as a dead snake. My old partner, Keith, now in the company of some bright-eyed young boy who was actually taking notes. Keith grinned and lifted his Styrofoam cup in salute, spilt a splash of tea on his chin, cursed and wiped it off with the back of his hand. Then, stifling a yawn, he looked back at the Onion.

'Might seem a long way off, but already we need to start thinking about Carnival weekend. I have before me the official figures –' the Onion was saying, turning a page of his notes '– and I know you will all be enormously relieved to hear that, according to these statistics, last year's Carnival went off without a major incident.'

Disbelieving groans from the crowd. The Onion glowered at them from under thick eyebrows, playing it straight.

'There were six stabbings, forty-eight robberies, and a medium-sized riot around the Boombastic Dancehall Sound System when it was asked to reduce the volume at 3.45 a.m. Happily, the environmental health officer who asked them to turn down the Bob Marley –' mocking jeers from some of the younger officers '– is expected to be out of hospital within a month. The council tell us that the loss of his spleen will not prevent him carrying out his duties. Fortunately, and rather wonderfully, none of these incidents were Carnival-related, so citizens should feel free to bring the wife and kiddies for this year's fun-packed extravaganza.'

Keith's new partner busily wrote it all down. I watched the Onion's briefing, feeling like a man with no fruit and nuts in a knocking shop.

I didn't know why I came here every morning. No, that's not true – I knew exactly why I came. As the Sergeant went through his shopping list of stolen cars, burglaries, muggings and knife crime, it made me feel as though I was still chasing the wicked, still part of the war on crime, and still the man I wanted to be.

But when the parade was over, I went up to my desk, forbidding myself a glance at my watch. If I could only stop myself from looking, then the time would pass more quickly. So I lost myself in checking MG3s – reports that officers make to the Crown Prosecution Service, who then get to decide which naughty people to prosecute, and which naughty people to pat on the head and release back into the wild.

When I looked over the top of my computer screen Keith was standing there, dabbing at the tea stain on his shirt.

'Fancy running a few red lights?' he said.

Keith's young partner was waiting in the passenger seat of their car. He looked up from his notes with a shy smile as Keith stuck his head in the window.

'DC Bailey and I are on an undercover operation all day,' Keith told him. 'So sling your hook.'

The young man got out of the car with a bewildered look. 'But – but what am I supposed to do while you're under-cover with DC Bailey?'

Keith erupted with exasperation. 'I don't know, do I? Go and do a bit of face painting. Do what you like.'

I slipped into the passenger seat and settled myself. It felt good.

Keith eased himself behind the wheel, red-faced and muttering about a lack of initiative among the younger generation. We left the kid standing in the car park, staring after us with a wistful look.

Out on the road, Keith pulled out a couple of packets from under the dash. Zestoretic. Amlodipine. He pushed out a pill from each and washed them down with a swig from a can of Red Bull.

'Goes a treat with your blood-pressure medication,' he smiled.

'We're getting old,' I said. Keith was forty-two, five years younger than me, although he looked as though he had even more miles on the clock. 'In fact, we are old.'

Keith just laughed and pulled out a packet of cigarettes with a skull on the front. Then with one hand on the steering wheel and the other on his high-tar snouts, he pulled his car on to the wrong side of the road and really put his foot down, as if he was trying to outrace someone.

We came across a woman crying.

'Pictures of my children,' she sobbed. 'It had all the pictures of my children.'

'Someone thieve your phone?' Keith said, and when the woman nodded, he motioned for her to get in the back of the car. 'Hop in, love,' he said cheerfully. 'We'll get your phone back for you.'

This was what Keith was good at. This was where he excelled. We drove around slowly, the lady still upset on the back seat, until we were passing a tube station where some kids in school uniform were talking to a skinny guy in his twenties. He had a scabby pallor about him that marked him as a heroin addict.

'He's not eating his greens, is he?' observed Keith, stopping on a double-yellow line. When we got out of the motor and moved closer to the little crowd, I could see how scared the school kids were. The suspect had one hand in the pocket of his shabby parka, and held the other palm outstretched to the school kids. One of them was giving him an iPod. Keith chuckled as he put his arm around the suspect's shoulder.

'What's going on here then?' he said.

The suspect looked at him with a start. 'Just listening to some music, officer.' He handed back the iPod and made to bolt, but Keith's friendly arm held him in place.

Keith was nodding. 'Downloading a few banging tunes, are we?' He nodded at the iPod. 'What you got on there? Bit of garage? Bit of Shirley Bassey? I'm a Clash fan myself.' He looked at the frightened faces of the schoolchildren. 'Never heard of The Clash? What do they teach you at these schools?' He made a small gesture with his head. 'Better run off and do some homework.'

They scarpered. The suspect made one last effort to get away. Keith embraced him tighter.

'Not you, moonbeam,' he said. 'You've got detention.'

With his free hand, Keith reached into the parka and pulled out a screwdriver. The metal had been sharpened to a vicious point.

'That's what he waved in my face,' said the woman. She wasn't crying now.

Keith considered the screwdriver. 'Planning a bit of woodwork, are we? Knocking up a few dovetail joints?'

I went through the rest of his pockets. Each one produced a mobile phone. When the lady found the one that belonged to her, Keith told her to get into the car and wait. She didn't move.

Keith pulled the thief under a sign that said NO ENTRY and into the tube station. The lady and I followed them. I could hear the trains rumbling far below us. Keith slammed him back against the wall and gave him a slap across the cheek.

'Stealing someone's pictures of their children,' he said. 'I don't think that's very nice.'

'You can't do that,' the suspect said. 'That's police brutality.'

'I can do what I like if you resist arrest,' Keith said. 'Did you see him resisting arrest, DI Smith?'

'It was appalling, DI Jones,' I said.

'I know my rights,' the suspect said. 'I want my lawyer.'

'Yeah, call your lawyer,' Keith agreed. 'Get him down here from the EU Court of Human Rights.' His face was getting red again. 'I'll give him a good hiding too.' Then he thought of something. 'But you can't call your lawyer, can you? You haven't got any stolen phones left.'

The lady was standing by his side. 'Can I have a go?' she said.

Keith was expansive. 'Be my guest!'

He held the suspect's collar while the woman's open palm crashed against his unshaven cheek. For the first time, she smiled.

'How did that feel?' Keith said. 'It looked like it felt pretty good.'

'It felt very good,' the lady said. 'Thank you very much.'

'Oh, you're welcome,' Keith said politely. He began dragging the suspect to the car. The lady went back at him for seconds, but I gently restrained her. I was already thinking about the Himalayas of paperwork we were going to have to climb, but when we got to the street Keith let him go, like a fisherman throwing back a little one, chuckling as the suspect dashed into the crowds.

'Not taking him in?' I said.

Keith shook his head. 'What's the point? So in six months' time some judge can give him community service? It's not worth the wait.' He pulled open the driver's door and I went round the other side. 'He's not going to show his face around here again,' Keith said over the roof. 'Probably going to devote himself to good works.'

And when we got into the car, the lady opened up her mobile phone and showed us the pictures of her children.

By the middle of the afternoon, I was kidding myself. By the middle of the afternoon, I thought that I was a real policeman again. And that's when we saw the patrol car.

It was parked in front of a derelict building, its yellow-and-blue Battenburg markings the only splash of colour on the street. I recognised it as a BMW 530iD, an ARV – armed-response vehicle. There were three cops in uniform crouching behind it, looking up at the building. Keith parked the car and we strolled over to them.

There were two constables, one of them a girl, and an inspector, the double silver pips of his rank shining on both epaulettes. He looked at us and then looked away, unimpressed. Keith and I smiled at each other.

It is a popular misconception that plain-clothes policemen are somehow higher-ranking than coppers in uniform. In fact, we all operate within exactly the same command structure as everyone else. So Keith and I outranked the two young police constables, but our balls were no bigger than the ones on the uniformed inspector. And didn't he want to let us know it.

'I bet he knows his way around a stapler,' Keith said to me, making no attempt to lower his voice. 'Bloody chimps.'

Chimps were coppers who were Completely Hopeless In Most Policing Situations. 'Do you think the chimp's got his own biro?' Keith cackled.

'There's a man in that building with a firearm,' the inspector said without turning round. 'Name of Rainbow Ron. You might want to get your heads down before he blows them off.'

'Who's Rainbow Ron when he's at home?' said Keith.

I looked at the uniformed inspector. He probably had a degree. I had five O-levels from my local comprehensive and Keith might have had a certificate for swimming his width, although I wouldn't swear to it. I coughed for a bit and then pulled out my cigarettes. Keith and I were just lighting up when there was the crack of a shot. We scooted down behind the patrol car. The inspector was screaming.

'He's got a gun! He's got a gun!'

'Get away, Sherlock,' Keith muttered.

Seeing us all hiding behind the Beemer, a young man at the end of the street began shouting abuse. Pigs this and filth that. The usual material. He was what we in the trade call a hundred-yard hero: a citizen who hurls insults at the police from a safe distance. Keith and I stared at him for a bit and then I noticed something glinting in the gutter. I crawled across to it and picked it up. It looked like a tiny silver mushroom. I handed it to Keith and he began to laugh.

'That's a pellet from a .22 air rifle,' I said.

Keith wiped away tears of mirth. 'So do you think we can rule out al-Qaeda?'

We stood up. Keith handed the pellet to the uniformed inspector. 'A souvenir of your first shoot-out,' he said. We began walking towards the derelict house. 'Come out with your hands up,' I shouted, as though I was not a canteen cowboy. 'Or I'll stuff that pop-gun right up your rectal passage.'

A bearded man appeared in the doorway of the house, gripping an air rifle by its stock. There were a few steps leading up to the front door and he stopped there, staring down at us. His hair was wild and matted and he was wearing an old trenchcoat. We stopped.

'Rainbow Ron,' said Keith. 'Probably an alias. Drop your water pistol, sonny.'

He could have been a vagrant or a runaway from a funny farm. Either way, he looked like someone with hardly anything to lose. Then, just as I started to feel the fear in my breathing, he threw the air rifle down the stairs. Keith stooped to pick it up. I kept my eyes on Rainbow Ron, and saw his gaze sweep down the street and fix on something. I turned to see what he was looking at. It was some old dear coming slowly down the street, on her way to the supermarket to blow her pension on two cans of cat food. Rainbow Ron started down the steps. I took a quick look over my shoulder; the uniforms were still behind their motor, peeking out at the action. The old woman kept coming, muttering away to herself. I held up my hand. She didn't see me. She was getting closer. I held my hand up higher and shouted a warning. She must have had the volume on her deaf-aid turned down low, because she didn't stop. Rainbow Ron reached the bottom of the steps as Keith straightened up, looking at the air rifle in his hand, and the old lady shuffled between us. I saw Rainbow Ron slip one of his dirty paws inside his trenchcoat.

And I thought – *knife?*

'Ah, that's not a gun,' Keith said, smiling affectionately at the air rifle and looking up to see what I saw at exactly the same moment – the snub-nosed handgun that Rainbow Ron had magically produced from somewhere inside his coat. 'But stone me,' Keith added, diving sideways. 'That is.'

Then Rainbow Ron had the old lady by her fake-fur collar and he was screaming at us to stay back, waving his black handgun in her face, and Keith and I had our hands above our heads and we were shouting at him to just calm down, calm down, and behind us I could hear the uniformed inspector calling for backup on his radio and in the distance the hundred-yard hero was going hysterical.

I looked at the eyes of Rainbow Ron blazing like the winner of a Charles Manson lookalike contest from behind his greasy fringe.

He looked stuffed and cuffed, jail no bail, going down for sure, and that made him dangerous. I took a step back. And then he flung the old lady forward, sending her sprawling, and I felt my blood surge to boiling point.

Then he was off. Back up the steps and into the house. We gave chase. He went up the stairs and he kept going. We followed. But by the time we reached the second floor, Keith was dropping behind, clutching his ribs and gasping for breath.

'I need a cigarette,' I heard him say, and so then I was on my own. Rainbow Ron certainly ran fast for a raving lunatic. I followed him all the way to the top of the house. A skylight was open. I stepped out on to the roof, the city buzzing far below, and he whirled round to confront me with the gun in his hand pointing right at my face.

And the anger was gone. All gone. All I could feel was the fear. I did not want to die on this roof. And when I tried to speak, almost cross-eyed from looking down the short black barrel of the terrible thing in his hand, nothing came out.

It looked like a toy. A cruel, ugly toy. The cheap shoddy banality of the thing. That's what I noticed. A toy from hell.

It was just a stubby right angle of black metal held in a red-raw, sweating fist. And it looked like the end of the world.

Pointing at my face.

Rainbow Ron came forward, sure of himself now, seeing my terror, encouraged by it, as if it proved he was making all the smart moves, and he pressed the barrel against the bridge of my nose. It looked like a toy, but somehow I knew it was real.

He squeezed off the trigger and I felt it at the same terrible moment – the shock of pain in my chest.

It was a dam-break of pain, obliterating everything, surging in the centre of my chest and spreading out, claiming me, a new and unexpected kind of pain, a pain to rob you of your senses.

It felt like everything was being squeezed. The pressure was unbelievable, dumbfounding, and increasing by the second as the pain consolidated its ownership of me and my chest felt like it was being held in a giant vice, as though the life was being forced out of me, as though the pain itself intended to kill me, and I knew that this was it, the end of all things.

I blacked out.

When I awoke, eager hands were lifting me on to a gurney. Rainbow Ron was flat on his face and the female constable was cuffing his hands behind his back. Then we were moving. Through the skylight and down the stairs. The squeezing in my chest was still there, but the fear was stronger than the pain.

I thought of my wife. I thought of my son and daughter. They needed me. I didn't want to die. Tears stung my eyes as we clanged into the back of an ambulance and immediately pulled away. And through the blurry veil of tears I saw Keith's face.

'It's a replica,' he said. 'Can you hear me, George? It's just a fake. It was never going to work. You understand what I'm saying?'

Not really.

Keith was talking about the gun.

But I thought he was talking about my heart.

three

Think of death as the ultimate lie-in. Think of death that way. A lazy Sunday morning that goes on for all eternity, with you just dozing away until the end of days. That's not such a bad way to think of death. Come on – it's not all bad.

What stops us thinking of death that way? I opened my eyes and I knew.

My family were there at the stations of the hospital bed. It felt like a lot of time had gone by, and that they had not slept, or had any sleep worthy of the name, and that things had got worse. My wife, our boy, our girl.

The great gawky Rufus, who had grown so extravagantly and yet still had so much growing to do. And Ruby, my darling girl, her face perfectly and incredibly poised between the child she had been and the woman she would become. And Lara, my wife, who I was planning to grow old with, because why would I ever want to be anywhere else? And now I never would, and now I never could.

Those three were what stopped me from thinking of death as a Sunday morning that I would never wake from. Lara,

Rufus, Ruby. The ones I would leave behind. They changed everything and made it impossible to let go, and made me want to weep, for them and for myself, because I loved them with all of my clogged-up, thoroughly knackered, pathetic excuse for a heart.

A doctor came and fiddled about. Glancing at charts, squinting at me over the top of his reading glasses. And when I paid a bit more attention, I saw that there was an entire herd of doctors with him. Baby doctors, learning their trade, looking at him as though he were the font of all medical wisdom, and me as though I was a specimen in a jar.

'Male, forty-seven, history of heart disease, had a myocardial infarction – let's see – three days ago.'

Three days? Was it already three days? The doctor held up a floppy black picture and pointed at some ghostly images. The baby doctors leaned forward with excitement.

'See that? The coronary artery was already damaged by atheroma. Can you all see? Blood will not clot on healthy lining. Looks rather like the fur in a kettle, doesn't it?' The baby doctors eagerly agreed. 'That's what caused the thrombus – the blood clot – which blocked the artery, depriving a segment of the heart muscle of oxygen, and quite literally suffocating it.' He put down the floppy black picture. 'And that was the heart attack.'

He was talking about me. For some reason I listened to all this with total indifference. It might have been the drugs. The doctor peered at Lara over the top of his reading glasses. 'How long has he been on the NTD?' he said, and she looked bewildered. 'The National Transplant Database,' he translated, and a light dawned in her eyes, a terrible light. Because of course she knew what he was talking about. It had become a big black chunk of our lives.

'Three months,' she said. 'That makes it sound as though it's a new problem, but it's not.' She was talking too fast, almost babbling. She held my hand as if that would make things a bit better. And funnily enough, it did. 'The problems have been going on for years,' she said.

I looked at Rufus and Ruby, who had retreated to the walls when the doctors came in. They were in the chairs pressed up against the corner of the little room, frightened and uncertain, and I saw that at seventeen and fifteen, they were suddenly children again. They did not seem like teenagers now.

No wry superiority in a hospital ward.

No knowing smirks in here.

'What are the odds?' Lara said to the doctor, and one of our children whimpered at the question.

The boy.

'The odds get better the longer he holds on,' the doctor said, getting ready to leave. He was smiling at Lara now, even as he edged towards the door. 'Thousands of men die before even making it to the list. One in ten waiting for a transplant don't make it because there's no donor.' He gave her a smile, and it wasn't much of a smile, but I saw that he wasn't such a bad guy, it was just that what was the end of the world for us was merely another day at work for him. And it was a big enough smile for my wife to cling to, and I could see that she was grateful. Some of the baby doctors were already out of the room. The big chief doctor was ready to say goodbye. 'So the longer he holds on,' he said to Lara, and it was as if I wasn't there, or in a coma, or invisible, 'the better the odds.'

It was good news.

Sort of good news.

So I couldn't understand why it made Lara unravel. She hugged me, making my IV drip wobble dangerously, and she told me the thing that was always between us though never spoken. And I regretted it now, leaving it unspoken through all those years, not telling her more often, and it seemed like such a stupid thing to have forgotten. And such a waste.

'I love you,' she whispered, stroking the back of my head. 'It's okay,' she smiled. 'You don't have to say it back.'

Then she straightened up. She was tough, my wife. She was brave.

'Say something to your father,' she commanded, and Ruby immediately threw herself on me with a 'Daddy!' that came out like a sob, the impact knocking the wind out of me for a second, and I held her with the arm that didn't have an IV drip stuck into it, and I could smell the shampoo in her long brown hair.

Then it was her brother's turn.

Rufus reluctantly shuffled towards me, uncomfortable in this hospital ward, uncomfortable in his troubled skin, uncomfortable with the whole thing. He didn't want to do it, he recoiled from it all, probably wanted to run away and hide in his room. But Lara gently led him to the bed where he touched the top sheet and held it to his mouth. He began to cry. Pulling my sheet up like that made my feet stick out the end of the bed, and I felt the air conditioning chill my toes.

There was something unbearable about his tears. He was not a child any more but he cried like one and I recalled a playground accident, a split head, blood all over the happily coloured climbing frame, and then the mad dash to the emergency ward. That is the worst thing about having children.

You want to protect them more than you ever can. You try to endure that unendurable fact. But it is always there.

I patted the back of his hand and I was amazed to see the amount of hair sprouting there. It was practically a rain forest. It must have been years since I had touched his hands.

'Rufus,' I said, 'when did you get so hairy?'

He pulled his hand away as if he had been scalded with boiling water. Then I needed to rest. I had to close my eyes immediately, and the pain punched a big hole in the morphine, and yet still I slept.

How George met Lara.

Twenty years ago I was walking down Shaftesbury Avenue, heading south towards Piccadilly Circus, the early-evening crowds making that bit of space they create for a uniformed police officer, even one who was just a year out of training and still raw like sushi. Then I heard a woman's voice.

'Excuse me? Hello there. Oh, excuse me!'

I turned to see a blonde, not tall, with that swingy hair that I suddenly realised I liked – hair that *swings*, do you know what I mean? Hair that doesn't just sit there but swings about with mad abandon. She had that hair. Not long, not short – just down to her shoulders. And swinging. On such details we build our lives.

And she had – I couldn't help but notice – a hard little body inside her training gear. She was quite small, and looked very fit, and she had a sexiness about her that was hard to define. I mean, there wasn't much of her, but it was all good. Far too good for me, in fact, and so I thought she must be shouting to someone else. A boyfriend who had walked past their meeting place? A friend she had just spotted in the crowd? One look at her and I could see she was out of my league. And also, she didn't seem to be in any kind of distress. Most people – all people – who run towards a uniformed police officer want him to help.

But Lara didn't want help. She wanted to give me something. She stood there laughing, and catching her breath. And I recognised her now, just as she handed me the tickets. She was one of the dancers.

I had just spent an hour in the theatre where she worked. There had been widespread thieving in the dressing rooms, both male and female. It took a couple of hours and all my powers of detection to work out that there was something suspicious about a caretaker with a locker containing seventeen Prada bags, some lovely watches and credit cards in twenty different names. He was nicked, and they were grateful. All those good-looking boys and girls radiating future stardom. I looked down at the tickets in my hand, as though I had never seen tickets before.

'For tonight,' she said. 'Bring your girlfriend.'

I brought Keith. Police Constable Keith Rooney, as he was in those days. We sat in the front row of the circle, still in uniform, and at first it was difficult for me to spot her. She was one of the Peasant Women who wanted to lynch Jean Valjean when he was caught nicking the old priest's candlesticks, but I lost sight of her for a bit until she was one of the Lovely Ladies urging Fantine to solve her problems by turning to prostitution. And then, as Keith chomped his way through a bag of Revels, I finally got a fix on her. Because nobody in that show moved like Lara.

She was a dancer. Most of them could do a bit of everything, and do it very well. But – I learned later – she never had much of a voice, and didn't really have the confidence to sing if she wasn't hiding in a group of seventeenth-century

French peasants or prostitutes. But she could move. Lithe, springy, a natural grace. I don't know what it was, but I knew I had never seen anything like it.

Not a lot of call for dancing in *Les Misérables*, of course, apart from the wedding of Cosette and Marius. It is mostly people dying tragic deaths while the survivors mooch around sadly. But the way she moved still held me. After the massacre of the posh students, she was one of The Women singing the song about how nothing ever changes, and nothing ever will, and by then I couldn't take my eyes from her. In the end, Lara hovered on the edge of the stage, like an angel in her newly laundered nightgown, as Jean Valjean died in the arms of his heartbroken daughter and by my side Keith gently sobbed into his bag of Revels.

I woke to the darkness and the smell of alcohol. I groaned and shifted in my bed, feeling the tug of the IV drip in my arm.

It was the middle of the night and the television was on with the sound turned down. At first I thought I was alone. And then I saw Keith. Under the light of the sports channel, he was slumped in one of the chairs, the bottle of vodka in his lap sticking up like a codpiece.

My eyes drifted to the TV. It was a highlights show. Nothing but goals. All the boring bits cut out. I didn't recognise any of the players or any of the teams. It was some sort of Third World league. I watched a big lean striker nod the ball over a flailing goalkeeper and then run towards the camera. And just before his kissy-kissy teammates reached him, he did a back flip, and then another back flip and then one more. His body violent with health and vitality and youth. His teeth bone-white in his grinning face.

Mocking me.
Mocking me.
Mocking me.

When I awoke again there was a light and I didn't know what was going on. I didn't know if it was just a vision caused by billions of brain synapses shutting down or a chemical hallucination or something else. I did not know if it was my dope-addled imagination or some new unimagined reality. I didn't know if it was the drugs or heaven.

Lara's voice held me.

'You never have to say it back,' she was saying, and now everyone was crying, including me, although I was getting beyond tears, and that was why it seemed so strange when the doctor burst into the room, laughing like a nutcase and his face all shiny with delight.

'We've got one,' he said.

four

In my dream I was in this field.

It was as unfeasibly smooth and green as a billiard table, my dream field, and as I jogged across it I was aware of the crowd watching me. Getting excited, they were, as if they knew what was coming before I did.

I smiled to myself, because suddenly I knew too, and then I was in the air and upside down – hanging there for that magic second in the middle of a back flip when the crown of the head is just inches from the ground and the soles of the feet are pointing at heaven. And the world is upside down.

I had once seen a photograph of a fifties actor on a New York street with his girlfriend and the camera had captured him at just that exact moment – hanging upside down in the middle of a back flip, his blond curls almost scraping the city sidewalk, his right-way-up girlfriend smiling at the camera, beautiful and proud. His name was Russ Tamblyn. He had been in *West Side Story*. Or maybe he hadn't been in *West Side Story* just yet, and that was still ahead. But he was a dancer. Like my wife. She was the one who showed me the photograph.

And then I landed and the crowd gasped with astonishment. It was pretty obvious that they had never seen such a perfectly executed back flip. They made that very clear. So I gave them another one. And then another. And every back flip only seemed to make them gasp louder, and clap harder, and go madder.

I can do back flips, I thought. Good ones, too. Like Russ Tamblyn in the fifties. Him in *West Side Story*. Bloody hell.

Then I saw the face in the crowd. All those faces, but that face was the only one I could see. I started running towards the special face, and then I was sliding across the impossibly green grass on my pain-free, highly flexible knees and into the arms of Lara, as the capacity crowd roared their approval.

When I woke the following morning I was breathing on a ventilator and Lara was holding my hand. We were in the Intensive Care Unit and she was wearing a mask, gloves and a gown, looking a bit like a superhero. Everyone in there was dressed the same way. But I knew it was her.

It could not be anyone else.

'You don't have to say it back,' she was saying.

I wanted to tell her that she looked like a superhero, but instead I went back to sleep, wondering if I would ever wake up again. Even in my heavily drugged state, I knew this was the dodgy bit.

They had filled me with immunosuppressant drugs so that my immune system was weakened, and my new heart could squat in my old body and have a chance of not being annihilated. But by deliberately weakening my immune system, by sucking the life out of all the blood and tissue and good stuff that fights bacteria and viruses, they had given me a good chance of being croaked by some killer infection. So it's Catch 23. Which is like Catch 22, but worse.

They had given me the first dose of immunosuppressants when I was sparko in the operating theatre, in the night, which is when all transplants take place. Now I would have to take them for the rest of my life. However long that might be.

I slept. I woke. Lara was still there, dressed as a super-hero. This went on for quite a while. Slept. Woke. I wanted to ask her, Haven't you got a home to go to? I wanted to say to her, Sorry about all this, I know it's a bloody pain. I wanted to say, I like you, you're nice.

But instead I slept, and if there were dreams then I couldn't recall them.

I was in the ICU for three days and then they moved me to my own little room on what they called a step-down ward. The ventilator had gone. By then Lara had stopped dressing like a superhero and stopped telling me that I didn't have to say it back, and I sort of missed it.

But that was a good thing.

Because it meant she thought that I was going to live.

When they give you a new heart, your body tries to destroy it.

Bit stupid that.

But the body really goes crazy trying to annihilate what it sees as this invader. They call it rejection but it is actually a lot more than that. Rejection sounds as though your body is snubbing the new heart, refusing to acknowledge its presence, not wanting it to move into the neighbourhood and lower property prices.

And it's not like that at all. Your body really wants to kill it.

40

It is like you wake up in the middle of the night and there is an intruder in your home. You chase the stranger around in the darkness, slashing at it with kitchen knives and broken milk bottles and anything else you can get your hands on. You feel like you are fighting for your life. You feel that your survival depends on killing this stranger.

Then you turn on the light.

And the stranger is you.

When I woke up my dad was there.

I automatically scanned the room for my mum – the kind, smiling, tea-making moderator between my father and me for these last forty-seven years – but there was no sign of her. Our five-foot-high buffer was gone, no doubt in search of tea, and my dad and I looked at each other.

'You're all right,' he said, the familiar voice soft and gruff. It wasn't a question. And I found that I was pathetically grateful for his optimistic diagnosis, even if it was coming from a retired copper with no formal training in heart surgery.

I could feel the pain in my chest flexing with every breath.

'It hurts,' I said, wincing as the breath came out of me. I arched my spine and the tube in the back of my hand pulled at me, as if urging restraint. I sank back into a pillow that was far too soft, like a giant marshmallow.

My father pulled his chair closer and took my hand. The one without the drip. The touch of his hand felt strange. Soft and rough at the same time. Like his voice.

'Close your eyes,' he said. 'Have a kip. Have a little kip now.'

And I wanted to sleep. The mere act of waking seemed to exhaust me. But instead I stared in wonder at my hand in my father's hand. I suppose he must have held my hand before. Walking me to school. Taking me to the park. Did he ever do those things? Once upon a time? I had no memory of it. Maybe he had never done those things because he was working. This felt like the first time he had ever held my hand.

'The pain will go,' he said, and he squeezed my fingers, and gave them a gentle shake that meant, *Be brave*. And it didn't feel like the first time that he had told me that.

I closed my eyes and my dad kept holding my hand. I felt the sleep of the heavily drugged come sliding in, and still he held my hand.

Then Lara and my mum came into the room with tea and coffee and I opened my eyes.

'There he is,' my mum said, as if I might have slipped out for a spot of bungee jumping while she was at the vending machine.

And that was when I felt him let go of my hand.

They wanted me to exercise. The doctors. The nurses. They wanted me up and about. They could see that I was becoming quite comfortable in that overheated bubble of my little room, regular food and affection being delivered to my bed as if I was a newborn. And that is not a million miles from what it felt like. The sheer fact of being here at all made me feel like laughing out loud.

Because I should have been dead by now.

But I was getting too attuned to the delights of daytime television. The recipes and rolling news and screaming family feuds. The hospital soaps and celebrity gossip. The fabricated drama of sport.

Time to snap out of it. Time to start thinking about my rehabilitation programme and physiotherapy schedule.

Time to take my first steps.

And after a few practice shuffles around my room, I was pretty much given the freedom of the hospital. They didn't have the time or the inclination to supervise me. They had sick people to worry about. They just got me out of bed and got my blood pumping. Then they let me get on with it.

And that was how I discovered the roof.

I walked down the hospital corridor, refastening the belt of my dressing gown, making it tighter, anxious not to expose myself in my stripy M&S pyjamas. I went past the nurses' station to the far end of the corridor and caught the service lift to the top floor. Porters with big rubbish bags and little English went about their business in this lift, and greeted my presence with polite indifference. When I got to the top floor, and said goodbye to whichever porter was lugging his bin bags around, I took a few steep steps up to a door that was never locked in case of fire. And when I walked through the door there was the roof, there was the city, there was the world.

Silence and the city's eternal hum. Fresh air and car fumes. Solitude and all those lives that I would never know.

The metal railing encircling the roof was so low that it made my breath catch, my head spin, my carpet slippers take a step back. Six floors below, the Marylebone Road flowed like a mighty river. I inhaled, smiled, and felt someone behind me.

'Dad?'

It was Rufus. I looked up at him. His eyes were red and his shoulders sagged. If it wasn't for my dressing gown and stripy pyjamas, you might have thought that I was visiting him.

'Looking on Google,' he said, and his voice caught. He closed his eyes and composed himself. The sob settled somewhere deep down inside him. 'Me and Ruby. Reading about – you know. What happened to you.' He closed his eyes. Controlled his breathing. And looked at his father. 'Half of transplant patients are dead after ten years.'

I smiled at him.

'So that means half of us are alive.'

His body twisted with discomfort. 'Yeah, but . . .'

'Don't be one of those guys,' I said, and it came out harsher than I wanted it to. 'One of those glass-half-empty kind of guys.'

We stood there awkwardly for a bit, the city flowing far below. Then he said that he might go back inside and I told him that was a good idea. I would be down in a while. All this without a second of eye contact.

I watched him go, wishing that I had the words to make him feel better, to make him understand that you don't whine and quibble and go on Google in the face of a miracle.

How could I explain it to him? I was feeling stronger. Feeling good. Feeling happy. Feeling young again.

Feeling – what's the word?

Alive.

'Uncle Keith,' Ruby said, and she got up to hug him as he came into the room.

I was glad that she still called him Uncle Keith, even though he wasn't her real uncle or any kind of blood relation. I was glad that she wasn't too cool or grown-up for that.

'Hello, gorgeous,' he said. 'How's the patient?'

The pair of them smiled at me sitting up in bed. 'He's all right,' she said. 'I'll leave you two alone.' A flurry of anxiety crossed her lovely face. 'I'll just be in the café,' she told me.

I nodded. It was fine. I didn't want her to worry so much,

even though I knew that was asking a lot. When Ruby had gone, Keith pulled a chair up to my bed and began eating the grapes he was carrying.

'Not dead yet then?' he said.

I looked at my watch. 'It's still early.'

He smiled. 'We need to get our story straight,' he said.

'Our story?' I said.

Keith nodded his enormous head. 'Why you were on that roof. Why a canteen cowboy was out chasing naughty people. Why you were in the car instead of my twelve-year-old partner.'

I thought about it. 'We were going to lunch and we saw uniformed officers in need of assistance.'

He leaned back in the hospital chair. It creaked in protest, not really designed for the likes of Keith. 'Yeah, that might work,' he yawned. He popped a fistful of grapes in his cakehole, and ran his weary eyes over me.

'Nice grapes?' I said.

'Not bad,' he said. 'Sorry, mate – you want one?'

'No, you're all right.'

And then he got this sly grin, and pulled out the unwrapped packet of Low Tars.

'For emergencies,' he said, and I nodded my appreciation as I slipped them deep inside the pocket of my dressing gown. He held out the grapes.

'So – how are you feeling?'

I chewed a grape and it tasted of nothing because of the drugs. Under my stripy pyjamas I could feel the scar on my chest pulsing. It was not the heart that I felt. You would think it would be the heart. But it was the scar.

'Never better,' I said.

Keith laughed, shook his head. 'Hard, aren't you?'

45

I smiled. 'Harder than you,' I said.

He snorted. 'Yeah, right.' He was cutting me some slack. Apart from eating my grapes, he had a lovely bedside manner. I appreciated him coming. I knew it wasn't just about getting our story straight. But I was a bit sick of people feeling sorry for me. I rolled up the pyjama sleeve on my right arm. Keith narrowed his eyes.

'Don't provoke me, shiny-arse,' he said.

I laughed and started to roll down my sleeve. 'More chicken than Colonel Sanders . . .'

He was on his feet, rolling his sleeve right up to his shoulder. I had said the 'c' word. There was a tattoo of barbed wire around his biceps that had blurred with the years. We pulled the table that sat across my bed between us. As we placed our elbows on it, we could feel it sagging. It wasn't really built for arm wrestling.

'Bit springy,' Keith said.

'Stop moaning,' I said. 'Best out of three?'

He was on the verge of beating me for the second time when Lara walked into the room, carrying flowers and a portable DVD player. Her smile faded as she watched Keith force my arm down on to the little hospital table with a triumphant roar from him and a yelp of pain and defeat from me. Keith only stopped laughing when he saw my wife.

Lara stood in the doorway of the hospital room, holding the flowers and the DVD player, and staring at us as if we were a pair of big stupid kids. I looked at Keith, his meaty head hung low, and felt like blurting, *'Best out of five, Granddad?'*

But I stifled my anarchic laughter, and said nothing.

five

There was a soft knock on the bedroom door and Ruby came in with a look of shy delight, carrying a breakfast tray.

I blinked back the fog of sleep as the smell of fried bacon filled the room. I could have sworn I had been awake all night long, fretting about how much time the doctors had given me, but I suppose I must have slept just before I was due to wake up. Ruby placed the tray on the empty side of the bed, where her mother slept. Orange juice. A still steaming mug of tea. Bacon. Two fried eggs. An incinerated sausage. 'Welcome home. I cooked your favourite,' she smiled.

Lara came into the room, already dressed, rubbing some sort of cream on her hands. The smell of my wife's hand cream mixed with the smell of my daughter's breakfast. They did not mix very well. We all looked at the tray, Ruby's smile slowly fading.

'That looks really good, darling,' Lara said briskly. 'But your father's not meant to eat –'

'No, it's fine,' I said, cutting her off as I snatched up the knife and fork. I grinned at my daughter and her face brightened. 'You're right. My favourite. Best meal of the day.'

Ruby frowned at the plate. 'The sausage is a bit . . .'

'Looks like a good sausage,' I said, sawing into it.

'Sausages are difficult,' Ruby said. 'Because they're so thick.'

I nodded, not looking at Lara. But I could sense her folding her arms and choosing her words and getting ready to restore order. I didn't need to look at her face to know what I would see there. And of course she was right. But she was also completely and totally wrong.

'Any brown sauce?' I asked, spearing my cremated banger.

'Ah,' Ruby laughed. 'I knew I'd forgotten something.' And she went off to get the brown sauce. Daddy's Sauce, they used to call it when I was her age.

I looked at Lara as I chewed on my sausage. She smiled thinly at me. It was difficult for her. I knew she had my best interests at heart. When she spoke it sounded like the voice of reason in a screaming nuthouse. Calm, rational, quietly infuriated.

'Have you been listening at all to these doctors? Have you heard a single thing they've said? Do you really want to clog up your arteries with the same old junk that you've been –'

'It's fine,' I said, gulping down the badly burned banger. It left the taste of ashes in my mouth. But the bacon looked good. Tender, juicy.

'It's not fine. It's stupid. It's self-destructive. It's just . . .' She shook her head, as if she was giving up on me. But I knew she would never give up on me. 'Is it because you're afraid of hurting her feelings? Her feelings will be a lot more hurt if . . .'

She turned her face away.

'Lara,' I said, 'come on.' But she didn't respond as I morosely sawed a piece off the bacon. Ruby came back with the brown sauce in one hand and little transparent shakers in the other.

'Salt and pepper,' she said. 'I forgot that too.'

Lara turned on the pair of us. She put her arm around Ruby's shoulder.

'Your dad can't eat this stuff, Ruby.' Her words were gentle but insistent. 'He can't put salt on his food. Never again. Do you understand? He might as well put rat poison on his meals.'

'Come on,' I said. This was too much. 'Salt's not quite the same as rat poison.'

She gave me a frosty look. 'You're right, George. Rat poison would probably be healthier. There's more fibre in it.' She gave Ruby's shoulder a gentle shake. 'It's great you made a meal for your father to welcome him home. It's such a lovely thing to do. But, darling, you have to understand that things have changed.' She looked at my breakfast plate and sighed. 'He can't eat this kind of stuff any more.' The hand she had around our daughter dropped to her side. 'It will kill him,' she said quietly.

And I laughed. I had stopped eating, but now I began again. It was a bit cold by this time, and it got even colder when I smothered it in brown sauce. 'One big breakfast is not going to kill me,' I said, really tucking in.

'You don't want the salt, I guess,' Ruby said, clutching the transparent pots to her chest, as if I might suddenly try to snatch them away from her.

'Not necessary,' I said, picking up a slice of toast, and feeling the slither of lavishly applied butter running across my wrist.

My wife and daughter stared at me as I jauntily consumed my big breakfast. As if they were obliged to watch this ritual. As if it was important.

As if they were witnessing the condemned man eating his last meal.

Ruby was in her bedroom.

I knocked, of course, and knocked again until I was given a half-hearted invitation to enter. There she was, at her desk, her head bowed before the computer screen as if in prayer.

'Thanks for my breakfast,' I said.

She nodded in response, not looking at me. I looked around for somewhere to sit. There was only her single bed and the chair.

'You all right?' I said.

She nodded again, her brown hair falling over her face like a curtain.

'Can you shove over a bit?' I said, and she automatically shuffled her bum sideways on her chair. I am a big man but she had always been a skinny kid and there was still just about room enough for two of us on that chair. Luckily she is built like her mother, the dancer, rather than her father, the fat bastard.

'Something bad is going to happen,' she said, so quietly that it felt like she was saying it to herself. Because she did not look at me.

I touched her shoulder, patted it. We were so close that I could smell the shampoo she had used in the shower.

'Nothing bad is going to happen,' I said. 'I promise you, Ruby.'

She shook her head, not believing a word of it. 'Something bad. Something very bad. It's coming.'

'Look,' I said, really needing her to believe me. 'I have great doctors. I am on the best medication that they can give me. And I feel good.' I leaned back in the chair and looked at her profile. Her mother's face, but with hints of me – a big forehead, the long upper lip – that somehow looked better on her than they ever did on me. 'I'll be fine, angel.'

And she looked at me.

'Not you, Dad,' she said. 'The planet.'

When the house was finally empty I went into the living room to retrieve the pack of cigarettes that I had hidden.

I was grinning like a maniac, all pleased with myself, because I was finally about to get the hit I was craving, and because the pack was secreted in such a good place – behind the coals of the fake fire that we had at the bottom of our chimney. Nobody would ever look back there.

My smile didn't fade until I stuck my hand behind the coals, felt around the gas pipe and fished out my fags, seeing the tiny holes that someone had drilled through the pack, destroying what was inside.

Whoever had done it hadn't bothered to take out the cigarettes. They had just pushed a pin, or whatever it was, into every corner of the packet, the way a magician shoves swords into his magic box, in a careful, all-encompassing frenzy.

Because they didn't want me to die.

I took out one useless cigarette and examined it. It sagged as if in submission, lovely golden tobacco spilling out of its pierced white paper. I tossed the pack in the rubbish bin and went upstairs, wondering who cared that much.

The floor of Ruby's bedroom was scattered with clothes,

schoolbooks, and random bits of technology. Tiny head-phones. A battery charger. An electric toothbrush, still vibrating. I picked it up, turned it off and placed it on her desk. The movement jolted her computer to life, and a screen-saver appeared of our blue planet seen from space.

You could still glimpse the earlier stages of her childhood on the walls. Scraps of posters of grinning actors and long-disbanded boy bands were just visible beyond the more recent additions of the planet in flames, or alternatively, in deep-freeze. BECOME PART OF THE SOLUTION, one of them urged. I stared at the slogan for quite a while.

Then I had a little look in her desk, and there was more archaeological digging to be done in there. Did she keep her *High School Musical* ruler and her Barbie pencil sharpener for nostalgic reasons, or just because she couldn't be bothered to throw them out? I had a good rummage around but there was nothing that could obviously be used to destroy her dear old dad's emergency fags.

So I thought it was probably my wife.

A pin, I thought. A brooch. Something sharp. She kept her jewellery in the bedside table on her side of the bed. There was not much. Just a blue Tiffany box with the bits and pieces that I had bought her over the years. A gold charm bracelet with two lonely heart-shaped charms, one that said IT'S A BOY and the other that said IT'S A GIRL. And there was a string of pearls with a broken clasp. And a silver heart on a chain. So nothing in there.

But there was another box of jewels that had belonged to her mother. I didn't feel good about looking in there, but I looked anyway, suspecting that the deed could have been done with the pin on one of those old-fashioned brooches that women used to wear.

52

It was a red plastic box with this sort of carpet material on top, in the design of some roses. Even I could see it was corny.

The lid was half-broken, and inside were indeed lots of old-fashioned brooches. There was one in the shape of a butterfly, another made out of some greyish metal, pewter maybe, with a picture of a deer looking over its shoulder, and another featuring a gold model of Concorde. This last one had a long sharp pin, but somehow I knew that Lara wouldn't use her mother's jewellery to destroy my cigarettes. There were also three rings. An engagement ring with the tiniest diamond I had ever seen. A plain gold wedding band. And what they used to call an eternity ring.

I closed the box, taking care with the damaged lid, and I put it back where I had found it, feeling the eyes of my wife's dead parents on me. And then I went to my son's room.

It didn't look like a teenager's room. It looked like the room of a forty-nine-year-old accountant. Nothing on the floor. A neat stack of schoolwork on his desk. His computer turned off. Tomorrow's white shirt waiting on a wire hanger on the handle of the wardrobe. Bed made with military precision. A small bookcase with neat rows of paperbacks. I pulled one out and flicked through it. A phrase leapt out at me, stopped me in my tracks. *The ragged and ecstatic joy of pure being.* I looked at the cover. Blue skies. A fifties car. Two men, smiling, their faces half in shadow. *On the Road* by Jack Kerouac. I put it back, noticing the Swiss army knife sitting on top of the books. I began pulling it open.

It had a tiny screwdriver and assorted thin blades and sharp points that could be used for removing a stone from a horse's hoof, or for destroying someone's emergency cigarettes.

He really loved me.

The little bastard.

Then I saw the hat. It was hanging on the back of the door, with the leather jacket that Rufus wore when he wasn't wearing his school blazer. It was a woollen hat, but with a little rim at the front, so it looked like the kind of hat that a jockey would wear. Except it was made of wool, so it wouldn't be much good if you fell off a horse.

I put it on and looked at myself in the mirror.

I looked pretty good.

Raffish. Devil-may-care. And younger. It definitely made me look youngish. Young.

The rest of my clothes didn't really match the jockey's hat. My baggy polo shirt. My dead man's chinos. Socks the colour of pewter. They were shown up by the hat. They were humiliated by the hat. They looked old and tired. Over and done. Ready to be chucked out. I was going to have to do something about my wardrobe.

Then I heard a key in the front door and I quickly headed for the stairs, smiling innocently as Lara came in. I helped her carry the shopping bags into the kitchen. She hugged me and kissed me and made me a cup of tea.

'Why are you wearing that ridiculous hat?' she said. When we had finished our tea she took me out for a very gentle walk in the park. As if I were a toddler, or a dog.

Or as if I might break.

In my dream I was sleeping by the side of a woman who was wanted by a million men. This phenomenal woman, this fabulous creature, this prize.

And when I awoke it was true.

'George,' Lara said. 'No, George.'

But I would not be denied. She knew that look. Even in

the darkness of the early hours, with only a drop of moon-light creeping around the curtains, she recognised that look in my eyes.

Cunning, amused, slightly bashful.

The look of love.

I edged across to her side of the bed and took her in my arms. I kissed her on the mouth. I knew that mouth and I had missed it. I had missed all that side of things, I realised. Our mouths did not want to let go. They fit well. Somewhere Lara's mother radar searched for the sound of our children.

But Rufus was out and Ruby was sleeping.

'George, George,' she said, offering one last chance of a cooling-off period. 'Are you sure that we should be doing this?'

I was sure.

Then she didn't say anything else, not even my name, and we loved for the first time in months. And that would have been fine, that would have been great, that would have been enough, but then later we woke, or at least came halfway out of sleep long enough for another slower, easier, less desperate meeting.

And then – somebody pinch me – yet again when it was just before morning and the room was still full of night, and now the urgency of the first time was back again – and I mean both the first time that night and the first time ever. And it was the way it is at the very beginning, when you just can't get enough of each other, when you can't believe your luck, and the night goes by in a blissful blur of heat and exhausted sleep and gathering light.

I was sleeping on her side of the bed when she got up and went to the bathroom. I could hear the birds and see the white edge of dawn around the windows. I needed to sleep now, I really needed to sleep. I was worn to a frazzle. But I opened one eye when Lara came back and turned on the bedside lamp.

'What?' I said.

She touched my face. 'Just checking.' She smiled.

I rolled over to my side of the bed and closed my eyes.

'Checking what?' I said into the pillow.

That made her laugh.

'Checking it's you,' she said.

six

A few people stared at us as we walked into the Autumn Grove Care Home. An old lady in a chair who had just been taken for a Sunday afternoon wheel around the park. Her middle-aged son and his two teenage children. A porter I didn't recognise.

Then the woman on reception smiled and said hello, and they all looked away. But we got that all the time. My wife and I were one of those couples that people take a second look at, without ever really knowing why. But I knew why.

It was because we didn't seem to fit.

Lara was so small and pretty, and she still had that dancer's grace, that ease in her own body. Whereas I was so big and lumbering and, well, not exactly ugly, but my nose has been broken twice – once by a Friday-night drunk who threw a traffic bollard in my face, and the other time while we were rolling around on the pavement as I arrested him. It gave my face a bent, damaged look, as though there were a lot of miles on my clock and I was likely to fail my MOT. Actually, now I think about it, ugly is exactly the word.

But Lara had retained some indefinable air from her dancing days. People once paid money to see this woman perform, to see her dance, to see her shine. She would be forty years old on her next birthday, and she was a working mother with two teenage children, but she still had that showbiz glamour. Whereas I was stolid. I wasn't like the other men she had known. I wasn't like the one she went out with before me. Her previous boyfriend. I wasn't a dashing young suitor racing back from Stratford after playing the Prince to rave reviews. I was from a different West End – chasing after glue sniffers and bag snatchers and mouthy drunks waving around traffic bollards so that PC Keith Rooney could give them a slap and tell them to stop being naughty. I was a big, uncomplicated man with a broken hooter who had no fear of the physical world. And that was what she liked about me. That meat-and-potatoes dependability – something that might have put off other girls. Women, I mean. She knew I would never stop loving her. She knew that it wouldn't even occur to me, that I would always be sort of grateful, because she was so clearly out of my league. Men, especially, looked at us. And the look they gave said, *Wow, if the bar is set so low* . . . And then I would stare at them and they would turn away. Because they noticed something about me. It wasn't a cop thing. It wasn't my size. It wasn't even the fact that I tried to carry myself like my father. They sensed they were stepping on sacred ground. Because she was everything to me. And so they took a step back.

It might have been different if her parents hadn't died in a car crash when she was twelve years old. They were on their way to pick her up from the airport after a school ski trip – seven days of laughter falling over on some French mountain – on a road slick with rain, ploughing into the back of a lorry stopped in the fast lane with a flat tyre.

If they had lived . . .

But they didn't.

And you never really appreciate the other side of glamour, the quiet comforts of home and family, until life has taken them all away from you.

'Have you got my book?' Lara's grandmother said, as I helped her from her bed to her chair. When she said *book* she meant *magazine*, and by that she meant her favourite TV listings supplement.

'Right here, Nan,' Lara said, and she placed it on her lap, already opened at today's page, with her selected TV programmes circled in red, like fences around her loneliness. Lara sat on the bed and smiled. 'Anything good on this afternoon?'

'*An American in Paris*,' Nan said, her watery blue eyes gleaming behind her glasses.

Lara was interested. She wasn't just being polite. 'Gene Kelly and – who?' she said.

'Leslie Caron,' said Nan, smoothing the TV listings page with her hands. 'And music by Gershwin.' She nodded emphatically. 'I like him, Gershwin,' she said, as if George Gershwin was a promising newcomer and her tip for the top.

Lara and Nan smiled at each other, their mouths almost watering at the thought of *An American in Paris*. It still mattered to my wife, the dancing. It never went away. The dancing never goes away. It had always been more than her livelihood. After she lost her first family, and before she got her second family, the dancing was her life. And she got that from Nan. She hadn't just taken the young Lara to lessons and auditions, the way her mother had. Nan had shown Lara that you could get lost in it – just lose yourself in the dancing, if that was what you wanted, or needed. And for years, that was exactly what she needed.

Twice a week she went to see Nan in the Autumn Grove. Usually not with me. She felt it should have been more often. I watched Lara settling the old lady in front of the TV, getting her a drink, holding the glass as she took a tiny, sparrow-like sip, and I saw how much my wife loved her. It wasn't just the normal love that you feel for a grandmother. Nan had done so much. She was one of those special grand-parents who brings up two generations. Nan had not brought Lara up all the way, but as much as anyone. As much as her parents, she always said.

What happened to Lara's mother and father is surpris-ingly common. I have met a few people who lost both their parents in a car crash. Married couples travel in cars together all the time, and sometimes they die together. So it wasn't just Lara. Although for many years I think it felt as though it was just her. Still does, on her bad days. She once said to me, dry-eyed and thoughtful, *I don't know what would have happened to me without my nan. She took me in. She loved me. She helped me on my way. She stopped me falling through the cracks.*

Nan loved MGM musicals. Fred and Ginger putting on the Ritz. Gene Kelly and Debbie Reynolds sparring. And when Lara went to live with her nan, it was the early eighties, the age of video rental. For the first time ever, you could watch *Singin' in the Rain* or *West Side Story* or *Oklahoma!* whenever you felt like it.

And Nan and little Lara felt like it most of the time.

They loved Gene, Ginger, Fred, Debbie and the rest, but

they loved Cyd Charisse above all. They loved her dancing with Gene Kelly in the great Broadway dream sequence in *Singin' in the Rain* – Kelly on his knees before Cyd the gangsters' moll in her green dress – and they loved Cyd with Fred Astaire in *Bandwagon*, dancing in a seedy, smoky bar, doing the kind of dancing that starts fights.

Although she had done her childish ballet and tap, that was where the dancing really began for her, those wet Sunday afternoons watching MGM musicals with Nan. Those other Sundays, long ago, where the colours seemed brighter than real life. Better than real life. And as I watched Lara and her nan watching their film, I wondered if anything had changed. It felt to me as if the dancing still measured out her dreams.

'One day I will dance the tango in Buenos Aires,' she said, sitting on the arm of Nan's chair, one arm lightly draped across the old lady's thin shoulders, neither of them taking their eyes from Gene Kelly. 'You can take lessons when you get down there. To BA, I mean. They call it BA. I looked it up on the Internet.' She laughed, and glanced over at me. 'That's the final frontier for an MGM musical nut,' she said. 'Dancing the tango with your husband in some little *milonga* dance hall in Argentina, with the music and the crowd and the sweat, and all the colours better than the real world.'

Might be a bit tricky, I thought. I put on my dancing shoes during our courting days, but these days Lara had her work cut out getting me to dance at weddings.

When Lara went to place the order for Nan's dinner, the old lady gestured for me to come closer. I thought she was going to tell me something about George Gershwin or Gene Kelly. But instead she hissed a warning in my ear.

'Don't get old,' she told me.

* * *

61

My parents wore matching kit at their self-defence class. They were a couple of trim seventy-somethings in their Adidas tracksuits, red for her and black for him, their uniforms as shiny as an oil slick. Accompanied by around a dozen other pensioners, mostly women, they shuffled across the floor of the gym on the instructions of their trainer, their kindly faces frowning with feigned violence.

'Dogs don't know Kung Fu,' the instructor told them. 'Dogs don't know Karate or Tae Kwon Do or boxing. Yet every dog can protect itself.'

The class smiled benignly at him. Their footwear was as white as their hair. It looked box fresh. It looked as though it would never get old. The instructor clenched his fists and his teeth.

'What did he say, dear?' one old lady asked my mother.

'He said, "Dogs don't know Kung Fu", dear,' said my mum, and she gave me a delighted smile. She was happy to see me. I didn't see them enough. I was always too busy.

'Dealing with the frontal bear hug,' the instructor said, motioning my father to step forward, 'you are gripped around the arms and the waist.' He proceeded to embrace my father in a way that I had never embraced him. Perhaps my mum had never embraced him like that either.

'First – knee your opponent in the testicles,' said the instructor.

'What's that?' said the old lady.

'Testicles, dear,' my mum said. 'Knee your opponent in the testicles, dear.'

My dad gamely lifted his foot a few inches off the floor as he mimed crushing the instructor's testicles.

'Next,' the instructor said, 'with the inner edge of your shoe scrape his shin-bone from just below the knee to the ankle.'

My father traced the assault in slow motion.

'Then – stamp on his foot,' said the instructor, and – playing to the gallery, as always – my dad pretended to bring his heel down on the instructor's foot.

The pensioners all chuckled. There was some mild applause. My mother beamed with amusement and pride. My dad looked very pleased with himself.

'If he still hasn't got the message,' the instructor said, giving a little jerk of his head, 'then smash your forehead as hard as you can against the bridge of his nose. And goodnight, Vienna. Okay, let's try that in our pairs.'

I sat on a bench and watched my parents and their friends, marvelling at their vitality and bravery, but most of all stunned at their heartbreaking innocence and trust in the world.

How could they feel so certain of being attacked by just one person?

At the end of the class they came over to me. My mum kissed me and oohed and aahed over some recent pictures of the kids taken at home after I got out of the hospital, and she said she couldn't believe how Rufus was turning into such a handsome young man and that Ruby, little Ruby, was practically a young lady already.

And my mum looked very hopeful when I said that we must have them round for Sunday lunch soon. But my dad saw right through me. My father, the retired policeman, always saw straight through me. He waited until my mum had gone off to the changing rooms.

'Still not back at work, then?' he said.

Sometimes I was down.

It was less a swing of mood – the heart doctor had told me to expect those – than a change of perception. I suddenly got it. The fragility of all things. Especially me. And our boiler. I could hear it spluttering its guts out in the bathroom. It will need a plumber soon, I thought with a sigh that was silent and endless, and I wondered exactly when my life had shrunk to a list of domestic chores.

'Do you want to talk about it?' Lara said, putting her arm around me.

But I didn't know where to start, or where to end, or what the middle should look like.

'I might be up for a while,' I said, and she took her arm away, and nodded, and soon I could hear her moving around in our bedroom. And then after a while I heard nothing, apart from the midnight hum of the fridge and the coughing and spluttering of the boiler on the blink.

The bottle of red wine was half gone by the time Rufus came home. He looked in a bad way. And he reeked of beer. Like something the cat had dragged in and washed in Special Brew. He looked at the AlcoHawk Pro sitting on the coffee table.

'Don't worry about that,' I said, suddenly seeing it for the ludicrous bit of plastic it was. 'I think we can skip that tonight.'

'I don't mind,' he said, and he bent his ungainly frame to pick it up. He looked at the shiny grey device in his hand. And then he looked at me. 'I didn't drink anything,' he said.

I smiled. 'Right,' I said. It was so blatantly untrue that I had to admire his front. 'Just try to get some in your mouth next time.'

Then there was that sudden flare of outrage, the easy outrage that is the natural habitat of the teenage boy. 'You don't believe anything I say, do you?' he said.

'Volume lower,' I said. 'Your mother and sister are sleeping.'

'Not a word of it,' he said, shaking his head at the AlcoHawk. 'Not a bloody word.'

I sighed. 'But, Rufus,' I said, shaking my head with wonder at his ability to stand there stinking like a brewery and lie to my face, 'I can smell it.'

'But I didn't drink it,' he said. 'They *threw* it. They chucked beer at me, Dad.'

He had lost me. 'They did what? Who are you talking about? Who are *they*?'

'It doesn't matter,' he said, although I could tell it mattered more than anything.

And I looked at my son, this great gawky monster, this thin-skinned stranger, and I willed myself to see the mop-haired boy he had once been, the boy I could hug and who would hug me back, and who would not pull away.

'What happened to us, Rufus? We were mates, weren't we? Do you remember when you were little? We went to the park. We went to the football. We went to Legoland. Remember Legoland?'

'Legoland? Yeah, I was carsick. Puked all the way to Windsor.'

'But you enjoyed yourself once you were there. Remember? Once we had cleaned you up a bit. What happened?'

He snorted, looked away. 'Yeah, well. I grew up.'

Was that it? Was that all it was? Really? The gap that opens up between the father and the son as the years go by? Was it really only natural? I couldn't believe it. I felt that somewhere along the line I had taken a wrong turn, and that's why I had lost him.

'It's not easy,' he said. 'Having a copper for a father. Somebody everyone seems to know. Always getting compared. Always getting measured. Being your father's son and nothing more. Always seen that way.' He smiled bitterly. 'Living in your famous shadow.'

I shook my head. 'I'm not famous,' I said. 'Bill Gates is famous. Brad Pitt is famous. The Dalai Lama . . . You should be grateful the Dalai Lama is not your father. I'm not famous.'

'Oh, but you are,' he said. 'On a local level. Everyone round here knows who you are. Or who you were, before you got ill. You're famous in that modern, micro-celebrity sort of way.'

'You're too kind.' I poured myself a large measure of red. Then suddenly there was concern on his face.

'What's wrong?' he said.

'Nothing,' I said. 'A bit of a rotten night. Probably the drugs. They tend to swing your moods around. Don't worry. Just a lousy night. Like you. Or did you think that you invented lousy nights?'

He still had the AlcoHawk Pro in his hand. I indicated what was left of the red wine.

'You want a drop of this? They told me not to drink. But I'm really tired of being told what to do. You ever feel like that?'

Rufus shook his head. 'I don't drink, Dad. It's not my thing.'

He put down the AlcoHawk Pro. I looked at him for a long time.

'Then where do you go?' I asked him.

And he told me.

When he had finished I gave him one of my clumsy hugs and he gave me one of his awkward squeezes in return and I left him in the kitchen, foraging for food and making a racket.

Upstairs in the bedroom the lights were all off, but my wife was still awake, and waiting for me.

I was jolted awake long before dawn.

This was not me. I had always slept like a baby. I don't mean like a real baby – waking up wet and screaming every two hours – but like the sleeping baby of myth, comatose from lights out to breakfast. Especially after sex. But not tonight. Not any more. And, I somehow understood, never again.

I lay there for a while, dry-mouthed from the red wine, listening to Lara's breathing, and then, knowing there would be no more sleep for me tonight, I silently made my way downstairs.

Hunched over my wife's laptop in the kitchen, the only light coming from the glow of the computer screen, I joined my brothers and sisters. All those people who had been in death's departure lounge, and then had their journey cancelled just before boarding. *God had thrown another log on my fire,* wrote one man.

Men and women, adults and children, in every corner of the planet. And as I bent before the computer's light, I learned what we shared was that we had all been saved by the unimaginable kindness of some unknown stranger. And we shared something else. We had not only been saved. We had been changed. Oh, how we had been changed.

Changed in ways that you can imagine. And changed in ways that were beyond all imagining.

'I am a Frankenstein,' cried Louis Washkansky upon waking as the world's first heart transplant recipient in Cape Town, South Africa, in the month of December, 1967. 'I am a Frankenstein.'

'Not a Frankenstein,' said his nurse. 'But an angel.'

I turned off the computer. There was still no light from the world outside as I went back up to bed. My family slept on. And my heart leapt to my throat when I saw him as I passed the darkened bathroom – the hair uncut and unkempt, the eyes bright and wild, not a gram of fat on his stubbled face, the flesh just fallen away. It was a face to make your heart leap in the middle of the night.

And it took me a long second to see that I was staring at myself.

seven

I was standing in front of the mirror in the bedroom, my shirt open, looking at the scar on my chest again. It was a long, livid, red wound, as though someone had tried to saw me in half, starting at the top. My fingers moved to touch it and I remembered touching the scar on my wife's stomach after the birth of our boy. The world had marked me, as it had marked her, as if to signal that one kind of life had ended and another kind of life had begun. I started to button my shirt and Lara appeared in the doorway.

'The cab here?' I said.

'We're not getting a cab,' she said, and got this little secret smile.

The bicycles were waiting in the hall, propped against the wall. Ruby's pink trekking bike, still caked with fresh mud, and Rufus' big black Saracen Dirtrax, three years old but shining like it had just come out of the box. Sometimes you give a kid a present and they have outgrown it before it is unwrapped.

I looked at the bikes and I looked at my wife. 'Oh, you've got to be kidding me,' I said.

'It's good for you,' she said, and squeezed my arm. 'And you're ready.' She gave me a wink. 'Know what I mean, big boy?'

'Just because I can – doesn't mean I can –'

'You take the pink one,' she said. 'It's easier to ride.'

'Ah, I don't know,' I said, watching Lara take the big black bike and wheel it out of the front door. Shaking my head, I took the handlebars of the pink bike and followed her. She was carrying two helmets. She placed one of them on my head, and began strapping it up.

'You'll be fine,' she said.

It was one of those big blue days when the whole city seems dipped in sunlight. We rode in single file out of Primrose Hill and past the big houses in St John's Wood. No – Lara rode, I wobbled. Every now and then she turned her head to see if I was okay. But I wasn't. I was scared. Scared of dying. Scared of having to say goodbye. Scared of falling off.

When we reached the entrance to Regent's Park I got off the bike and began to push it. Lara dismounted and walked beside me, and I thought that she could probably hear my breathing – these short, laboured gasps that had more to do with suppressed panic than physical exertion. I fought to get the air inside me under control. And I almost jumped when she touched my arm.

'George?'

'What?'

She lifted her chin and smiled. 'It's lovely, isn't it? The park. All those lovely houses.'

She gestured at the Nash architecture that circles Regent's Park like a mountain range in heaven. I grunted – a grunt that was meant to convey, Yes, it is indeed lovely, but I have other things on my mind right now.

'Why did you destroy my cigarettes?' I asked.

'Because I love you,' Lara said. 'Should we stop and get you a few packs? So you can carry on killing yourself?'

'No, you're all right,' I said, and sullenly pushed my little girl's bike through Regent's Park.

'Nothing bad is going to happen to you,' Lara said. We stopped and looked at each other. 'Because I won't let it.' She held my eyes. 'I promise, okay?'

Somehow I found myself getting back on the pink trekking bike. But now my sense of balance, or my confidence, or all of it, was just shot. I slid on to the little pink saddle and immediately slid right off. The bike toppled sideways and I shoved a foot out to stop myself falling, banging my shin hard against the pedal. 'I *can't* . . .'

She took my face in her hands. Her eyes blazing. And she didn't say a thing. I took a breath, getting the pain down, and I got back on the bike but with Lara holding the handlebars and the seat, as if it was a wild horse about to bolt. I started to pedal, and she kept holding on to the handlebars and the seat, and she didn't let go.

At first the bike trembled uncertainly and I could tell that it was taking all of Lara's strength to keep me upright, but then it got easier, and I could feel that light magic of balance starting to come, and then it got even easier because I felt safe, she made me feel safe, and it was like being with my son and my daughter in this same park on the day they took off their stabilisers. We were not going fast. It was not much more than a wonky snail's pace, and Lara had no trouble keeping up. Then suddenly she was trotting along beside me, still holding on.

'I've got you,' she said, and I found all at once that I believed in the magic of this bike, and my feet were pushing

71

down hard as I moved away from Lara with a fluid, easy grace that I felt I had borrowed from someone else.

And I laughed. It felt like the first time I had laughed, really laughed, with nothing dark behind the laugh, in a very long time. Then I was away and gaining speed all the time, the wind whipping my face as I veered off the park and on to the grass and then out on to Albany Street, skidding right into the path of a car full of young men with the windows down and music blaring. The car swerved to miss me and I glimpsed angry faces at the windows. One of them hurled a paper cup of coffee at my head. It missed. I laughed wildly.

'I love that tune!' I shouted at them, and I let go of the handlebars, allowing my hands to trail by my side, as happy as a twelve-year-old paperboy at the end of his Saturday job. Then I heard someone cry out in protest as I jumped a red light, zipped across the miraculously empty Marylebone Road, and entered the West End. I pulled my elbows back and yanked the bike on to its back wheel. A voice behind me was screaming faintly. I could just about make it out.

'I've got you,' the voice said.

'Hmmm,' said my cardiologist, Mr Carver, examining the pathology results as if they were a rather fine wine list, and wondering what he should order with the duck. 'I like the Cyclosporine with the Prednisolone but I am tempted to try it with the Azathioprine.'

'More bloody drugs,' Lara said from the passenger seat in front of the heart man's big, empty desk. 'Still more drugs. And are there any side effects to all these drugs?'

My wife was not afraid to confront him, and returned his frosty gaze as he eyeballed her over the top of his half-moon reading glasses.

'Indeed,' he said, getting up. 'The side effect of all these drugs – this veritable smorgasbord of immunosuppressants – is that they are keeping your husband alive.'

I was standing up, taking my shirt off, and my mind was wandering. Drifting down to Harley Street where I could hear the diesel rumble of the black cabs. Drifting north to the great green expanse of Regent's Park. I caught my breath when I felt his long, cold fingers on my chest. 'That's a good heart you have there,' he said, peering at my scar. 'Strong. Healthy. Young. A young man's heart.'

He sat on his desk and watched me.

'I want to thank them,' I said. 'The family of my donor. I saw stories on the Internet. People write to their donor's family. Sometimes they write for a lifetime. And they even meet.'

'Indeed,' said Mr Carver. 'And it can be a very emotional experience. Giving the gift of life. Receiving it. Knowing your deceased loved one gave someone else the chance to live.' His long, bony fingers brushed non-existent dust from his empty desk. 'But your donor's family have requested anonymity. That happens too. So you just have to accept the gift you have been given.'

'I want to thank someone,' I said.

'Of course,' he said. 'That's natural. But the donor's family have the right of anonymity. All I can tell you is that your donor was a nineteen-year-old male who died in a London hospital. He was a registered organ donor and I can reveal that he also donated his lungs, pancreas, small bowel, blood, tissue and bone marrow.'

And I wondered: How does a young man with a strong heart suddenly die?

And somehow I knew: Violently.

'Sometimes I feel different,' I said.

'Like a new man.' Carver smiled.

I nodded. 'As though – I don't know – as though I am living another life.'

'Change is natural,' Mr Carver was saying. 'Change is to be expected. Many patients suffer from mood swings because of the high dose of steroids given after the operation. And everyone changes after what you have been through. The formerly obese run marathons. Ex-chain smokers climb Everest.' He gave me his Harley Street smile. Calm, reassuring, wise; £450 an hour. 'Being that close to death would change anyone.'

'More than that,' I said. 'I read about a woman who had vertigo and then, after a transplant, she started climbing mountains. And a little girl who started having terrible nightmares after she was given the heart of a murdered child. And a woman who went from reading celebrity magazines to Dostoevsky and Jane Austen. And –'

He held up his hand to stop me.

'You're talking about cellular memory phenomenon,' Carver said, his voice honey-smooth with professional calm. 'Transplant recipients taking on the characteristics of their donors.'

'The Internet is full of it,' I said.

'The Internet is also full of people who have been abducted by aliens,' he said. 'The medical and scientific community only recognises one case of inexplicable change – a fifteen-year-old Australian girl who had a liver transplant.'

'And what happened to her?' Lara said.

Carver looked at her as he slipped back behind his desk. Then he looked away. 'Her blood type changed,' he said, and for a while none of us said a thing. Then my heart man chuckled.

'Look, some people remain transplant patients all their lives. They never learn to just accept the gift they have been given. And some move on. They claim their own life back. Or a new kind of life. I strongly suggest that you count your blessings and concentrate all your efforts on getting well. It is your heart now.' His hands were like big white spiders on his empty desk. 'You have been given something that men have dreamed of through the ages – the chance to live your life again.'

And I saw that he envied me. He was fascinated by me. He wanted to know what it was like to have that second chance. But I wasn't really listening to him. My mind was out there – out in the beautiful day.

And when I got back to it, and back to my bike, I rode it as if I owned this glorious morning, rode it with the wind and the sun in my face, rode it like a madman who knew with total certainty that he was never going to die.

God had thrown another log on my fire. And the faster I went, the more I felt it burn.

I was expecting something resembling a nightclub. I don't know – tables with little lights on and cocktail waitresses. Maybe a dance floor. But this was just an East End pub, everything stained brown from ancient nicotine and spilt ale, with a small stage that had a fireman's pole in the middle, for Wednesday and Saturday when the floor show was pole dancing, not comedy.

It was open-mic night and the place was packed. That surprised me. There was no one famous on the bill. As far as I could tell, there was no one who had ever even appeared on TV, and any idiot can get on the telly these days.

But the place was full of young men and women with beer

bottles in their hands, grinning and loud and halfway to drunk. They were all pointing their eager faces at the stage and its parade of human sacrifices.

There was a compere leering on the edge of the proceedings. He was dark-skinned, Middle Eastern-looking, wearing a white T-shirt that said, *Don't freak – I'm a Sikh*, on the front and *Don't panic – I'm not Islamic*, on the back. When the mob got too hostile, he killed the electric on the microphone, and wheeled out the next one.

A fat boy in a shiny suit was on stage, smiling and sweating. 'I bloody hate London,' he said in his singsong Geordie accent. 'Bloody hate it, I do. You Cockneys are so rude, man. You dial 999 and the operator says, "This better be good, you slag."'

Someone threw a kebab and it hit him in the face.

The compere killed the mic and the fat kid shuffled off in disgrace, still smiling and sweating, with bits of tomato and lettuce dangling from his sharkskin lapels.

Then my heart seemed to slide into my stomach because Rufus walked on to the stage, wearing the kind of frozen smile that I had seen on his face long ago. On his first day at a new school, and when he was the last to arrive for some other little boy's birthday party, and when he was trying very hard not to cry. A smile with terror in it.

I applauded but I was the only one. There were a few sarcastic cheers – so much sarcasm in the world, where does it all come from? – and a couple of half-hearted boos. I felt his mother tense by my side. I took her hand and gripped it tight.

'Everything's got to be convenient these days, everything's got to be easy,' Rufus said, his voice too loud, the microphone too close. A blast of feedback howled through the little brown pub. Someone laughed uproariously, although it may have had nothing to do with Rufus, or it may have been ironic. There it was again – this mean-spirited urge to cut everything down to size, to keep it in its place. My son, I thought, hiding behind his smile in this merciless world, and thinking it might be enough to get him through.

'Speed dialling – what's all that about?' Rufus was saying. 'What – we're all too busy and important to dial a phone number?'

'Ah, get *off*,' someone bawled, suddenly and irrationally furious, and from all around the pub there came the toadying weasel voices raised in agreement.

'Not funny!' cried someone else. There was a horrible self-consciousness about that awful crowd. As though the audience felt that they were the ones auditioning for something. I wanted to kill the lot of them.

But Rufus grinned, as though it was all in good fun, and ploughed on, and I felt this surge of love for him as a shower of lager sloshed across his shins.

Louder jeers, and all around the white faces raised, as if sniffing the fetid air, and smelling their kill.

'I've got,' Rufus stuttered, 'I've got these two numbers on speed dial – the Good Samaritans' suicide hotline and Dominos Pizza . . . I've lost count of the times I called the suicide hotline, poured my heart out and told them I was thinking of topping myself – only to have some nice Polish lady say, "Any drinks or dessert with that?"'

I looked at Lara and laughed. Her face was a mask, her eyes never leaving the boy.

Rufus ploughed on, not pausing to be abused.

'And I can't tell you how many times I called the suicide hotline and said, "I'm really upset, you forgot my chicken combo."'

Then there was a tsunami of beer descending on the stage

and on our son and Rufus was suddenly talking into a microphone that had been turned off. Seeing him standing there, still wearing his please-like-me-cruel-world smile, made my throat clench. The bloke next to me was laughing wildly, an empty beer bottle in his hand, and I turned on him, only to feel Lara pulling at my hand.

'Come on,' she said as Rufus slunk off. We pushed our way through the mob and went backstage, although that's too grand a term for what was beyond the tatty curtain at the side of the stage. There was a narrow corridor lined with battered silver barrels of draught beer, and it was crowded with nervous young men and a few nervous young women who were all talking to themselves, nervously rehearsing their doomed routines.

Rufus was in a room the size of a large coffin. Graffiti on the walls, no windows, no air. The smell of sweat and fear almost made me gag. He looked up as we walked in, his hair wet and matted from the beer they had thrown. Lara smoothed it down and said, 'Oh, just look at you.'

When I embraced him, he did not pull away.

'I'm so proud of you,' I whispered.

'Thanks, Dad,' he said.

I wanted us to go home. I wanted us to go for a drink – he could have had a mineral water. I just wanted us to be together. It did not matter where. But there was a skinny girl in spray-on jeans lurking in the doorway, looking at Rufus, and I realised that perhaps he had other plans. He did not introduce us to the girl. But he thanked us for coming, and I knew that our being there meant something, so I hugged him so hard that he groaned, and we both laughed, and he shyly patted my back.

Then we left him, and Lara and I did not talk about it

until we were back in the car, and she had checked that the central locking was on.

'I'm not sure you should be encouraging him,' she said.

And I sighed – an unfair sigh, a sigh that said she was always spoiling my fun. 'Oh, come on,' I said. 'At his age you were dressing up as a cat and prancing around to the tunes of Andrew Lloyd Webber.'

'But I was good,' she said quietly. 'By the time I was wearing that cat costume I had been dancing for years. Practising, learning, stretching. Being taken to classes and auditions by my mother and my grandmother. Ballet, tap, jazz. Years of it. Two decades of doing full splits.' Now it was her turn to sigh. 'I didn't just decide that dance was going to . . . I don't know. Get me out.'

I stared glumly at the dark East End streets. The towers of Canary Wharf were ahead, dazzling in the night sky. I wanted her to understand. I needed her to understand.

'He's at the age where you feel like a world beater. When you've still got dreams. What a great way to feel, Lara.' I looked at her, and smiled, wanting her to be with me. 'What a wonderful way to look at the world. To believe – to *know* – that you can own it.'

She laughed at me. 'But it's not real,' she said. 'You can't own it, can you? The world's not like that, is it?'

'No, the world's not like that,' I said bitterly. 'He'll get over it soon enough, right? You don't feel that way for very long. By your twenties you still think you can do anything, but you know you might have to wait for a while. Then by the time you're in your thirties it's dawning on you that the world can keep turning quite happily without you. And by then you're probably trapped with a marriage and a mortgage and a couple of kids.'

'Yes, sorry about that, George. Sorry about trapping you.'

I shook my head. 'I'm not talking about me.'

'Doesn't sound like it.'

'I just mean there comes a point when you know you are never going to be what you want to be . . . then you have your first health scare, and it's not serious. Then you have your second health scare, and it *is* serious. And a bit later – one, ten, twenty years – you die. What just happened? That? Oh, that was your life, mate. That was my life? Can I get a refund? Can I complain to someone? Can I go round one more time? Sorry, mate – no refunds, no letter of complaint, no second go at life.' I lightly banged my fist against the steering wheel. 'And that's why I am never going to be the one to take his dreams away from him. Because the world will do it soon enough.' I could smell the beer on us. 'He has to follow his dreams,' I said, looking at my wife and then back out the window. 'What else can he do?'

'Even if his dreams take him off a cliff?' Lara said, and I didn't bother to reply, I just kept my eyes on the congealed traffic on the Mile End Road, and my cakehole shut.

We were in sight of the Kentish Town lights of home when the scar began to throb like a madman. I welcomed the pain like an old friend. It distracted me from all the other stuff – our reluctance to see our children laughing at the top of the climbing frame, the anxieties about diminishing money and dying flesh, the boiler that was on the blink – the day-to-day confluence of ordinary life, and how in the end it bleeds you dry.

I stirred around dawn, creamy light seeping through the curtains, and before I was truly awake I was aware of that feeling, that glorious feeling of hardness unbidden.

Moaning, I rolled on to my side, smelling Lara's hair, freshly shampooed before bedtime, trying to wash that pub right out of her, and I pressed myself against her thigh – more moaning – my skin against her brushed cotton pyjamas, my hands on her curves, gasping with that feeling, that feeling of knowing more pleasure than is bearable.

What a woman. What a fabulous woman.

She pulled away from me with an exasperated sound that came from somewhere deep inside, a sound that was somewhere between a cluck and a tut, sent on its way with an exhalation of disapproval.

'Can't you think of anything else?' she said, and before she turned away she gave me this look.

As if she no longer recognised me.

I stood in the Never Too Latte coffee shop, waiting for my order, and I knew that Lara was right.

I found it difficult to think of anything else. It was true. When you get right down to it, what else is there? Really?

The girl in Never Too Latte had her back to me, and she was doing this thing with the silver spout that produced the foamy milk. Every time it had shot its load of milk, she gripped the silver spout in her right hand, and shook it. Her hand, wrapped in a white cloth, running up and down the full length of the shaft – giving it a good old rub. A single bead of foaming milk emerged from the spout.

I mean – really. What was I meant to think? What was it meant to remind me of? It didn't look much like someone making a cup of coffee.

And now she was doing it slowly – the little minx. Her hand in the white cloth, oh-so-slowly running up the length of the silver spout, finishing it off. Fantastic wrist action.

I gawped, then I snickered, and turned to stare at the customers behind me. Their faces were blank and miserable. Maybe it was just me.

The girl turned to look at me. She was saying something. Concentrate, George, must concentrate. She was this tired, pretty girl – the city seemed to be full of them – from the Balkans, or the Baltic, or Billericay. Her hands were on her hips. She was waiting for me.

'What?' I stuttered.

She just about stopped herself from sighing. Her perfect little rib cage rising and falling inside her dark blue Never Too Latte T-shirt.

'I said – how do you want it?'

I opened my mouth. Closed it again. Her lips were moving – those sweet lips from the Balkans, or the Baltic, or Billericay. I couldn't believe what I was hearing.

'Do you want it sweet and hot? I bet you like it sweet and hot, don't you, you dirty boy? And strong. Very, very strong. Is that how you like it? Is it, you gorgeous slag? And lots of foam – I bet you like it when the foam is all over our skin and running down . . .'

Wait a second. Did she really say that? Or did I just imagine it?

The man behind me rattled his *Evening Standard* with impatience.

A pair of weary blue eyes were looking at me. 'I said – do you want chocolate on top?'

I nodded. 'Yes, please.'

And then I staggered from Never Too Latte, my cheeks burning, consumed by lust and shame, the chocolate-smeared foam on my fingers.

eight

A dozen of us sat in a circle in a rented room above a florist's shop. We had the room for two hours, between Belly Dancing for Beginners and Narcotics Anonymous. It cost us a tenner each. Very reasonable. We were all men, and we were of all ages and races. But under our shirts we all carried the same scar.

'Let's start by expressing our gratitude for this new life,' said Larry, our leader, and we all joined hands and closed our eyes.

I wasn't crazy about the hand-holding, to tell you the truth, or the thought of having to stand up and talk to a bunch of strangers. But my cardiologist, Mr Carver, thought that it would be good for me to meet people who had been through the same experience, it would help me cope with what he called the psychological stress associated with a transplant. And I liked Larry. He was a large, gentle man, his big, bald head as smooth as a baby's bottom, and there was a warmth and certainty about him. I could use a second helping of that, I thought.

'We are grateful to our families for their support,' said Larry, that big head bowed, making it feel like a kind of prayer. 'We are grateful for the gift of life. We are grateful for the skill of the doctors. And we are grateful to the donors who made it possible.'

Larry opened his eyes and suggested we share some of our stories. They were happy stories. How could they not be? These were men who had stared death in the face. Men who should be buried by now, not sitting above a florist's shop on Hampstead High Street.

It was a dumbfounded kind of happiness these men shared, a happiness that was full of wonder and the awe of people who could not quite believe their impossible luck. The men in that circle spoke of miracles.

'I abused my body for years,' said the small man in glasses to my right, getting to his feet. 'I smoked, I drank, I filled my body with junk. My body wasn't a temple, it was a waste-disposal unit.' A nervous ripple of laughter around the circle. 'And now I am about to run my third marathon.'

He let the words hang there for a bit and then he sat down.

'Thank you, Geoff,' said Larry. He nodded at the man to my left. Tall and thin. The youngest guy in the room. He slowly stood up.

'My wife was six months pregnant when I had a heart attack,' he said, his voice shaking. He looked across me at Geoff. 'I never smoked. Was never a big drinker.' He wiped his eyes with the back of his hand. There was silence. We didn't look at him.

'It's okay, Paul,' said Larry, taking control. 'If it's too difficult . . .'

Paul sniffed, nodded furiously and took out his wallet.

He flipped it open and displayed it to the room. There was a photo of a grinning toddler on a sunny beach. 'That's Yasmin,' he said. 'She will be three next week.' He shook his head, closed the wallet. 'I don't know what else to say.'

He sat down. Larry got up and went over and hugged him. When he returned to his seat, he looked at me and smiled, giving me a nod of encouragement. So I took a deep breath and stood up.

'Sometimes I stay up all night on the Internet,' I said, stuffing my hands deep into the pockets of my new Diesel jeans. 'And I learn things. I learn about people like us. People who have had transplants. And I learned about a man in Georgia who received the heart of a suicide victim – and twelve years later he killed himself in exactly the same way.'

I raised a hand to my forehead as the little guy to my right – Geoff? – snorted with disbelief. But I ignored him. I ploughed on.

'And I learned about a woman who received a man's heart and suddenly she started walking like a football player, and she wanted to drink beer and eat Kentucky Fried –'

Geoff laughed out loud. He touched his hand to his mouth and pulled a face. 'Sorry,' he tittered.

And I still ignored him.

'She suddenly had all the cravings and quirks of her donor,' I said. 'And it's not just hearts. There was a fifteen-year-old Australian girl whose blood type changed after a liver transplant. It *changed*.' I shook my head. 'Dozens, maybe hundreds, thousands of people all over the world, transplant recipients like us, say that they changed after the operation. They *changed*. A little girl of seven started having nightmares after she was given the heart of a murdered child. An American woman who was terrified of heights became a mountain climber . . .'

Geoff raised a hand.

'Don't tell me,' he said. 'Her donor was a mountain goat.'

'But I don't need to stay up all night reading about this stuff,' I said. 'Because I *know* it. I *feel* it. It's *real*. And it's not just change. It's as if they – we – have become someone else.' I pushed the fringe out of my eyes. I was growing my hair. 'A new man,' I said, and sat down.

Geoff stifled a fake yawn.

'You're talking about cellular memory phenomenon,' he said. 'And it's a fallacy. In fact, there's a medical term for it – bullshit.'

Laughter. I felt my face reddening.

Larry raised his hands.

'Well, I think it's important to remember that the heart is no more than a pump,' he said gently, addressing the room but looking directly at me. I liked him but he was parroting the standard line – exactly what my heart man always told me. But if you changed the blade of a sword, and then you changed the handle – is it still the same sword? Answer me that, Geoff.

'Organs are only removed for transplantation after a person is dead,' Larry said, smiling at me with infinite kindness. 'A transplant does not change your personality or behaviour.'

'You get your mood swings because of the high doses of steroids,' Geoff said abruptly, and I swung on him, showing my teeth.

'*I don't get mood swings!*' I screamed in his face, my fists clenched in sudden fury, and he reared back in alarm.

Larry raised his hands to calm things down. 'George,' he

said, as if he knew me. And I suppose that in a lot of the ways that matter, he did. Never met me before that night, but you would never guess it. 'It *is* George, isn't it?'

I hung my head and my fringe toppled over my eyes. I did not brush it back. My face was burning with shame. I wanted to have a happy story, too.

'First of all,' Larry said quietly, 'why don't you say sorry to Geoff here for shouting at him, George?' He waited, like a kindly teacher pleading for common sense to prevail in the playground. 'There's no need for raised voices in this room, is there?'

I shook my head, bit my lip, and shuffled my trainers. I couldn't get it out. I squirmed in my seat. I wanted Larry to like me.

'Sorry, Geoff,' I eventually mumbled.

'Apology accepted,' sneered Geoff, the little creep.

'Organs don't have a genetic memory,' said Larry, and I looked up and saw his scar peeping at me from the open neck of his green Lacoste.

But that's just it, I thought. They do. How could I explain it? There were other people in that rented room above the florist's shop. There were ghosts. The ones who had saved us. The ones who had made the miracles happen.

It was as if I could actually feel their presence, urging us to live the lives that had been stolen from them. I could hear the beating of their hearts, hear their low voices, sense them rattling at the door. But it was just the reformed cokeheads from Narcotics Anonymous waiting to come in. I thought I recognised one of them. He had those black Irish good looks, almost Spanish looking, and his face was definitely familiar. An old collar? It was quite possible that I had once nicked him, if he had been a hardcore druggie.

When our hour was up, and we were leaving and the next lot were coming in, our eyes met for a long moment and then he quickly looked away. I had to laugh. Sometimes naughty people know what I do just by looking at me. My wife always said that it's the size of my feet. I reckon there's something in the way I look at their kind. But it is real.

They have a nose for a copper.

I sat with Larry in the pub next door and I watched him sip his Guinness.

'Mmmm,' he said, 'I bet my donor's enjoying this.'

I shot him a look and he laughed.

'Sorry. Bad joke.' Then his big soft face got serious. 'Of course there are side effects. Chemical, psychological, emotional. People who have been sick for years, and completely reliant on their partners, suddenly find they are independent.'

I saw Lara's face. 'I don't want things to change,' I said. 'I want things to be the way they were.'

'Exactly,' he said, not getting it. 'That new-found freedom can cause incredible problems.' He took a long pull on his beer. 'Look at it this way – your new life is a gift. And doesn't it beat the alternative?'

A woman and two kids were coming towards us. She was a small, pretty redhead and the children were twins, a boy and a girl, about eleven, and Larry wrapped them all up in his big arms. When he went to get their drinks, his wife looked at me and smiled.

'Larry tells me you're a policeman,' she said. 'That must be very exciting.'

Then he came into the pub. The one with the black Irish good looks and the nose for a copper. He moved quickly, as if he knew exactly where he was going. There was a man at the bar. I watched them go off to the toilets together.

'I'm not really that kind of policeman,' I said.

I kicked down the door to the toilet stall. It's really not that hard. What you have to do is kick directly behind the lock. It just comes flying off. They were in the process of cutting up some white lines on top of the cistern. Now what were the odds of that? The Irishman was bending over to have a good hoover, one finger placed against his hooter, and the other guy had a razor blade and a rolled-up note in his hand. He looked at my face and quickly dropped the blade. I smiled at the Irishman.

'I know you,' I said.

'Rufus about?' I said, kissing my wife on the cheek. 'Up in his room,' Lara said, kissing me back as she exchanged polite smiles with our guest.

My wife recognised him immediately, I thought. Or at least she registered that modern sort of recognition – where you know the person, but you have absolutely no idea where from. Ten years ago the Irishman had enjoyed the perfect comedy career: a little bit of radio, a little bit of TV, a little bit of rehab. But it had been a while since Eamon Fish had been properly famous. Somewhere along the line, somewhere between the Edinburgh Festival and the Priory, he had been replaced by the younger, the edgier, the more sober. But I was honoured and excited that he was in our house. He followed me upstairs like a dutiful pageboy going down the aisle.

You need luck in this world, I thought. The other guy's knife stays in his pocket. The drugs are cut with artificial sweetener rather than rat poison. The oncoming car swerves at the last moment and misses you. Just that little bit of luck. And that was what I was bringing home to my son.

'Rufus,' I called, knocking once as we crowded into my son's bedroom. He was sitting on the bed reading a paperback called *Love All the People* by Bill Hicks. He looked up at Eamon Fish and his mouth sagged open.

'Okay,' Eamon sighed, shaking hands and nodding curt acknowledgement at my introductions. 'Show me what you've got.'

He sat down on Rufus' bed as the boy stood up. I also sat on the bed, but at the other end, almost on the pillow, very careful that we did not touch, as if I was leaving space for a companion who was about to join us. Rufus looked at me and grinned miserably. I can't pretend that it wasn't embarrassing for all of us. But there are worse things than being embarrassed.

My son took a breath.

'I really want to meet the right girl but the problem is there's no romance in the world these days,' Rufus said. 'The other night – the other night I was holding a girl in my arms. Her body was trembling all over, her lips were on fire.' He paused and we waited. 'Turns out she had malaria.'

There was a knock on the door. 'Do you want a cup of tea?' Lara called.

'No, thanks!' I shouted, too loudly, as if she was a Jehovah's Witness who would not go away. I looked at Eamon. His face was immobile. There were no tears of helpless mirth coursing down his cheeks, he was not slapping his thighs with delight. I thought it was very funny myself. But then I was my son's greatest fan.

'Sometimes I think, sometimes I think that love is what happens to a man and woman who don't know each other,' Rufus said, pacing in front of us for a few steps, and then turning back. It wasn't a large bedroom. 'Guy my age – at my sexual peak, right?'

I chuckled and nodded.

'People think a guy like me is doing it all the time,' Rufus continued. 'But all I get is social security sex . . .'

'A little every week but not enough to live on,' Eamon said. 'I've always liked that one.' He raised his thick black eyebrows. 'Don't stop now,' he said.

Rufus rubbed his hands together. He licked his lips. There was a thin film of sweat on his forehead.

'My sex life is really lousy,' my son said. 'If it wasn't for the pickpockets, I would have no sex life at all.' He was rushing on now, speaking too fast, wanting it to be over. I could feel a touch of rigor mortis setting in with my smile. 'I bloody hate being single,' my boy said. 'Sometimes I wash up my dish and make my bed and think – oh God, I am going to have to do this again next month.'

'Rubbish,' Eamon snarled, and Rufus stopped pacing, his face reddening. 'You're crap. Total drivel. Get off the stage.'

Rufus looked at me, and back at Eamon. He held up his hands, and shook them, like a fisherman measuring the one that got away. But he was silent. He looked as though speech was impossible from this moment on.

'Off!' Eamon shouted. 'Off! Off! Off! Next, please! You suck, mate! Boring!'

'Steady on,' I said, placing a restraining hand on Eamon's leather jacket. He angrily brushed it off.

'Is that what you do?' he asked Rufus, standing up. 'When you get a heckler, is that what you do? You just stand there

91

with your mouth open, looking like you're going to burst into tears? Is that the way you handle the haters? Is it?'

'Well,' Rufus said. 'Usually.'

'Look, you control two things,' Eamon told him. 'Your material and the audience. It's your show, right? This is your world. You have to crush the hecklers. Destroy them like ants. And it's easy. They're all drunk. They're all idiots. They're all losers. They wouldn't go to the ballet and try to trip up the dancers, would they? They wouldn't go to the golf and try to stop Tiger Woods from getting his ball in the hole – would they?'

Rufus shook his head. 'They would never do that,' he agreed.

Eamon indicated the bed and my son sat down next to me.

'You are the one holding the microphone,' Eamon said. He looked around, snatched up a hairbrush, held it like a hand mic. He nodded at us. 'Go on,' he said. 'Heckle me.'

Rufus grinned with embarrassment.

'You suck,' I told Eamon, with feeling that was not so hard to summon. 'You really suck.'

'What's that?' Eamon smiled. 'Young man at the back? What was that, sir?'

'You, er, suck,' I repeated, more mildly now, and disarmed by the smile that was starting to split Eamon's dark good looks. 'What?' He cupped a hand to his ear, almost laughing.

'You . . . suck?' I squeaked, and Eamon looked triumphantly at Rufus.

'You can do that,' he said. 'Get them to repeat what they say. Chances are the audience didn't hear it in the first place. Chances are they're trying to impress some girl who will think they're a moron by the time you get them to repeat it a third time. Or you can use a bog-standard comeback: "Listen, if you keep telling me how to do my job, I'll come to your workplace tomorrow and start abusing you just as you're saying, Do you want fries with that?"'

Rufus and I looked at each other and laughed.

'That's pretty good,' I said.

'Yeah,' Rufus said happily. 'I could use that one.'

There was a pen and notebook by the side of his bed. He picked them up and scribbled something down.

'Never panic,' Eamon said. 'Never get angry. Never feel fear. Never lose control. Never show weakness. Never show nerves. Visualise success at all times. Anticipate glory. Expect laughter – mad, uncontrollable laughter in your adoring audience. And if you get a hater – and you will – then remember that they have entered *your* world, and all you have to decide is their moment of total annihilation.' He nodded. 'Stand up,' he said to Rufus, and when they were facing each other, Eamon placed his hands on my son's shoulders and looked into his eyes. 'They are not as funny as you. They are not as smart as you. They are not as brave as you – remember that most of all. There are no cowards on a stage, only in an audience. And promise me one thing . . .'

'Anything,' Rufus said quietly.

Their faces were very close now. Eamon was gripping his shoulders, demanding that he take this in. And I wished that my son would look at me that way sometimes. And I wished I could talk to him like that. And I wished I could hold him like that.

'Promise me that you will never burst into tears,' Eamon said. And then he smiled. 'The audience may perceive it as a sign of weakness.'

They both laughed, and Eamon said, 'Ah, come here, you big lunk,' and they embraced each other like friends, like brothers, like father and son. And the feeling I had grew stronger – that feeling of being grateful and jealous all at once.

And then Eamon's face got deadly serious.

'But above all there is one thing you must always remember,' he said. 'Everything will unravel if you forget this one thing. It is the key, it is the secret, it is the final piece of the puzzle. Forget this one thing and you place everything in danger. *And it is this*,' Eamon said, just as there was a polite little knock-knock on the door and Lara came in with a tray of tea and Jaffa Cakes, smiling happily, and saying, 'Is everything all right? I heard some shouting.'

Eamon's pocket began to vibrate and he took out his phone. 'Got to go,' he said. He shook Rufus' hand and wished him luck and thanked Lara for the offer of tea and Jaffa Cakes, and said to me, 'It's been a real pleasure being abducted by you, and I would love to stay chained to your radiator for a while longer, but there's a car waiting outside.'

It was true. From the bedroom window I could see a big silver Mercedes idling at the kerb, the driver waiting on the pavement sneaking a cigarette as he waited for his semi-famous passenger to emerge.

'But what's the one thing?' I was saying. 'The one thing that, if you forget, puts it all in danger?'

But by then Rufus was thanking him and Ruby was there and Eamon was turning on the charm as a means of escape. So the one really important thing – the key, the secret, the final part of the puzzle – got forgotten among the thank yous and goodnights.

And my family looked at our guest with affection as he took his leave, waving to him as he slid into the silver Mercedes, all smiles, all three of them, as if there was nothing waiting out there on the other side of luck.

nine

They clapped me when I went back to work. All of them. The canteen cowboys and the ones with medals. The gangbusters and the pen pushers. I walked into the morning parade and they stood as one and put their hands together. The young and the old, the uniforms and the suits. The lean, hard and scarred, and the shiny-arse station cats with bellies like award-winning marrows. They all laughed and cheered and slapped my back. I hung my head and blushed and choked back the tears.

I had never loved them more.

Then I went up to the office, and when I was settled at my old desk, time just seemed to congeal. I had forgotten the mind-numbing monotony of processing charge sheets, witness statements and the edited highlights of police interviews. I had forgotten what it was like to feed the Crown Prosecution Service's insatiable appetite for pointless paperwork. Or perhaps I had never realised it until now. But my chores seemed drained of all meaning, and my head reeled with the stupefying boredom of it all. How could this be how I spent my day? My first day back at work would last for the rest of my life.

So I slipped away to a place that Ruby had introduced me to. It was like one of those web sites that will beam you to any address in the world, and your head spins with all the dazzling possibilities of life as you watch the planet turn, racing across oceans and mountains and deserts and cities and rain forests. This site was even better because it propelled you into outer space.

Soon the office had faded away and I was falling through the stars. I watched solar systems being born and planets dying. I travelled light years into the infinite blackness, only pausing for a cup of tea and a Jaffa Cake when I was staring at the remnants of Crab Nebula, a star that had collapsed one thousand years ago with the radiance of ten billion suns. Then I realised that someone was standing by my desk, and with a guilty touch of my thumb and index finger, I hit *quit*.

Keith was standing there grinning at me, an unlit cigarette stuck in the corner of his mouth. He placed a brown paper bag from a coffee shop on my desk and it landed with a soft metallic clunk. I picked it up and was surprised at the weight. I glanced quickly inside at the dull oily gleam of the replica gun and then put the bag in my desk.

'I want to show you something,' he said.

Keith's partner was waiting by the car. When he saw us coming he got into the back seat without being told, giving me a deferential nod of welcome. Keith got behind the wheel and gunned the engine. He knew exactly where he was going. When we were on the road he shook his head and gave me a wonky grin. 'You're not going to believe this,' he said. 'Because I can't believe it myself.'

We headed south. We crossed the river. All the tourist land-marks dropped away and we were suddenly in darker, shabbier streets. And then we saw him. Matted beard, tatty coat, and looking like a soup-kitchen Jesus. Exactly as I remembered him. Standing on a corner on Borough High Street, rocking back and forth as he had an animated conversation with himself.

Rainbow Ron.

'But he had a bloody gun,' I said to Keith.

'No,' Keith said, savouring the insanity of it all. 'He didn't have a gun. He had a toy gun. A replica.'

'Didn't they bang him up?' I said.

'He was sectioned under the Loony Bastard Act of 1814,' Keith said. 'Something like that. And later released back into the community awaiting psychiatric reports.'

'History of mental illness,' murmured the boy on the back seat. 'Paranoid schizophrenia. Manic-depressive psychosis. Self-harm. Personality disorder.'

'The whole raving nut-job package,' sighed Keith, and he swung the car up on to the pavement, making Rainbow Ron look up with alarm.

'And he hadn't been taking his medication,' said the boy in the back.

'Stop,' Keith said. 'You're breaking my heart.'

He kicked his door open and got out. Rainbow Ron had not moved. He stared intently at Keith, as if trying to place him. Keith took his arm and gently guided him to the back seat. The boy shuffled over. Then we were off again, Keith steering with one hand and moaning about the grime on his other hand, and telling us to open all the windows. He glared at Rainbow Ron in his rear-view mirror.

'What a whiff,' he said. 'You should be bloody ashamed of yourself.'

Rainbow Ron sniffed the air once and declined to comment. He looked at me briefly and then turned away, his matted face impassive as the world slipped by.

We drove back to the river. Even now, with the Thames bordered by shining towers and fancy apartments, parts of the old London docklands somehow remained. Keith turned into a labyrinth of streets that snaked between buildings that had been abandoned decades ago, only to somehow miss out on the future. He put his foot down. He knew where he was going. He had done this before.

There was an old warehouse right on the river. There had been a padlock on the big doors but someone had sawn through it and one of the doors had been pulled off its hinges. Keith drove straight inside. It was dark, but spears of sunlight came through the shattered roof. There was a flurry of movement in the shadows and half a dozen hooded figures dashed for the door.

'Little rascals,' Keith said, and we all got out. I looked down at the sound of running water. Between the floorboards you could see the river, as grey as a battleship.

The boy went to watch the door. Keith stood facing Rainbow Ron, whose eyes were wandering to the ceiling. I saw the tail of a rat as it scuttled across a rafter. When the rat had gone, Ron looked back at Keith, just in time to see him throw the first punch – a short uppercut, Keith bending his knees for leverage and bringing his fist up like a shovel into Rainbow Ron's midriff. With a shocked little gasp, he sunk to his knees. Keith took a step forward and pulled back his hand to hit him again.

'No, Keith,' I said, as Rainbow Ron looked up and Keith threw a left jab into the middle of his face, the snapping motion of his hand so fast it looked like he was catching a fly.

Rainbow Ron bent his head, like a man saying his prayers, a hand clutching his broken nose.

I went behind Keith and threw my arms around him and held him. He cursed me and struggled, sinking to drop his centre of gravity, and then pushing up to throw me off, slinging his head back, trying to nut me. But I didn't let go. And I was stronger than him.

'This is for you,' he said, twisting his head sideways to look at me.

'But I don't want it,' I said. And I let him go. He immediately aimed a wild kick at Rainbow Ron's head, which just missed, and we had to go through it all again – me with Keith in a bear hug, Keith trying to headbutt me. Me telling him to stop. Keith telling me to fuck off. Locked in this mad waltz.

I let him go again and this time he didn't attack Rainbow Ron. I put my hand on Keith's arm. I wanted him to understand.

'He's sick,' I said. 'And giving him a good hiding won't change anything.'

Keith furiously threw off my hand. He tugged at his jacket and then stuck an index finger in my face. 'No,' he said. 'You're the sick one.'

Then he was off, the boy at the door falling into step behind him as he strode to the car. I helped Rainbow Ron to his feet and felt in my pockets for something to mop the blood streaming from his nose. But I had nothing, so Rainbow Ron bent his head, and delicately used his sleeve. At the sound of the engine I looked up to see Keith pulling away, as the boy leaned across cradling the flame of his lighter, holding it steady for the cigarette in his partner's mouth.

*   *   *

I sat at my daughter's computer, falling through the stars.

Ruby was at school. It was after nine, but her brother had yet to stir. I could hear Lara softly knocking on his door, calling his name. Perhaps he didn't come home last night, I thought, as I sipped my tea and wandered through space.

I was travelling through Messier 101, better known as the Pinwheel Galaxy – a trillion stars, a billion suns and twice the size of our Milky Way. So there was plenty to look at.

I took a bite out of a Jaffa Cake, letting the giddy cocktail of dark chocolate, sponge and orange jam melt on the back of my tongue as I zoomed into the golden core of Messier 101, and felt my breath catch, and my Jaffa Cake dissolve.

Slowly, pulling back out, I shook my head with awe and wonder at the full, mind-boggling majesty of Messier 101 – a Catherine wheel of space dust, galactic gas and new-born stars, white and blue, looking like a sprinkling of heavenly frost as they spiralled and danced out into infinity.

'Rufus? Are you up?'

I could feel her hesitate and then go inside, and even from the bedroom next door I could sense the suffocating fug of young manhood. Opening his door was like pulling off a giant's sock. I caught the smell of ancient pizza and forgotten clothes and some terrible sweet perfume that he probably used to make him irresistible to women, or to kill flying insects. I heard him stirring under his tangled duvet as Lara pulled back the curtains.

'You're late again,' she said, moving about the room, trying to restore order. I heard her throw open the window. And heard our son groan as the sharp morning air flooded the room.

I tensed, imagining him sitting up in bed, bleary-eyed and scratching himself, hair everywhere. Because I somehow knew what was coming.

'I'm not going in today,' he said sheepishly.

His mother said nothing. But I could feel her eyes on him. Waiting.

'What am I doing wasting my time in school anyway?' he said. And then the punchline. 'Dad's right.'

I took a deep breath. Before my eyes new stars were being born, and old suns were dying.

'What is your father right about?' Lara said, very quietly.

'About everything,' Rufus said, and I could imagine his eyes shining with belief, and I felt a surge of love for him that almost overwhelmed me. 'About following your dreams,' he said. 'About being, you know, true to yourself. And sort of doing what you want.'

I waited for her to laugh. But Lara was silent.

'You have to find something you love, don't you?' Rufus said plaintively. 'What's it all about if you don't do something you love?'

There was silence. And then Lara spoke.

'Get dressed,' she said. 'Go to school. Get an education. Get a job – get a bloody *job*, Rufus – and if you can pay your way in the world doing something you love, then I salute you, and I'm happy for you.' She moved towards the door. 'But save the I've-just-gotta-be-me stuff until you're doing your own laundry.'

She left the room and shot me a look as she came past the open door.

'You,' she said. 'I'm not even talking to you.'

And then she tripped over the jeans that had been left on the landing for someone to fall over. Oh, bloody hell, I thought.

Lara picked them up, went back into Rufus' room and threw them at his head.

'And if you are going to live in this house,' she said, her voice rising, my little spitfire, 'then show some respect and pick up your own bloody clothes, will you?'

I could almost hear Rufus scratching his head as he examined the crumpled denim.

'But, Mum,' he said, 'these are Dad's.'

ten

I lay on my back in a field of wild flowers. Above me the sky was a cloudless blue dome.

I thought about the strangeness of being inside my own skin, about how absolutely mind-boggling it was that I was me and nobody else. And I thought about the enormity of the sky, and how it is nothing really, just mankind's back yard, and just as my senses were reeling with all this stuff – guess what? A 747 roared across the heavens and made me gasp out loud with shock and joy. Then I heard the voice.

'Sir?' it said, that special kind of *sir* – the kind of *sir* where you feel that the person calling you sir wants to give you a slap in the kisser. I sat up and saw the two cops standing above me. Both uniformed, both young, but one looked neutral and one looked mean, and I thought that I would have to be careful with him.

They had pulled up beside my car. Aggressively close, right up tight against the front bumper, barring any sudden break for freedom. And although their siren was silent, the blue light on the roof was lazily revolving. The mean one pointed at the hole in the wire fence.

'You make that hole, sir?' he said.

I got to my feet, brushing off the petals of wild flowers. They were purple and white. 'No, officer,' I said. 'It was there already. I just crawled through it.'

He held out his palm. 'Let's see some ID,' he said, making this impatient gimme-gimme gesture with his fingers.

I took out my wallet, flipped it open and gave it to him. He took it from me, stared at my face and laughed. Then he showed it to his friend.

'Why didn't you say?' said the mean-looking one, closing the wallet on the plastic window of my Met ID card.

I took the wallet and put it back in the pocket of my jeans. I said nothing. We began walking back to the hole in the fence. The mean one held it open for me as I squirmed through.

'Security's being stepped up, mate,' he said, slipping effort-lessly from the threatening sarcasm of *sir* to the unearned familiarity of *mate*. I think I preferred it when he called me *sir*. I'm not your mate, I thought. 'We got a barrel load of loonies coming in.'

All at once I saw what he meant. On the far side of the road, there was already a gathering of the tribes. Coaches, tents, banners. PLANE BARMY, said one of them. PLANE MENTAL, said another. PLANE MAD. PLANE STUPID. NO MORE PLANES.

'The new runway,' said the mean-looking cop. 'They don't fancy it much. They want to change the world, but they can't change their pants.'

'You all right?' said the other one, the nice one. 'You look funny.'

I smiled at him. I knew what he was talking about. I was on so much Cyclosporine, Prednisolone and Azathioprine that I rattled. But it was more than that. He was right. I looked funny. How could I not look funny? I was not myself.

On the far side of the wire there were caravans of women and children and dogs, men with dreadlocks erecting portable toilets, women with shaven heads hammering in tent pegs. And I thought they looked like they were at the beginning of something momentous. I thought they looked like – I don't know – history. They looked like history, about to be made.

'They must go on holiday by canoe,' said the nice cop, and both of them laughed.

Ruby was at her computer, her solemn face reflecting the shifting lights of the screen. I sat next to her, the pair of us squeezed on to the same chair but me taking up most of it. We sat in silence and in front of us were images of the end of the world.

Dead fish floating in brown rivers. Factories belching black smoke so thick that it covered the sun. And a ten-lane highway full of furious cars, none of them moving. Lara appeared in the doorway.

'Penne arabiatta,' she said.

Ruby looked at her and frowned. 'Penne arabiatta?' she said flatly. 'Right.'

'You can save the world after dinner,' Lara said, and she looked to me for support. But I found I couldn't place dinner above the fate of the planet. Lara folded her arms and leaned against the doorjamb.

'They all used to come running for my penne arabiatta,' she said, to no one in particular. 'Whatever happened to the old days?'

Then she clapped her hands. My little spitfire.

'This is *important*,' Ruby said, in those exasperated italics that were so often the overture to screaming scenes and slammed doors. 'Don't you *understand*, Mum? Don't you *get it yet?*'

Lara stared at the pair of us and said nothing. She didn't need to. I knew exactly what she was thinking. She felt like wrapping that mouse-cord around our throats, and then listening to us beg for mercy as she told us how long it had taken her to cook the dinner that was now getting cold and hard on the table downstairs. But what she said before turning away and going off to eat dinner alone was, 'And you need a haircut, George.'

I looked at her and then back at the screen. The end of the world continued to unfurl in front of us.

'I was thinking of growing it,' I said.

I was sitting at my desk eating a sandwich when Keith approached me. Avoiding my eyes, his meaty fingers fluttering over the stacks of files before me. He coughed, took the unlit cigarette from behind his ear and then put it back. I set down my paperback.

'What you reading?' he said shyly.

We both looked at the cover. The hood of a big fin-tailed fifties car was pointing down an empty desert highway, aimed at a distant range of mountains.

'*On the Road*,' he said carefully, as though he were translating from the Hindi. 'Any good?'

'Brilliant,' I said. 'It's about these two friends, Dean Moriarty and Sal Paradise, and they travel across America and down into Mexico.'

'Hmm,' Keith said thoughtfully. 'And then what happens?'

I stared at him for a moment. 'Well, that's it,' I said. 'That's what happens.' Keith looked doubtful. 'You should read it,' I told him. 'Everyone should read it. I'll get you your own copy. Or you can borrow mine.'

'Yeah,' Keith nodded. 'Well. All right.'

'Yes,' I said. 'Okay then.'

Then he wandered off, and before I went back to my sandwich and my Kerouac, I called out to him.

'Read it, man,' I said, and without turning round he raised one of those big red hands in acknowledgement, or farewell.

'The news is on,' Ruby said, and we quickly cleared the dinner table and legged it to the living room. But it wasn't the first item. There was trouble in the Middle East and a politician on the take and caught with his trousers down before they got to the latest report from the airport.

There was not much happening. Protestors being held back by lines of relaxed-looking coppers. Shots of distant aeroplanes lazily snaking across the runway. Everything under control.

Lara came into the room and placed mugs of hot chocolate in front of us. I smiled my thanks and Ruby said, 'Brilliant, Mum,' and gave her mother a smile that was like watching the sun come out. Then she turned back to the TV and groaned. 'Wish I could go to this,' she muttered, already knowing the answer.

Lara perched on the arm of the sofa and kissed her head.

'You're just a little too young, angel,' she said.

'It can't *wait*,' Ruby said, in the same voice that not so many years ago had begged for a pet horse. 'It's so important to do something *now*.'

Lara nodded. 'I know you care, and it's great to care, but

there will still be things to make right next year, and the year after, and all the other years. Come here.'

Lara held out her arms and Ruby sank into them. Sometimes they were fine. My wife and daughter. Sometimes they seemed to remember the old love, and realise that it was still there, unchanged and as strong as ever. And sometimes they forgot. Now they watched the news together, and they sipped their hot chocolate, and they held on to each other.

Rufus came and sat on the other arm of the sofa. I knew I wasn't allowed to hold him the way that Lara held Ruby. It is different for fathers.

When they are babies you can revel in them, you can kiss their cheek as hard as you dare and get drunk on their smell and the velveteen sheen of their skin. When your children are babies, you can get stoned on the incredible living fact of them. That all changes as they grow. You hold them. And then one day you realise you have stopped holding them.

I watched my son's face as he watched the news and I realised that by the time they are in their teens, you can let years drift by without really touching them. The physical expression of your love – the hugs, the kisses, the way you are allowed to touch their hair – all disappears. When Rufus and I came into shy, fleeting contact now – the hurried hug, the awkward kiss, those gestures of habit more than feeling – it was like an electric shock from the button of a lift, and we immediately recoiled with alarm. He saw me looking at him.

'What's wrong?' he said, rearing away, and I shook my head and quickly looked back at the television. Long before your children are grown, you grow out of the habit of touching them.

He was about to go out, and he was wearing a leather jacket covered in pockets. Some kind of biker's jacket. It had a small Union Jack on the sleeve and a belt tied up at the back, and it said *Belstaff* on a discreet metal tag. It looked like the kind of jacket you would wear for riding a motorbike in the 1940s. And I could smell him inside that leather jacket – the very essence of him, just as I had when he was a baby.

Now the milk and puke and sugar smell had been replaced by the scent of cheap aftershave and musky body odour and nights spent in boozy little clubs. It was a different perfume from another life.

But it was still him, and it was still me, and the years fell away.

There was an old lady on the news. Around Nan's age. She was talking about her childhood in a hamlet called Heath Row, torn down at the end of the Second World War to make way for an RAF base.

'I never knew that,' I said. 'Did you know that? About this little place called Heath Row?'

But my family didn't hear me. They were listening to the old woman talking about spending a lifetime a few hundred yards from the airport's perimeter fence. She had grown up, got married, and raised a family in a village called Sipson. But she wasn't going to die there. Her home, the hospital where her children were born, her local church, the little neighbourhood of seven hundred houses – it would all come down if they built another runway, another terminal.

'I've no idea where I'll go,' she said. 'I don't want to go into a home. I've written to the Queen.'

My daughter turned to her mother as they cut back to the bulldozers. Lara rubbed her back and smiled. There was nothing left to discuss. And I looked at my daughter's face, numb with the intolerable unfairness of this world.

'I'll take you,' I said.

'I don't want to be the one who always says *no*,' Lara said, as we lay in bed, on our sides, facing each other. Her voice was soft and our faces were almost touching. 'I don't think any parent should be put in that position. Being the bad one. The one who forbids everything. The voice of bloody reason. Do you know what I mean, George?'

I reached out and touched her face. It was the same face as the one I had first seen on Shaftesbury Avenue. The face of the girl who was the dancer, going out with someone far cooler, more handsome, more dashing, than I would ever be. Unchanged by the years, by marriage, by motherhood and all the rest of it. The face of the woman who chose me. How to thank her?

'Just be careful,' Lara said. 'I know she's a great kid. A smart kid.' She rolled on her back and sighed at the ceiling. 'It's just that they do really stupid things when they're young.'

I know, I thought. I'll get a tattoo.

All at once the fence came down, and I was falling forward, bodies pressing behind me and pushing me on before I even had a chance to think about it. The cheers and screams were rising until they were obliterated by a plane suddenly filling the sky as it came in to land.

It was like being at the head of some great human wave, and we were all surging forward. The police fell back, and their mates who had been in the front line were scrambling out from under the collapsed fence as we stumbled and fell across it.

I looked back and saw Ruby's face, and I saw her shouting something to me, but the air was full of the noise of planes and people and I was always being carried away from her.

Only one section of the fence had come down, and now the police were regrouping around this breach in the perimeter and I felt myself shoved up hard against a wall of rough blue serge, the breath squeezing from me and the fear of dying today coming out of nowhere. The crush of bodies. The smell of sweat and aftershave. My scar throbbed against the chest of a young policeman.

And then a helmet fell across a face, a baton flashed in the sunshine and somehow there was a gap and I was through it, past the line of police and sprinting across scrubby open grass, no idea where I was going, glancing from side to side and seeing that I was on my own. It was as flat as a field in a dream. In the far distance I could see a 747 taxiing towards the terminal. I began to jog towards it.

Suddenly I was knocked sideways and down, tackled hip-high by a copper who had probably played a bit of rugby in his youth. But that must have been a while ago now, because as we lay side by side on the ground he moaned in agony and furiously patted his knee as if he was trying to put out a small fire. I got on my knees and then on my feet and the fallen cop had a fistful of Rufus' Belstaff jacket and he would not let go. So I shrugged off the jacket – let him have it, I would buy Rufus a new one – and began once more to jog towards the runway, one hand on my sore ribs.

I felt quite peaceful now. The sounds and the crush of the protest were far behind me and the airport's cacophony of air and metal was still some distance away, although even from here the 747 looked gigantic, like some great ocean liner washed up on the surface of the moon.

I was running at a calm, measured pace. I could see little faces at the portholes of the 747 and I raised a hand in salutation. I was on tarmac now and I heard footsteps pounding behind me, getting closer, and then someone punched me hard in the back of the neck and I went down face first. After that I did exactly what I was told to do and I did it quickly.

I had been in the holding cell for a couple of hours when Keith turned up. He settled his great bulk next to me on the bed and sighed.

'Who's a naughty boy then?' he said.

eleven

There was a stag party in the audience. Maybe a dozen of them, right at the front but with their backs turned to the stage as they howled and cackled in each other's faces. Foaming beer bottles in their fists. One of them was being held up by a couple of his mates. They were playing this game where they'd let go of him, allow him to start sinking to the floor, and then hoist him up before he hit the ground. A stag party was never good news. They always wanted to be the funny men. And I couldn't help considering them with the cold eye of a seasoned professional. *Pick the biggest one and stick your baton in his lughole,* I thought, remembering my training days in Hendon. It seemed a lifetime ago.

'Old man walking down the road and he comes across this talking frog,' said Rufus. He could cross the little stage in three paces, then he had to turn and go back again. He looked trapped. 'The talking frog says, "Old man, I am not really a frog at all, but a beautiful princess who has had a spell cast upon her by a wicked witch. If you kiss me I shall be free of this enchantment, and I shall reward you with one night of wild, passionate love."' There was wild laughter from the stag party, completely unrelated to Rufus. The legless one had sunk to his knees, causing much hilarity. 'The old man keeps walking and the talking frog looks shocked. "Old man," it says, "I don't think you heard my offer. I am a beautiful princess –" The old man holds up his hand. "I heard," he says. "But at my age I would rather have a talking frog."'

There was a ripple of laughter around the pub and the stag do seemed to take this as a personal affront. They looked up at Rufus as if noticing him for the first time. One of them – squat, overweight, with the kind of shaved head that is meant to hide baldness and promise violence – looked like trouble. But when he began his half-cut heckling, Rufus was waiting for him.

'What's that, sir, what's that?' He had that smile, the vicious smile that Eamon Fish had lent him. 'Speak your mind, sir – if you'll excuse the overstatement. Yes, sir – you. The man with the head like a giant boiled egg.' Rufus cupped a hand to his ear, and kept getting the man to repeat the insult, screaming the same two words until they were drained of all their sting, and turned to ashes in the mouth of the man with the head like a giant boiled egg.

He did it, I thought, and my heart filled with pride.

'Maybe I'll come down to where you work tomorrow,' Rufus said, turning away, his borrowed smile still in place, 'and shout at you while you're asking everyone if they want fries with that.' He laughed shortly. 'You ugly bastard.'

Pub gigs were always bad. The comedy clubs had their share of haters, hecklers and lager-chucking nay-sayers, but the pubs were the worst because there were always men who resented a bunch of show-offs taking the stage for a night, demanding attention and applause, a procession of smart-arses who couldn't wait to move on to better things – and almost anywhere would be better than one of these dying pubs. But this was different.

We came out of the pub and the stag party were there, unsmiling and smoking and waiting. They looked up and with the precision of synchronised swimmers they threw down their cigarettes, sparks flying and dying on the pavement as they walked towards us, the one with the head like a giant boiled egg at the front.

I shoved Rufus back and placed myself between the men and my boy, although it did not make any difference in the end. But he is my son and I love him.

And as they got stuck into us, I suddenly understood that this was the missing lesson of Eamon Fish.

Don't provoke the bastards.

I opened the garden gate of my parents' house and there it was – the perfect blue rectangle of my father's swimming pool, glowing and shimmering in the heat like the window to another, better world, some suburban Narnia.

My father was at the poolside with a black man around his own age. Winston, the pool guy. They were peering into a little fishing net that Winston was holding. My father suddenly turned with eyes blazing, and then calmed down when he saw it was me.

'Oh,' he said. 'I thought you were one of them.'

'They don't come in daylight,' Winston said. 'They too scared of the old man!'

Winston and I grinned at each other, but my father wasn't smiling. He was at war with the local youth. They sat on his wall. They dropped empty crisp packets and half-eaten kebabs in his roses. They made noise. They breathed in. They breathed out. And, worst of all, when the summer came they sometimes sneaked into his back garden in the middle of the night and frolicked in his pool. He took something out of Winston's net and showed it to me. An empty can of Red Bull.

'What happened to your face?' he said, crushing the can in his fist. 'Walk into a door, did you?'

I nodded. 'Something like that.'

'You got to watch those doors,' Winston laughed.

I waited by the edge of the pool as the pair of them fell into a debate about organic chlorine. Such a thing exists. The sun turned the surface of the pool to a sheet of molten gold. When Winston had gone my father stood by my side and stared at the water.

'So they're not charging you with anything?' he said.

I looked at him. 'What would they charge me with?'

He skimmed the water with a leaf rake, even though it was completely clear. Then he shrugged. 'Illegal trespass. Obstructing an officer. Resisting arrest. Being daft as a bloody brush.'

I shook my head. 'They're not charging me with anything,' I said. And then I could not resist. I held my arms wide, like a child pretending to be a plane, and dropped face first into the pool. It was surprisingly warm. My dad liked to keep the temperature turned up, and I suspected that this was one reason why his pool was such an after-dark sensation.

I lay on my back with the sun on my face and the chlorine stinging my eyes. I felt good. Like a new man. When I climbed out, my dad was still standing in the same place. I sat by the side of the pool, my clothes heavy and sticking. Already my magnificent gesture was starting to seem a little rash.

'Have you lost your job, sunshine?' my dad said. 'Chief

Super tell you to do the decent thing and fall on your truncheon?'

I thought of my meeting with the Chief Superintendent. How understanding he'd been, how kind. How I'd thought he might offer to help me fill my little cardboard box. There wasn't much to put in it. My family photos. My copy of *On the Road*. My fake gun. Then the embarrassed handshakes with a few colleagues. And no sign of Keith.

'Six months' leave,' I said. 'They gave me six months' leave. Full pay.' I thought about it. I was a bit fuzzy on the boring details. All I knew was that I was getting half a gap year. 'And pensions. Something about pensions.'

'Lucky boy,' said my dad. 'I would have got a toe up the arse.'

He knew that wasn't true. The police have always looked after their own.

'But I might not go back,' I said, knowing it would provoke him. 'At the end of the six months I might want a change of direction.'

My dad nodded thoughtfully. 'Fancy a change of career? Something more fulfilling? More in touch with the real you?'

'Yeah.'

He stroked his chin. 'Rock star? Premiership footballer?'

'I don't know,' I said. 'What's the money like?'

My mum came into the garden and stared at us. 'Why are you all wet?' She turned to my dad. 'What happened to his face?'

'He walked into a door,' my dad said. 'And after that, all hell broke loose.'

'You'll catch your death,' she told me, and went back into the house to put the kettle on.

My dad sat by my side, tapping at the water with his leaf net, as if he might catch something.

'What about your family, George?' he said. 'What about your responsibilities?'

I stared sullenly at the water. I was starting to feel very cold.

'I love my family,' I said, and my dad had a good chortle at that.

'With that and two quid,' he said, 'they can buy a cappuccino.'

I threw open the wardrobe and began pulling out clothes. Circus-tent chinos. Sad corduroy. Dead and dying pants. Terminal T-shirts with amusing phrases that made my spirits sink.

'But what happens at the end of the six months?' Lara wanted to know. 'Is it the kind of six-month leave where you get your job back at the end of it? Or is it the kind of six-month leave where they never want to see your face again?'

'I don't know if I want my old job back,' I said. 'I hated my old job. My old job was killing me.' I began stuffing the clothes into a black bin bag.

'Then what about money?' she said. 'What happens if you don't have a job after six months? Because we will still have bills. That boiler is on the blink. What's going to pay for all that – my ballet class?'

'We've got money,' I said. 'Six months' money. Think of it as a sort of mini-gap year.' I took her in my arms. She was as welcoming as a sack of spuds. So I released her and continued tossing out depressing clothes. But I really wanted her to understand that this was a good thing.

'Don't you see what this means? It's a chance for me to do something that I really love. A chance to start again.'

My wife exhaled a married sigh.

'Nobody starts again,' she said, rescuing a pair of sludge-coloured cords from the bin bag. 'You can't collect some money and return to *Go*. That's not life. That's a board game. All you can do is get up after you get knocked down and carry on.' She ran one of her hands over the cords. 'There's absolutely nothing wrong with these trousers, George.'

I stared at them for a moment and then returned to the deforestation of my wardrobe. 'There's everything wrong with those trousers,' I said, reaching for an anaemic-looking polo shirt. And then I stopped. 'What's that sound?'

We both listened. It was coming from Rufus' room. Seeping through the wall. A guitar that sounded like – I don't know – a waterfall made of beautiful jewels, jangling and shining as they fell. Johnny Marr, I thought. Johnny Marr on guitar. And a voice that was a miserable drone and yet somehow strangely hypnotic and lovely. The Smiths, I thought. 'How Soon Is Now?' by the Smiths. From that jeans commercial.

I used to love that song, I thought. And I still do.

The bin bag was full. I began tearing off my clothes. On the bed my new clothes were waiting. A black All Saints polo shirt with an even blacker ram's head. A pair of brand-new Diesel Black Gold paint-spot jeans. Why were they different from my old clothes? Because they were tight. They clung to me. As if to say that they would not tolerate fat or old age. Although, ironically, the jeans looked as though they had already seen thirty years' service in the decorating business.

I stripped down to my pants and advanced towards the bed. But Lara took me by the elbow, stopping me. She spat on her fingertips and rubbed at the tattoo at the top of my right arm. She sighed when it didn't come off. 'What the hell is that?' she said.

We both stared at the two Japanese characters.

'That's my tattoo,' I said.

She thought about this for a while. Her face was impassive. 'Why is it upside down?' she said softly.

'It's not upside down,' I said, pulling away from her. 'You're looking at it wrong. You're looking at it upside down.'

I sat on the bed and began pulling on my paint-spot jeans. Lara watched me for a while, and then turned away when I put on my ram's head top, and the tattoo almost disappeared. You could just make out the bottom of one of the Japanese characters peeking out from the cap sleeve.

'Don't you think you're a little old to be getting your first tattoo?' Lara said. 'Don't you think you're a little too old for all that?'

She walked away before I could reply, before I could tell her: But I did it for love.

And how can you ever be too old for all that?

My children smiled at me as I came down the stairs carrying my black bin bag, breathing with some difficulty in my ram's head shirt and my new old paint-splattered jeans.

'Yeah, Dad,' Ruby said. 'You rock.'

I reached the bottom of the stairs and looked at them. 'Do I?' I said hopefully. 'Do I rock? Do I really? Am I rocking?'

Rufus snorted. The bruises on his face were fading to a dull yellow now, and they gave him a slightly malarial look. 'Nobody says "you rock" any more,' he told his sister.

She punched his arm and smiled at me, that smile that was like watching the sun come up.

'We do,' she said.

*   *   *

Under the blackened arches of Waterloo Bridge, the van served soup and sandwiches from ten until midnight.

I found Rainbow Ron sitting by himself, cradling a polystyrene cup of minestrone, watching the steam curl off it. I stood near him, but not too close. His beard had been roughly hacked off, or at least most of it. There were still tufts of hair clinging to his face where the nail scissors or garden shears or whatever it was had missed. But he no longer looked like some ageless Jesus. He looked like a young man.

'Looking good,' I said, and he glanced at me quickly with those eyes and looked away. 'Really,' I said, afraid he thought I was making fun of him, and afraid he might throw his boiling vegetable soup in my face. 'Losing the beard – a good idea. It takes years off you.'

I held out the bin bag, but he made no move to take it. I opened it up, showed him the clothes, waited for a word of gratitude. Some recognition of goodness. But he would not touch the clothes. And by now the rest of them were gathering round, mistaking me for the Red Cross, rummaging in the bag and spilling their soup as they yanked out cords, and shirts and the clothes of my old age. Rainbow Ron just stood there buffeted by the men, but otherwise not moving. When the bin bag had been picked bare, the others wandered off.

'I'm trying to do you a favour,' I said.

He looked at me and smiled. If you could call it a smile. It was more like an involuntary spasm of the mouth, revealing teeth like a graveyard full of ruined tombstones. He looked me up and down, as if he had placed me at last, and I felt as though he saw right through me.

*   *   *

At first I thought she was sleeping.

She was lying on her side of the bed, with her back turned towards me, perfectly still. But I should have known. Her breathing didn't have that soft little sigh in it that she always got when she was sleeping. And her body was too unmoving for sleep. When Lara was sleeping, that dancer's body just seemed drained of all tension, loose-limbed in her rest, completely at peace.

'Now she wants a party,' she said without turning round. 'For her sixteenth birthday.'

I sat on the bed and began pulling off my paint-spot jeans. 'I know,' I said. 'She told me.'

A bitter little laugh. 'Of course she did. I should have guessed you two would talk it over before approaching the old battleaxe.'

'It's not like that.'

'It's exactly like that.'

I thought about folding my new jeans, but it seemed a bit pointless. They were so riddled with holes and frayed with wear that it already seemed too late to be taking undue care of them. So I just chucked them on the floor.

'And what did you tell her?' I said.

She was quiet for a bit. 'I'm not going to be the one who always says no. But there have to be some rules. You have to have some *rules*, George.'

'Thanks,' I said, 'it will be fine.'

'It's hard to be the parent who always says no. It's hard to be the one who always spoils the fun, who always urges caution, who always tries to keep their family out of the emergency ward and the police cells and the mortuary. But that's the role that you seem to have forced upon me lately. I never wanted that role. You lot made me take it.'

'Right,' I said.

'*Everybody* has their sixteenth birthday party without their parents in the house. *Everybody* does it.'

I smiled in the darkness. She did a very good impression of our daughter's use of italics.

'Everybody being a few spoilt brats in her class whose parents were happy to have them off their hands, and had always been happy to have them off their hands. I wonder why these people bother having children. They seem to spend their lives trying to escape them.'

I slid into bed and lay on my back. Between you and me, I felt like a cuddle – a really good cuddle, maybe two – but I knew this wasn't the moment. Then Lara's voice broke the silence.

'What does it mean?' she said. 'The smudgy thing on your arm? Those upside-down squiggles?'

My fingers flew to the top of my arm. 'My tattoo?'

'Is that what it is? Your tattoo?'

'Yes.'

'What does it say?'

What does it say? What does my tattoo *say*? I didn't understand how she could ask me a question like that.

It said *Lara*.

What else would it say?

twelve

It was like a date.

We had decided that we were not going to lurk in the Rat and Trumpet for a few hours. We were not going to be the old folk who didn't know what to do now that the youngsters didn't need us around. Let them have their fun. Why not? Toss the rule book out the window. While Ruby was having her birthday party, we were going to have some fun of our own. Dinner, and dancing, and everything. Just like the old days. Just like a real date.

And when Lara came down the stairs, and I couldn't stop looking at her, then it was even more like a date. And I knew that I had done one thing right in my life when I married this woman.

Guests were starting to arrive as we prepared to leave. Guests I had known for ten years, since they were little girls with no front teeth. That lost pink-and-purple world of childhood. Horses in high heels. It was not so many years ago.

Now they were almost grown but still young enough to

get excited about the chocolate fountain, and they were still young enough to look at Lara as though she had the key to some other, more glamorous world. They were so sweet to us – Mr and Mrs Bailey. Or perhaps they were just looking forward to getting shot of us.

There were a few boys – gentle, well-mannered lads with soft, self-deprecating ways. Boys who had longer hair than the girls. But the girls ruled in here. These self-confident, decent, not-quite-grown young women like Ruby. The product of good state schools and loving homes.

Music began to play in the living room. Lara smiled at me as girls started dancing together. The boys smiled self-consciously and lurked on the edge of the room, hiding behind their fringes, hoping they would not have to suffer the humiliation of dancing.

'Let's go,' Lara said.

'Wait,' I said, and I stared at her because I wanted to remember how she looked at this moment, and to never forget it. And she could tell that I loved the way that she looked, and the old feelings were still there, and that looking at her made me happy.

'What?' she said.

'Nothing,' I said. 'Everything.'

And I grinned at her like a different kind of boy to the gentle souls that Ruby had invited to her birthday party. I grinned like the kind of boy who knew he was going to get lucky tonight.

There was a mix-up with the restaurant booking. The table wasn't ready when we arrived and a queue of would-be diners were double-parked at the bar. We were told that our table had slipped into the black hole of pre-theatre dining, and that we should have a drink at the bar until it was ready. I looked at Lara.

'Or we could just go dancing,' I said.

When I met Lara, I needed to be drunk to dance. And I was one of those Englishmen who danced as though I was celebrating a goal. Arms above the head, not much movement of the feet. She got me over all that, she made me relax, and she gave me a few technical tips – like the one about opening your eyes. And she told me that there was more snobbery about dance than there is about art or wine or almost anything. She said people thought that dancing was for the young, or the cool, or the technically proficient.

And one of the things I always loved about Lara was that she thought dancing was about as elitist as breathing.

As midnight approached in the Africa Centre, I could tell by the smile on her face that she was impressed I still had all my old moves, as well as a few new moves that I was introducing into my repertoire.

Lara and her mates used to come here after work in the eighties. They would pretend to be peasants during the French revolution or prostitutes in Saigon or cats, and then they would come to the Africa Centre to dance the rest of the night away. So they would dance for their job, and then they would dance for fun. When we started going out, Lara took me to the Africa Centre and it was a bit of a struggle for me. Because I could see that, if I didn't dance, then I wouldn't stand a chance.

So I danced. And she helped me. And it became the most

fun I had ever had. And we had some great nights at the Africa Centre. They played funk and soul and African music. We saw Soul II Soul a few times when they were starting out.

But tonight was the best night.

Tonight was the best night of all.

When we came out of the Africa Centre it was raining and there were no cabs. I threw my jacket over Lara's head and took her hand, and we headed east, out of Covent Garden and across the Charing Cross Road. The neighbourhood was strangely unchanged from twenty years ago. People were still falling out of clubs and drinking double espressos at one in the morning and necking in doorways. We strolled through the rainy night in Soho and twenty years fell away.

I thought that it wouldn't take us so long to walk home, and that nearer to the park we might find a taxi heading back to the West End. We didn't, but it hardly seemed to matter. We stopped under an old-fashioned gas lamp by Regent's Park and I took Lara in my arms.

'Someone will see us,' she said.

'We can do whatever we like,' I said.

And then a miracle. A black cab with a yellow *for hire* light shining bright was coming out of the rain and I was in the middle of the street, waving it down.

We climbed in the back and our dripping bodies huddled together, wet and warm, the engine a soothing rumble as our mouths searched for each other and found each other and couldn't get enough of each other.

Lara whispered in my ear, afraid the taxi driver was

listening, and then she said, 'You don't have to say it back,' and the black cab played its diesel lullaby all the way to our home.

Or what was left of it.

Police lights.

Packs of people in the street.

And lights on in the windows all the way down our road. Neighbours watching the show, some of the braver ones in their doorways, but mostly peeping from behind their curtains. I paid the cab driver with a pounding in my head and then a beer bottle exploded between my shoes.

There were kids I had never seen before in our front garden. One of them was being sick into the recycling bin. The rest of them were arguing with a young policewoman, telling her about their human rights.

Our front door was hanging off its hinges. Someone had tried to kick it in. They had succeeded. I looked at Lara's face and then I looked away. We went inside.

There was a girl I didn't recognise sitting at the foot of the stairs with puddles of vomit on the knees of her embroidered jeans. There were crowds of people standing around as though they were in a club. Young and not so young. The average age had shot up. Some of them were ten, fifteen years older than the birthday girl.

A couple of cops I didn't know held up their hands for calm as they were angrily lectured about their fascist behaviour. There was assorted music, all at top volume, coming from different corners of our unrecognisable home.

Lara began pushing through the mob, calling Ruby's name.

I ran upstairs.

The landing was covered with random debris. It looked like the aftermath of a bomb. There was a single shoe. Scraps of clothing. A bloody handprint on the wall. A pair of furry pink handcuffs. And everywhere the crumpled cans and empty bottles, and everywhere it stank of cigarettes and wacky baccy, and everywhere the carpet was pockmarked with black burns and crumpled stubs.

I called her name.

I kept calling her name.

Condoms were scattered around like dead eels. I opened the door to Ruby's bedroom. Two boys were asleep on her bed. There was blood on the walls. No, not blood – pizza. I moved on.

In Rufus' room some guy about thirty was urinating in the wardrobe. As he turned round, zipping up his jeans, I hit him in the mouth with my elbow. He went down and stayed down.

Rufus was in our bedroom. He was death-white and sober, bending over his sister on the bed, stroking her hair. No, not his sister. One of her friends. One of those nice, well-brought-up girls who'd been so excited about the chocolate fountain. She seemed quite peaceful, but her face was streaked with make-up and tears. Bodies were collapsed all around the room. The smell of beer and puke and sweat and smoke was overwhelming.

'She took a pill,' Rufus said. 'But apparently it didn't work. So then she took another one. And then they both worked.'

'Did you call an ambulance?' I said. 'Call an ambulance.' I stepped up and felt for a pulse.

He placed a palm on the girl's forehead. 'She's better now that she's got it all out.'

'Call an ambulance, Rufus. Where is she? Where's your sister?'

'It's not her fault, Dad. Somebody posted something on the Internet. And some DJ started talking about it on his radio show. And then all these older guys, these guys in their twenties, they all heard about it. And this is what they do. They crash other people's parties. Don't blame Ruby.'

I looked at the girl on the bed. 'I'm not going to blame her. I just need to know she's all right. I just need to see her.'

'Last time I saw her, she was in the garden shed.'

'What's she doing in the garden shed?'

'She was hiding.'

Lara was waiting at the foot of the stairs. There was a policeman with her. From somewhere in our house came the sound of breaking glass, followed by cheers and laughter. My wife stared at me as I came down the stairs. She had found a terrible calm. Or perhaps she was just in shock.

Then there was the rumble of a black cab in the street, the one that had brought us home, and we went to the door.

As it pulled away we saw someone turn to look out of the back window, and the revolving blue lights illuminated our daughter's face.

And then the cab reached the end of our street and she was gone.

'It's not her fault,' I said, and I was about to blame the blabbermouth DJ and all these old guys in their twenties and careless chatter on the Internet, but Lara cut me off.

'That's right,' she said. 'It's not her fault.'

And she didn't look at me as if she didn't know me.

It was much worse than that.

Because my wife looked at me as if she was seeing me, really seeing me, for the very first time.

I stood outside the florist's and moved my face close to the glass.

Among the tulips and the lilies there were flowers I could not name, flowers that looked like they came from another planet – extravagant blooms, orange and spiky, exactly like some exotic bird, and also delicate white blossoms on the end of thick green stems, as intricately carved as a French horn. But my eyes kept coming back to the roses. I knew I had to have the roses. She would love the roses.

There were a dozen of them in a simple bowl of green glass. They looked too perfect to be real. A lush deep red, they were, the colour of wine, the colour of blood. I went inside the shop, and a man in a green apron looked up at the sound of the bell.

'Help you with anything?' he said with a smile.

'The roses in the window,' I said, and his smile grew broader at my exquisite taste. He went to the window and fished them out, casually mentioning the price as we made our way to the till. Eighty pounds for a dozen roses? I fumbled in my pockets for every last grubby note and forgotten coin, placing them on the counter next to the roses, as we stood there with our smiles plastered on our faces like slowly peeling billboards. I was about seventy quid short. The roses were carted back to the window and I got out of there as quickly as I could, the bell dinging behind me, the man staring at me through the window, unsmiling and wiping his hands on his apron. I walked away with my face burning.

But there were more roses in the park. On a bed next to the playground, ringed by a low green fence. They were very much the poor relations of the roses in the shop. They lacked the deep, vivid hue of the shop roses. They looked a bit anaemic in comparison, these poor municipal roses; knackered and knocked about by the patrons of the park, two-legged and four-legged. Most of all they lacked the glorious uniformity of the shop roses. But it's the thought that counts, I reflected to myself as I looked both ways to make sure nobody was around, and then climbed the little fence and started past the KEEP OFF – NO BALL GAMES sign.

I had just picked the dozen I needed when the park keeper spotted me, giving me a head start with his outraged cry of, 'Oi!' I could not run very fast with the roses clutched to my chest, but he only chased me to the park gates before he pulled up and stood there shaking his fist, like a sheriff watching an outlaw cross the Mexican border.

'I know where you live!' he shouted.

On the surface, the life of a dancer resembles the life of an actor. Dancers go to auditions, they grow up on a diet of rejection, and they have periods of intense activity followed by longer spells of unemployment. In reality, dancers are different. They never audition alone, they always audition in packs. Unless they are completely deluded, they do not harbour dreams of stardom. And once you get beyond the footlights, once you get backstage, you see that dancers are treated like respected manual workers, more like electricians and carpenters than stars.

Then there is the physical element. Dancers live totally in the physical world in a way that no actor ever does. Julia

Roberts will never have to end her career because she keeps tearing her hamstrings. Brad Pitt will never have to retire because he ruptures his anterior cruciate ligament. But that happens to dancers all the time. And that was what happened to Lara.

It's strange how bad injuries happen. It can be the toll of the years, or it can be a single moment. You could be working up to it for years, or it could be an instant of bad luck. A stab of blinding, mind-numbing pain and suddenly you have a different life. That's all it takes. An awkward landing, a fall, something suddenly tearing, and it changes everything.

This is what I learned from my life.

Some injuries you never get over.

Lara was sitting at the kitchen table, rubbing her leg, when I came in. There was a broom leaning against the table, a dustpan on the floor. She was massaging the area round her kneecap with her thumb, and digging her fingers into the back of her leg. Her face was white with pain. She didn't look up.

Ruby was down on her hands and knees, scrubbing the floor, her hair tied back with an elastic band. She glanced up at me and grinned at the flowers, then went back to her scrubbing. I could see Rufus in the back garden, emptying a rubbish sack into a recycling bin. Crumpled beer cans clattered down. When it was full he carried the recycling bin into the kitchen, and said to his sister, 'Come and help me with this, Rube.'

Our children melted away.

I placed the flowers on the kitchen table. 'Lara? I got these for you.'

She picked up a flower and absent-mindedly pulled a clump of dried mud from its stem. 'Thank you,' she said.

'That's okay,' I said, and wondered if I should sit down, or just leave her alone for a bit now that I had given her the flowers. But then she began to speak before I could decide, so I just stood there listening.

'There comes a moment when you don't recognise them,' she said, and she still didn't look up, so it was as if she was addressing the dirt-encrusted rose in her hand rather than me. 'At the start, you have all this unconditional love. It's as if you never knew you had that kind of love inside you, that you were capable of feeling that strongly, that deeply. That much love.'

'I know what you mean,' I said. I thought it was right for me to say something at this point.

'But then it changes,' Lara said, ignoring me. 'It changes almost without you noticing that it's changed. Suddenly it feels like the connection to the past has been broken. It's as brutal as that. As final as that. You just don't recognise them any more. It's as if they are a different person – I mean, quite literally someone else. And that's the big problem.' She held the rose in both hands. A pinprick of deeper red welled on her thumb where a thorn had pierced her. 'How do you keep loving someone when they are no longer the same person?' she said. 'It's not that you don't *love* them. It's worse than that. You don't even *know* them.'

I pulled up a chair and sat down.

'Lara, they grow out of it,' I said. 'I know it's tough – and I know exactly what you mean. You love them as babies, and you love them as children, but suddenly it gets harder to love them when they become teenagers and start driving you nuts. But – and this is what I really believe – they are still the same child that you loved. That baby, that toddler, that ten-year-old – they are still in there somewhere. And you get them back. You really do. You get the mad years out of the way and then you get them back.'

She put down the rose and looked at the blood on her thumb.

'Lara?'

And now she looked up at me.

'Not the kids,' she said. 'I mean you, George. I'm talking about you. Do you want to help bring up these kids? Or do you want to be one?'

I shook my head.

Face burning. Heart pounding. Eyes stinging with self-pity and shame. I fought the urge to say, I got a tattoo for you.

'That's not fair,' I said. 'It's really not fair.' She stared at me as I got up from the table and backed out of the kitchen. *'It's not fair!'*

And I could still feel her eyes on me as the front door of our home slammed behind me.

She had made me a bed on the sofa.

The sofa of shame.

A makeshift bed where I would toss and turn and atone for my sins. I shook my head and almost laughed.

Lara walked into the room.

'Have we got a guest?' I said, nodding at the sofa of shame.

She stopped and stared at me, the sofa between us. 'Don't you get it yet?' she said. 'I don't want to be around you right now.'

I felt the self-pity swell and rise and break the banks.

'After all I've been through,' I said.

'No,' she said, 'after all you've put me through. It was

bad enough when you were encouraging Rufus to drop out of school.'

'I didn't –'

'You were the one who was always banging on at them about getting an education. Having the chances that you never had.'

'He will get an education if he does stand-up,' I insisted. 'It's the University of Life.'

'The University of Life?' she said. 'Telling jokes to a bunch of drunken bums in some grotty East End pub? That's not the University of Life. It's not even a polytechnic.' A derisive snort. 'And it was bad enough when you were encouraging Ruby to think she was some kind of eco-loony.'

'She already –'

'But this is *our home*, George. This is where we've raised our children. This is where we live our lives. Do you remember how excited we were when we moved in? Do you remember how happy we were, and how worried about if we could really afford it? Do you remember any of that?'

Of course I did. I remembered all of it.

'This is our home, George,' she said, and I saw how tired she was – tired of clearing up somebody else's mess, tired of me, tired of everything. 'Our home,' she said. 'And look what you did to it.'

We looked at it together. The four of us had done a good job of clearing up. But there were still ugly black cigarette burns on the carpet. Assorted stains had not quite come out of the furnishings. And out the window I could see where the flowerbeds had been trampled flat by people having sex, throwing up or passing out. Or perhaps just destroyed for fun. We had worked hard, all four of us. But it was not the same. And it would probably never be the same.

'So if you have to sleep down here for a bit,' Lara said, 'then I reckon you're getting off lightly.'

That brought my resentment – which had been simmering quietly as I stirred it with a generous serving of guilt – back to the boil.

'After all I've been through, I'm expected to camp out in my own house,' I said.

'Fine,' Lara said, exhaling a sigh full of such exhaustion that it chilled me. 'You take the bed. I'll have the sofa.'

'You love me,' I said, and it sounded like I was accusing her of something.

She hung her head. 'I love the memory of you,' she said. 'I love the way you were. Kind. Strong. Responsible.' She looked back up, her eyes roving, and I could see that she was sneering at the length of my hair. Bloody cheek.

'I loved you when you were a real man,' she said. 'Not just one more pathetic, middle-aged *boy*. Did you get a Porsche yet? Isn't that that happens with you lot? Shouldn't you start fancying a Porsche about now?'

'A Porsche?' I said. 'That's not a bad idea. I can see myself in a Porsche.' I shook my head. 'Is that what you think this is – some kind of mid-life crisis? I don't want a bloody sports car. I don't want to roger some WAG.' I reached across the sofa of shame and took her little hands in mine. 'I just want to *live*, Lara. I just want to remember what really matters. I feel like all the juice has been sucked out of my life. And I want the juice back.'

She pulled her hands away.

'Don't worry about juice,' she said. 'Worry about the lager stains on our bedroom floor. Worry about your children. Worry about our home.' She picked up the pillow from the sofa of shame and threw it at me. 'Just *grow up*, will you?'

I caught the pillow easily. She slumped on to the sofa of shame and covered her face with her hands. Her breathing was suddenly very fast.

'I can't stand it, I can't stand it, I can't stand it . . .'

I put my arm around her and she shoved it off with all the force she could muster. She began tugging at her wedding ring, and when she couldn't get it off she started cursing.

'Here,' I said, standing up. 'I've got one you can have.'

But I couldn't get mine off either. The band of gold scrunched up against the bony knob of my knuckle and stuck there, pressed into a barricade of flesh. I looked at Lara. She had given up and was just sitting there, one hand pressed against her forehead, her hair hanging down, trying to steady her breathing.

I went to the kitchen, opened the fridge and found a tub of I Can't Believe It's Not Butter.

I smeared some of it around my knuckle and my wedding ring came off in an instant. I went back into the living room brandishing my ring triumphantly.

'Ha!' I cried. 'Ha!'

Lara looked up. It was the face that I had loved for half of my life. She had never looked as old as she did today and I had never loved her more. Right here, right now. Never loved her more.

She took my wedding ring and looked at it, the yellow and the gold, the wedding ring and the more-or-less butter that had set it free. And she smiled. But it was a smile of such infinite sadness that it made my panic soar. I didn't want to lose her.

'But we're happy, aren't we? Most of the time? Nearly all the time? We've had fun, haven't we?'

I began to pace the room and she watched me, and it

was etched into every line on her face. More than the stress of my illness. More than the exasperation of living with the new, improved me. And more than the raging bitterness that she felt at having her home smashed up by a bunch of morons.

She surrendered. She had had enough. She was giving up on me.

'Yes, George,' she said. 'It's been fun.'

Mention of the *f*-word encouraged me to pick up the pillow from the sofa of shame and throw it at her.

I imagined that she would throw it back again, laughing this time, and soon we would be having a happy pillow fight and end up rolling around on the floor like a couple of pups.

But the edge of the pillow must have caught her in the eye, because she recoiled, crying with pain.

'Oh Jesus, Lara, I'm so sorry,' I said, falling on my knees before her as she pressed her fingertips against her wounded eye and then examined them for blood.

'Yes, you're always sorry,' she said, squinting at me with her good eye. 'And you always have so much to be sorry about.' She waved me away. 'Leave me alone. Can you just do that for a while? *Just please leave me alone, please.*'

I took back my wedding ring.

'For how long?' I said.

'How long?' she said, and it was as if I had asked her to unravel the secrets of the universe.

I nodded. 'Like – how long?'

She shrugged.

'A few days? Until things get better? I don't know. Can't you get a room or something?'

Get a room? Get a room?

I began wiping the butter off the third finger of my left hand.

Where was I going to get a room?

There were boys playing football in the park.

Hoodies for goalposts. Laughter and shouts and goal celebrations they had seen on television. A medley of club shirts on either side, unlikely allies, Liverpool and Arsenal and Real Madrid against Manchester United and Chelsea and Barcelona.

The dog walkers were giving them a wide berth, although for all their noise they were harmless. In their teens but only just, and still young enough to think that one day they would replay these same celebrations before an audience of billions. Still young enough to dream, or to kid themselves, or whatever you call it.

An overstruck pass brought jeers and the ball was suddenly coming my way. I half-turned, killed it on the top of my thigh and volleyed it back before it touched the ground. Some of the boys turned to each other and conferred. And it turned out that one side was a man short, and they asked me if I wanted a game.

So I shyly trotted on to the field of play, and soon I was dreaming too – *Me, me, over here, over here!!* Hanging on the wing, holding out my palms, to show that I was free. *Yes! I'm free!* My T-shirt soaked with sweat, the blood pumping and an exquisite ache in the back of my legs. *I'm free!*

It was a high-scoring game, although nobody seemed to be counting, and a match apparently without half-time or end. But eventually a midfield maestro from Real Madrid strolled off and collected his bike, saying his mum was waiting.

The numbers on each side began to dwindle as we got closer to teatime.

A few of us played on for hours yet, booting the ball between those makeshift goalposts, our limbs aching and our voices hoarse and our new hearts pounding, giddy with happiness in the fast-fading light.

part two

zen and the art of

swimming pool maintenance

thirteen

I awoke with music in my head.

It was coming from downstairs. Music that I knew. I could hear my mum singing along with the radio, doing a duet with Boy George as she prepared breakfast. There was the smell of frying bacon and the blaze of a summer's day beyond my bedroom curtains. Everything was as it had been long before. I had slept late again.

I sat up in bed and discovered that I was still wearing my jeans. There was confetti in the bed – no, not confetti but pieces of paper that had fallen out of my pockets.

Charlotte and a telephone number scrawled on a napkin. *Sara* and a number scribbled on a matchbox from a bar I didn't remember. *Tomoko* and an email address carefully printed on the back of a business card.

I scratched my head.

Who were these people?

My mouth felt like a plumber's rag, and I rolled out of bed with a moan, stood up and stared at myself in the mirror.

My scar began to throb the moment it caught my eye, as if bidding me good morning.

My room was a mess. There were clothes strewn all over the floor, stacks of books everywhere, some fossilised pizza in a box the size of a vinyl LP. My mum had placed a stack of fresh washing on a chair. Order among the chaos. I picked up a shirt from the clean pile, pulled it on and buttoned it up. The scar settled down.

Out in the garden, my father was talking to Winston, and I could hear their soft, conspiratorial laughter and the swish of Winston's net as it was dragged through the water. I went to the window.

It was a beautiful day. Shirtless and lean and tanned, my dad swaggered around his back garden like a Mediterranean beach bum on the pull for Scandinavian tourists. He nodded and chuckled with Winston, the small shining rectangle of turquoise water between them. My dad had worked all his life to own that little swimming pool.

I staggered on the spot, my head all woozy. Where was I? Oh yes.

I was home.

I went downstairs and my mum smiled at me from the cooker. 'You're missing this beautiful day,' she said, and began loading a plate with bacon, scrambled eggs and toast. At the open window another golden oldie played on the radio, 'Come On Eileen', tinny and perfect.

Everything was eerily as it was before. My mum at the cooker. Dexy's Midnight Runners on the radio. Me sitting there with a hangover and a big appetite and vague memories of yesterday's girls. All it needed for this day to feel like all the days of my youth was my dad to come in, moaning about some domestic disappointment.

He barged through the back door on cue. 'That filter's gone again,' he said, and then he stood there with my mum and they both watched me as I wolfed down my breakfast. It was as if they couldn't quite believe that I was back. I couldn't quite believe it myself. My mum took my plate and began to refill it.

'Got to keep your strength up,' she said, giving me a quick, meaningful look. 'You'll be all right. You and Lara. You'll be fine. You're just going through a rough patch. Everybody goes through a rough patch every now and then.'

My dad snorted, settling himself opposite me, armed only with the *Daily Express*. 'A rough patch,' he said. 'I've been going through a rough patch for forty-five years.'

'Oh, that's a lovely thing to say, George,' my mum frowned. He was called George too. 'And put a shirt on,' she told him. Then a song came on the radio and she lifted her head with a smile. A heavenly saxophone solo swirled around the room, and my mum waved her wooden spatula as if she was a conductor. It was another song that I knew. I knew all the songs this morning.

'Oh, I love this one,' said my mum.

'"Baker Street" by Gerry Rafferty,' I said. 'Taken from the album *City to City*, which knocked the soundtrack of *Saturday Night Fever* from the top of the Billboard 100.'

My mum began to make tea for everyone. When the middle sax break came in she gestured at the radio with a pint of semi-skimmed.

'That bit,' she said. 'That's a good bit.'

'The famous saxophone solo,' I said, 'played by top-flight session musician, Raphael Ravenscroft.'

'Aren't you clever, Georgie?' My mum smiled.

My dad didn't look up from the *Daily Express*. 'Knowing

a lot about pop music,' he sighed. 'There's a lot of money in that racket.'

I ignored him. 'Funnily enough, Mum, although it is one of the most famous singles of all time, "Baker Street" never made it to number one.'

My mum looked stunned at the news.

'You want a cup of tea, Winston?' my dad shouted, half turning towards the back door. Out in the garden, still skimming his net across the water, Winston didn't respond. He was the same age as my parents – cresting seventy – but he seemed much older.

'Deaf as a bleeding post,' my dad said.

'I'll take him one out,' my mum said.

'It's ironic that the song is named after a famous tube station,' I said, 'because at one point Gerry Rafferty earned his living busking on the London underground.'

We were all silent for a while, just listening to 'Baker Street' playing on the radio, and alone with our thoughts.

'I like it, it's nice,' said my mum.

'A very pleasant melody,' my dad said emphatically, as if that was the last word on the subject.

My mum sugared the tea and placed great steaming mugs on the table before us. She took one out to Winston and placed it by his side as he knelt before the clogged filter. My dad spoke without looking up from his paper.

'You'll be wanting a job,' he said.

'A job?' I said, as though it vaguely rang a bell.

He nodded. 'Paying for your keep,' he said. 'You want to pay for your keep, don't you?'

Then my mum came back. She picked up a shapeless pile of wool and came towards me. I squirmed away, laughing as she held it to my throat like a hangman measuring a noose.

My mum was knitting me something. I think she secretly liked having me back home.

'Your *hair!*' she said with appalled delight, slapping my flowing locks with her bad knitting, and I ducked and laughed as the summer blazed, the bacon fried and the big hits kept on coming. My dad just sighed, and rolled his eyes, and buried himself in the *Daily Express*.

My daughter looked at me shrewdly.

'If it's too much of a drag meeting me at home, you can meet me at school,' she said. 'I know she can be a bit of a bitch.'

I tried to look disapproving. 'Don't say that, potty mouth. That's not a nice way to talk. I don't know what you mean.'

But I knew exactly what she meant. And my treacherous heart secretly thrilled to hear Ruby openly criticise her mother. We were walking through the crowds on Camden High Street. A Range Rover crawled by our side, slowed down by pale-faced locals and pierced tourists strolling in the middle of the road. The woman at the wheel began tossing rubbish out of her window. Here it all came: a coffee cup, a plastic bottle, the remains of her lunch, splatting on the road before being lifted by the summer breeze. Some millionaire's missus in a fifty-grand motor chucking her garbage into the street, as unthinking as a Victorian fishwife emptying the family bedpan.

'That makes me so bloody angry,' I said. 'Wait here.'

'Oh, *Dad*,' Ruby groaned, and it followed me into the road. '*Daaaaad*.'

But I was on my way, weaving through the crawling traffic, and I collected the coffee cup, the bottle, a half-eaten panini, all of it. Then I carried it across to the Range Rover, reached in the open window and gently placed it all on the passenger seat. 'You dropped something,' I said, and even behind Chanel sunglasses the size of dessert plates, there was no missing the loathing in the woman's eyes. As I walked back to the pavement there was a smattering of applause from a *Big Issue* seller standing outside the tube station. But Ruby was shaking her head.

'The earth's dying,' she said. 'You think you can stop that by picking up after some Hampstead housewife?'

'That's exactly what I think,' I said, and she just laughed and took my arm, giving it a squeeze as we fell back in step with the crowds.

'We recycle our Perrier bottles, and we wave our little banners, and it doesn't change a thing,' she said, and sighed with the infinite wisdom of sixteen. 'We only do it to make ourselves feel better.'

'You've changed your tune,' I said, and I wondered if she was still coming out to the airport at the weekend.

We wandered into a clothes shop. Rows of T-shirts and denim. A woman approached me with a pair of jeans so worn and frayed that they looked as though they had been dipped in toxic waste. 'Do you work here?' she said, and I quickly shook my head. 'Well, you look as though you work here,' the woman said. Ruby was quite insulted. I took it as a compliment.

We moved on.

'I want to go in here,' I said.

It was one of those independent bookstores that always seemed on the verge of going out of business. I had decided that I wanted to give places like this my custom. And maybe Ruby was right. In the great big scheme of things maybe it didn't make any real difference. But if you are not part of the problem you are part of the solution. Or was it the other way round?

There was an intense young man with a wispy beard behind the counter. He looked alarmed when we came in, as if he hadn't been expecting company. 'Can I help you guys?'

'I'm looking for a book,' I said. '*Zen and the Art of Motorcycle Maintenance* by Robert Pirsig.'

He lifted his chin, making a small gesture with his wispy beard. 'In the back. Under philosophy-slash-spirituality.'

'Thanks.'

Ruby trailed after me, lazily running her fingers along the spines of the books. It felt more like a library than a bookstore. It was an airless maze, narrow spaces between shelves of books that didn't appear to have been touched for years. I found philosophy-slash-spirituality and the book I was looking for. I pulled it out and read the first paragraph.

> *I can see by my watch, without taking my hand from the left grip of my cycle, that it is eight-thirty in the morning. The wind, even at sixty miles an hour, is warm and humid. When it's this hot and muggy at eight-thirty, I'm wondering what it's going to be like in the afternoon.*

Wonderful stuff. Freedom. Adventure. The open road. Kerouac on a motorbike. I often felt like that when I was cycling around Primrose Hill. My heart raced at the words, and I could feel my scar pulsing with delight. For those few dreamy moments I was riding pillion with Robert Pirsig, heading towards the Dakotas on a warm summer morning in search of meaning, and truth, and everything, smelling the oil on the hot metal of the motorbike beneath us, my child and I.

I closed the book and turned smiling to look at Ruby, wanting to tell her how great this book was, and that she should definitely read it, and thinking that I might buy two copies, one for my daughter and one for me. And just as I turned I saw her slip two slim green paperbacks into her rucksack.

She caught my eye, gave me a grin and turned away, heading for the door, and I stumbled after her with my paralysed smile, thinking that I must have somehow got it wrong, that this was not what it appeared to be. I still thought that she was going to do the right thing.

'Cool shop, mate,' she trilled at the man behind the counter, but he had his back to her as he tore open a cardboard box, and merely grunted a response. A warning bell pinged as Ruby stepped into the street. I hesitated at the counter, stared at his back, and followed my daughter into the street. The door pinged again.

'Are you nuts?' I asked her.

She began to walk away. 'Don't know what you're talking about,' she said. A gang of boys in paint-splattered trousers walked past, all turning to check her out. I stared at them with death in my eyes. They didn't notice.

I took her arm and pulled her into a shuttered doorway. 'What did you just do? Come on, Ruby.'

With exaggerated languor, she fished two books halfway out of her bag. Penguin Popular Classics. *The Hound of the Baskervilles* and *The Adventures of Sherlock Holmes*.

I shook my head. The books were slipped back inside the rucksack. 'I didn't even know that you liked Arthur Conan Doyle.'

'Who's he when he's at home?' she said. 'It's just a bit of fun. You know. The fun of getting something for nothing. The fun of getting away with it. The fun of being smarter than they are.' She raised her eyebrows, which I suddenly realised had been plucked almost out of existence. 'Don't tell me you don't know what I'm talking about.' Then she placed a palm on my chest. 'Wait.'

The young man with the beard was standing outside the shop, his beady eyes scanning the crowded street.

'Now look what you've done,' I said.

'He's not looking for me, Dad. He's looking for you.'

And we both stared at the copy of *Zen and the Art of Motorcycle Maintenance* I still had in my hand. She took my arm and pulled me into the crowds, dragging me quickly away as she chuckled softly to herself.

'What are you going to do, Daddy?' she said. 'You can't give it back, can you?'

And by then I knew we were probably going to get away with it, and I was confused, and my scar throbbed like it had never done before.

'They budget for shoplifting,' Ruby told me as we slid into a booth at Marine Ices. 'It's like electricity or water or something. What do you call it? An overhead. To them it's just a business expense.'

We tucked into elaborate ice cream sundaes and then sat there, happily bloated, not talking much, just watching the crowds thin out as the sun went down over Chalk Farm.

The lights came on in the Roundhouse, all crimson and beautiful. And as the waitress cleared our plates, Ruby chewed her bottom lip until I could see the tooth marks.

'And when do you think you'll be coming home?' my daughter asked me, staring out the window.

'Soon,' I said. 'I'll be coming home soon.'

I walked her to the bus stop and when she was safely on

her way, waving from the top deck until she couldn't see me any more, I went to get my bike.

My spirits lifted at the thought of being on my bike. As I anticipated pedalling north up the Finchley Road, relishing the sensation of flight, I thought of Kerouac and Cassady driving through Mexico and never wasting one second worrying that their heads might go through the windscreen. Nobody wears a seat belt in *On the Road*. And nobody worries about their mortgage. And nobody frets about their pension plan.

Because there are times in your life when the possibility that you could ever get hurt simply does not cross your mind. Fleeting moments of freedom when you just feel immortal. When you know that nothing in this world can touch you. That, I thought, is the very best thing about being . . . Now what did I do with that bloody bike?

At first I thought that I had forgotten where I had chained it. Those Camden Town lamp posts all look alike to me. But I got there eventually.

Some rotten bastard had nicked it.

Rufus looked older.

There were dark smudges under his eyes, things on his mind. No colour in his face. I watched my son coming down the stairs of the club and, in those moments before he saw me at the bar, not being at home with my children weighed on me like a crime that I had never been punished for.

This was the strangest bit. The allotted time. Making a date to see your children. Finding a window to see my son and daughter. The scheduled, premeditated time of the rough patch.

He saw me and moved slowly through the crowd.

We embraced awkwardly. He wasn't an easy thing to cuddle, my son – all awkward arms and stray elbows. But I grabbed him and reached up on tiptoes to kiss his cheek, the baby bristles and the thin film of Lynx aftershave brushing across my lips. I held him for a moment too long and then I let him go, thinking that he was probably shaving twice a week by now.

'You all right?' I said. 'You look – are you all right?'

'It's just work,' he said. 'That night shift is a drag.'

'Want a drink?'

'I'll get them.'

He bought a beer for me and a fruit juice for himself, and we made our way to the side of the club. A smirking boy came on to the tiny stage. Low-slung jeans, carefully faded polo shirt – his clothes looked older than he did. I realised with a jolt that he was probably younger than Rufus. But already it felt like there was more than a year or so separating him from my son. It felt like the boy up there was from some other kind of life. He took the mic off the stand and it crackled in his hand.

'Sometimes I think I should just grow up,' said the boy. 'You know – get a proper relationship, commit to someone, embrace maturity.' He lifted his shirt and scratched his stomach. 'But then I think – wait a minute, *it's the middle of the conker season.*'

I looked at Rufus. He was smiling. 'He's not bad,' he said, and I wanted him to be up there, and I wanted him to never grow old, and I wanted everything to be restored to the way it had been.

Towards the end of the act a gang of women came down the stairs carrying a giant inflatable penis. They were wearing tiaras and torn stockings. A few of them had magic wands.

One of them stumbled and fell but landed on her giant inflatable penis, and bounced back up. Her friends lurched into each other and howled.

'Hen night,' I said. 'They'll move on in a bit.'

Rufus glanced at his watch. 'I'm going to have to go anyway,' he said, just as he was struck on the head by the giant inflatable penis. He smiled good naturedly and quickly finished his fruit juice. Then we headed for the exit.

At the bus stop the crowds heading for Leicester Square swirled around us and Rufus kept looking at his watch, and it didn't seem right that he had to worry about being late for work when everyone else was out having fun with a giant inflatable penis.

We went upstairs on the bus. The air was thick with the smell of chips. The bus lumbered through the West End's neon glow.

'Everyone goes to Edinburgh for the festival,' I said. 'Every stand-up in town. You know what that means, don't you? When it's Edinburgh, you don't go. You stay right here in London, because there's masses of work.'

'I thought I might miss Edinburgh anyway,' he said, looking at me quickly before glancing away. 'Just give it a miss.'

'That's what I'm saying,' I said, although I knew we were saying completely different things. 'Rufus?'

'What?'

'You were good,' I said. 'You *are* good. I'm not just saying that because I'm your dad.'

He looked hopeful. But only for a second. 'Yeah, well. Nobody else thought so.'

He got up. We were near his stop.

'Maybe later,' I said. 'Maybe it's something you could go back to.'

He gave me his shy grin.

'Yeah, Dad. Maybe later.'

There was a lorry being unloaded outside the supermarket where he worked. Rufus went into the back while I hung around just inside the entrance, looking at the front pages of tomorrow's newspapers. My boy came back buttoning a white coat, a little white hat on his head. A squat shaven-headed geezer in a bad suit was standing beside me, reading tomorrow's sports pages. He looked up at Rufus.

'Get a bloody move on, Bailey,' he said. The paper in his hands shivered with irritation. 'You're meant to start at ten. What are you – some kind of comedian?'

I followed Rufus out to the street. We went to the back of the lorry and I saw it was full of fruit and vegetables. There were men in the back talking in Polish and a pallet with boxes full of oranges was waiting on the tail of the lorry.

Rufus picked up two of the boxes.

'Let me help you,' I said, trying to take a box from him, and he laughed with embarrassment, turning his shoulder to me.

'I've got it,' he said.

I knew I couldn't stay. I knew I was in the way. I wanted to talk some more, to make our scheduled time last a little longer, to just be around him.

But he had to go to work.

I watched him carry the box into the supermarket. And I could smell the oranges. The dark and grimy street was full of the smell of oranges. When he came back I hugged him hard and whispered in his ear.

'Don't settle for an ordinary life,' I said. 'Please don't ever settle for the ordinary, Rufus.'

He pulled away. I think I had exceeded my hugging quota for the night.

'But, Dad,' he said, 'maybe I *am* ordinary.'

Not to me, I thought. Never to me. But I shook my head and said nothing. And then the shaven-headed geezer in the bad suit was at our side.

'Get your finger out, Bailey,' he said to Rufus. 'You're not getting paid to hang out with your bloody mates.'

And my son and I smiled at each other.

fourteen

I dragged the leaf rake across the surface of the swimming pool, skimming up the strays, watching the sun on the surface of the water as it shimmered and rippled with the tiny waves I made. It was a different kind of work from what I was used to, the kind of work where you could shut down your brain and just do it. That was a good thing. I had my shirt off and I could feel the midday sun on my shoulders. My career as a canteen cowboy had made my big hard body soft and weak. But now I felt it aching to fall away. The desk jockey weakness. The old man softness. The station cat pallor. The summer was waiting to take years off me.

Winston struggled with the filter at the far end of the big pool, and I felt myself drift away, with no awareness beyond the distant sound of a saxophone solo on a radio, and the smell of cut grass mixed with the smell of the chemicals that Winston used to turn the water a heavenly shade of blue.

He squinted up at the sun. 'Put your hat on,' he said.

I pulled on a baseball cap and looked up at the big house.

159

There was a woman watching me from one of the first-floor windows. She was young and unsmiling. I pulled down the brim of my hat, picked up my rake and went back to work, slowly dragging the rake across the pool. I liked the sound it made. It sounded like the beach.

When I looked up at the big house again the woman had gone. A housekeeper emerged from the French windows and I thought perhaps she was bringing us tea. She was wearing one of those old-fashioned maid costumes, a black dress with a white pinny, which you saw in a surprising number of these big houses. When she got closer I could see that she wasn't bringing us any tea. She walked straight past me without a glance and over to Winston. He stood up, holding his aching back, listening to her without expression. Then he nodded once and she started back to the house. Winston crouched over the water filter.

'Put your shirt on,' he told me.

For a moment I thought that it was some sort of archaic dress code that I was violating. Maids wore one costume and drivers wore another costume and the pool guys wore another. Or maybe he was worried about me getting sunburned – Winston was always worried about me getting sunburned. But then I got it, and laughed to cover my embarrassment. I pulled on my shirt and looked up at the empty windows of the big house.

She didn't want to see my scar.

We worked all day, travelling between the big houses in Winston's neat blue van. We were at a big white house in Holland Park, wrestling with a jammed pool cover, when Winston caught me stealing glances at my watch.

'Big date tonight?' he asked, his face impassive and shining with sweat. Then he laughed at me, and told me to go home, and that he would see me in the morning.

'Go get your girl,' he said.

'You didn't have to come,' Lara said.

'But I wanted to come,' I said.

When did this start? This sullen small talk? Creeping around each other like a pair of strangers? I preferred it when we felt like throwing things at each other.

I reached for Nan's hand to help her out of the cab, and she blinked with surprise at the lights and the noise and the teeming theatre crowds of Shaftesbury Avenue. The old lady seemed as fragile as a baby bird in all this bustle and grime.

With Nan in the middle, holding on to our arms for dear life, the three of us began heading towards *Les Misérables*, Cosette's face up on the billboard as big-eyed and vulnerable as a baby seal that was about to be clubbed to death.

The trip had been arranged months ago. We did it once every year, taking Nan to a show in the West End on her birthday. In truth, over the last few years it had become a bit of an assault course for all concerned. Nan had fallen asleep in *We Will Rock You* the year before last, and had made a number of homophobic comments about Freddie Mercury in the taxi home. But I knew that Lara did not want to give up this annual ritual, because it would be an admission that Nan's life had retreated to her musty cell at the Autumn Grove Care Home. I wondered if she was really strong enough for a few hours of pre-revolutionary France.

But I needn't have worried. As we settled in our seats at the front of the upper circle, the old lady still between us, I remembered how special *Les Misérables* was for Nan and Lara. And for me too.

'Which one were you again, love?' Nan said loudly, sucking on a boiled sweet as Jean Valjean toiled under the boiling sun of the chain gang.

'Ssssh!' hissed the man in the seat behind me, as Javert appeared, like the Marquis de Sade enlisted in the Metropolitan Police.

'Hmmm?' said Nan, oblivious.

'I wasn't in this scene,' Lara whispered, her mouth pressed against Nan's lughole.

'What?' said Nan.

'There's no women characters on the chain gang, Nan. I was a peasant and a prostitute.'

Nan reared back in alarm. 'Who's a prostitute?' she said, and the man in the seat behind leaned forward to bellow, *'Will you be quiet!'*

I turned to look at him, torn between the urge to apologise and the urge to throw him off the balcony. I had expected some miserable middle-aged man, but it was a young rugby-player type, all prime beef and Hackett casual, out with his leggy bird. I raised my hands in a plea for calm and attempted to smile. He didn't smile back. And then his phone went off.

It might have been the *William Tell* Overture. Or perhaps 'Umbrella'. But it went off, shrill and hysterical, a tinny babble that had half the upper circle turning towards him as he rose in his seat, a big man but out of shape, fumbling in his jeans for the offending mobile. Even Jean Valjean and Javert seemed to cast their eyes towards the heavens, wondering what kind of idiot forgets to turn off his phone.

The phone was fished from his jeans, but immediately squirmed out of his chunky fingers, like a ball slick from the scrum, and he caught it just before it landed in his girlfriend's popcorn. Cursing, he finally turned it off, but security had arrived by then. And we all turned to look, even Nan, ignoring Fantine doing her big number, as they led him out, the leggy bird trailing behind him in tears of shame, spilling her popcorn all over the gaff. And for the first time in a long time, my wife looked at me and smiled, reaching across Nan's boiled sweets to squeeze my hand in the darkness.

Lara stopped and turned on our front doorstep, the key in her hand, and a few houses down I saw a neighbour's net curtain twitching like a maiden aunt in a knocking shop.

'Beautiful night,' Lara said, and I followed her gaze beyond the yellow glow of the streetlamps and the orange pall that always hung over the city at night. 'Is that a star or a planet?' she said, pointing with the hand that held the keys.

'Where?' I said, trying to follow her finger, squinting into the fathomless abyss above our front garden.

She put her free arm around my shoulder and pulled me closer, close enough that I could smell her perfume and something else, the essence of her that was always there. It was so familiar, it made me catch my breath. I missed her so much.

'There,' she said, and I saw what she was pointing at, a white light winking at us from the other end of space.

'That's a star,' I said. I turned to face her, and watched her profile as she kept staring at the sky.

'How can you be so certain?' she said.

'Because it's sparkling.'

'You mean twinkling?'

'Yeah, twinkling. Stars twinkle. Planets don't twinkle. They just shine.' She turned her face to me and I kissed her lightly on the lips.

'George, don't,' she said, shaking her head and pulling away.

'Stars twinkle because they are so far away,' I said, lunging at her with my lips again. 'Their light gets absorbed by the earth's atmosphere, so –'

'I said no, didn't I?' she said, placing her hands on my chest. I could feel the keys pressed against my heart. 'I can't be that close to you right now.'

I took my own step back.

'I thought things would be better,' she said. 'Things would be good. That's what I thought. After what happened to you. I thought it would save us. Not tear us apart.'

'It did save us,' I said. 'Don't you get it yet? I nearly died, Lara.'

'Yes,' she said drily. 'I was there.'

'And yet you want – I don't know – you want me to act as though nothing happened. To fill in tax returns and fix the bloody boiler. Chastise the kids and kip in front of the telly. Sometimes you have to stop and pick the roses.'

'Smell the roses,' she said.

'What?'

'You don't pick the roses. You smell them.'

'Why can't you do everything? Pick them, smell them, take off your clothes and skip through them?'

She grimaced. 'We can't just skip through the flowers. That's not life. Life's not a laugh a minute.'

I could feel a sulk coming on strong. 'Yeah, well. It should be.' But then the thought of sleeping without her tonight was unbearable. 'Don't you want me back?'

'I want you back. The way you were. The way you are. Not some . . . extra teenager.'

'What's wrong with an extra teenager?' I said, trying to use my charm. It didn't work.

'Two's plenty,' Lara said, and she slipped the key into the lock. 'Good night, George. I'm glad you were there tonight.'

'Don't you see? This is my chance. To break free. To make a change.'

'What – you mean getting out of the rat race, and all of that?' I nodded. 'By clearing the leaves off of someone else's swimming pool?' she said. 'Very fulfilling. Very bloody meaningful. Let me know when you discover the secret of the universe in your leaf rake.'

'You think what I did before was more noble?'

'It paid the mortgage, George.'

'Don't you want more than that? Don't you want more than just meeting the mortgage payment?'

'No, I don't want more,' my wife said, and she gave me a look of married frustration. She opened the door, and the light from the hallway of our home flooded her face. 'I'm past all of that, George. I just want to hold on to what I've got.'

'But you're young!'

'I'm not young, George. I wish!'

'Seven years younger than me!'

'Yes, and forty next birthday.'

I frowned. She was right. Lara's big birthday. Of course. And yet this was somehow still shocking news.

'We should do something special,' I said. 'Go to one of our places.'

'I don't know,' she said. 'Do we still have places?'

'Forty next birthday?' I said. 'How did that happen?'

'Search me,' she sighed.

She kissed me on the forehead. A chaste and friendly goodnight. But the touch of her brought my blood from steady simmer to boiling point, and my hands somehow inveigled themselves under her top, gorging themselves on her smooth, warm flesh. Familiar and beloved and missed. I said her name and she said my name and then I said her name again. Her face. My hands. Her body. My Lara. And then she stepped back and punched me as hard as she could in the chest. I stood there coughing as next door's net curtains twitched with alarm.

'I don't believe it,' she said. 'You sperm-brained little slut, George. Did you just try to put your hand inside my bra?'

'If you're sick,' Keith told me, nodding at me in his rear-view mirror, 'you're going to clean it up, and I mean it.' He bared his teeth. 'You're acting like some stupid kid. Next time I'll let them give you a good hiding.'

That hardly seemed fair. It was the back of his bloody car that was making me feel sick. It was possible that all those bottles of Corona with a pointless wedge of lime stuffed in the top, necked in a dark, cavernous bar with Russian bouncers on the door, may also have had something to do with it. But Keith's car was not helping.

The Russian bouncers had been escorting me from their bar when Keith happened by. They were about to accompany me down an unlit alley to discuss my version of Whitney Houston's 'And I Will Always Love You' when Keith intervened and tossed me into his back seat.

Now I moved uneasily on the seat, breathing in the trapped air that smelled of all the drunks, no-goods and naughty people who had been there before me. Keith's partner gave me a snooty look from the passenger seat. He was growing a goatee. It looked ridiculous, as though something had crawled on to his chin and died.

'What now?' Keith sighed, and I saw the blue lights flashing ahead of us on a bleak stretch of the Camden Road. A car was parked across the street and a couple of uniformed coppers were tussling with a pair of bad boys. As their bodies moved and jerked in the changing light, it looked like chucking-out time at a cheap disco.

It wasn't going well for our lot. One of the bad boys – a short, broad refrigerator of a geezer – had one of the coppers in a headlock, making his superior upper-body strength count. He was attempting to get the copper on the ground. The other officer was doing better, and he had cuffs around one wrist of his suspect – a weasel-faced little runt – but he was holding him by the scruff of his hoodie, clearly torn between helping his mate and holding on to the one he had nicked. He could not do both.

Keith slammed on the brakes and him and goatee boy both leapt out, not bothering to shut their doors behind them.

'Need my help?' I said.

Keith jabbed a fat finger at me. 'You stay right where you are,' he said. They both jumped on the one who was built like a fridge-freezer, ramming his nose in the tarmac as they administered the cuffs. Then they went to the assistance of the other officer, who had managed to get the cuffs on weasel-face all by himself. A small crowd had gathered by now, drifting out of the nearby flats and a pub that looked as though it had closed down twenty years ago, and the mob were half-heartedly whining about police brutality and human rights. Keith barked at them and they backed away sharpish.

Cuffs on nice and snug, the two pairs of arresting officers stood there for a few minutes, having a chat, holding on to their collars like absent-minded dog walkers. Curious cars slowed down for a gawp at the action. Then Keith and goatee boy said their farewells and slung the one who was built like a refrigerator in the back of the car with me. He acted as though I wasn't even there. He was a lot younger than I thought. His pumped body and shaven head were meant to put years on him. And they did when he had a policeman in a headlock. But up close and handcuffed he looked like a scared kid. Then we were on our way again.

'That's a nasty little scam,' Keith said, narrowing his eyes in the rear-view mirror. 'Playing dead in the middle of the road and then robbing the poor bugger who stops to help you.'

The boy raised his eyebrows, a gesture of defiance so pathetic that I felt sorry for him, and then he stared out of the window as we headed down to King's Cross. With his hands cuffed behind his back, the kid had to sit forward, almost on the very edge of that cracked vinyl seat.

'Do I know you?' I said. 'I know you, don't I?'

He looked at me for the first time. 'I'm not saying anything without my brief,' he muttered, a voice thick with South London.

'How do I know you?' I said, and I knew it was just out of reach, and that he was as ignorant as me.

We got back to my parents' place. The kids stayed in the car and Keith fished me out. The fresh air immediately did something to my legs. They went from rubber, to jelly, to water, and Keith took me by the scruff of the neck and said, 'Easy, Tiger,' as he gently led me up the garden path. I stopped to lean against my dad's car, a red Ford Capri, and struggled to get it all under control. My stomach, my breathing, my life. I could see the blue glow of the swimming pool in the back garden. It looked beautiful.

Then my parents appeared in the doorway in their dressing gowns, my mum's eyes going to the black and uncaring windows of the neighbours, my dad staring at me with a total absence of surprise. The way he looked at me made it hard to concentrate on the medley of Soul II Soul songs I was singing.

'He can sleep in his own bed tonight,' Keith said, 'if you can stop him singing.'

My parents fussed around him, grateful and ashamed, and he shook his great bashed-in head, declining all thanks and offers of tea. Then he kissed my mum and shook my dad's hand and placed me in the custody of my parents. He patted my back and was gone.

'I'll make that tea,' my mum said, and my dad almost laughed.

'It's not tea he wants.' The old man shook his head and almost tutted. 'Is this the part where I tell you you're grounded?' he asked me.

I was ready to rise to the bait, but then he was up the stairs and gone and I looked up at the ceiling, listening to the soft fall of his carpet slippers on the bedroom floor. And then I realised that, just like all the other nights, my pockets were full of scraps of paper. I rewound the night after leaving Lara, trying to remember the girls and the women I had encountered. But when I began to empty my pockets, it was not the usual collection of names, numbers and electronic addresses. It was all Lara.

I held up a photograph of our wedding day. Then I pulled out a photo-booth strip of the pair of us looning around like a couple of kids about a year after we met, when it was still new but we knew it was going to last. And then there was Lara in an orange bikini on a beach with Rufus and Ruby when they were about four and two, and she was scooping up wet sand and the sun was going down over her shoulder, catching the collarbone and glinting with gold. Then Lara was smiling in our first home, wearing dungarees for decorating, a bit heavier after the birth of our second. And – folded in four – how could I be so stupid as to fold it in four? – there was an agency photo of Lara taken the year before we met.

I got down on my knees to smooth it and out tumbled more pictures. Lara unsteady on skis, Lara in our back garden, Lara in a hospital bed with a sleeping baby in her arms.

So it just wasn't true, was it?

We still had plenty of places.

The law had it all under control. I had to admire their crowd management. Even if I was now on the other side.

They had established a perimeter around the demonstrators, and corralled us into a crowded pen of protest, held in place by lines of orange barriers, hundreds of bored young cops and, beyond them, a lot of empty space before you reached the place where the meat wagons were waiting with their reinforcements and charges of resisting arrest.

The mood among the demonstrators was surprisingly upbeat. Perhaps now everyone was getting what they wanted. The law kept the peace. The demonstrators got to demonstrate. And the airport got to build its runway. In the distance I could see the diggers and the men working, but it was so far away it felt like I was watching it on the news.

I narrowed my eyes at the sun. The light from the sun takes eight minutes to reach earth, so I was looking at what the sun looked like eight minutes ago. Time travel, I thought. It's real. Here's the proof. And up in the roaring blue sky, the 747s were masters of the heavens, coming and going as if free of all human direction, taking off and landing, completely oblivious to the sign in my hands. PLANE BONKERS, it said, and I had made it myself.

I took out my phone, started calling Ruby and then hesitated. I was dehydrated and tired, staring at the world through an evil hangover, and just the tone of my voice would make her think that she had won the argument. *Nothing changes*, she had told me. *Don't bother. Do something useful instead. Something that really makes a difference.* Like a bit of light shoplifting.

I was not ready to concede that she was right. I believed that I would never be ready.

So I put my phone back in my paint-splattered jeans and wearily shook my sign at the heavens.

fifteen

I felt like just walking into his office without an appointment but I managed to restrain myself. After all, I didn't want him to think that I was some kind of nut-job.

But when the heart man came out of his Harley Street office at the end of the day, I was waiting for him. I thought that perhaps he would be off to do a spot of surgery before going home for his tea. But he was wearing black tie and looked like David Niven off for cocktails on the Aga Khan's yacht.

'Ah, Mr Bailey,' he said, covering his surprise quite well. 'How can I help you?'

'This is not my life,' I told him, and he nodded. I couldn't work out if he was humouring me, or if it was a perfectly reasonable statement and a sentiment that he encountered quite frequently in the course of his working day. 'I mean, this is not the life I am meant to have. There's been some mistake. I want my old life back.'

'Do you?' he said, and the late-evening sunshine made the shiny collar of his tuxedo look like the blackest thing in the world. 'Do you really want all that back? I wonder.

The constant fear of dying, the daily routine of serious illness, the inescapable knowledge that your body is failing.'

I furiously shook my head. 'But I don't know who I am,' I said. 'I need to know where it came from. My heart, I mean. I have to know more.'

He touched his bow tie. It was a real one, not the kind that comes on a bit of elastic. You can't beat a real one. The fake ones just look too perfect. The police are big on functions, and I always wore a real one.

'I'm not keeping a secret from you, George,' he said. 'I don't know myself.'

'I don't believe you,' I said.

'It's true. I don't need to know. And it doesn't matter to me. If your donor's family want anonymity – so what? You're my patient. Just be grateful for your life.'

'I am,' I said. 'But I want to know who it belongs to.'

My hands clawed at my hair. He said my name, and touched my arm, and he did it in such a subtle way that I almost missed it when he glanced at his watch.

'Sorry,' I said. 'I'm keeping you from your dinner.'

'*Madama Butterfly*,' he said. 'You're keeping me from Puccini.'

Then I saw why his bony finger kept touching his bow tie. It was coming undone. That was the trouble with the real ones. They were always coming undone. I smiled and nodded.

'Your tie,' I said.

He laughed and touched it self-consciously. 'My wife usually does it,' he said. 'She's not coming tonight.'

'Let me help you,' I said. 'I'm good at this.'

He flinched very slightly as I reached out to him, but then he stood there with an embarrassed, grateful little smile as

I tugged the tie apart, and confidently took the black satin between my thumbs and index fingers.

I pulled it so that the end in my left hand was a couple of inches lower than the end in my right hand. I crossed the longer end over the shorter end, passed it up through the loop, and then formed the front loop of the bow by doubling up the shorter end and placing it across the collar points.

And it looked like a car wreck.

I tried again. And then I tried again. And by now he was looking worried, and staring at his watch more openly, and taking a step away from me. And I felt the sting of failure burn my eyes.

'I used to know how to do it,' I said, and the crumpled black material hung forlornly from his neck. 'Honest I did.'

He looked like he really believed me.

I watched Larry flip the burgers, his big face smiling through the smoke as he waved his hand above the grill.

'Enjoy every sandwich,' he told me. 'The likes of us, we have a ninety per cent chance of living for a year, a fifty per cent chance of living for ten years.' With his free hand he cracked open two cans of beer and handed one of them to me. 'We've been given a great gift, you and me.' He took a deep breath and exhaled with a sigh. At the neck of his shirt, the first few inches of his scar were showing. 'All of us,' he said waving his spatula to indicate the other guests. And the rest of the group was all here. Paul, tall and shy, with his young family. Geoff, small and rat-like, with his young girlfriend. All the rest. All the guys who should be dead by now. 'We don't see you at the meetings any more,' Larry said.

I felt the stab of guilt. I didn't want to let Larry down.

He was the one who made us feel as though we were a community. He was the only one.

'You know, George, your life is not different because you have been given someone else's heart. Your life is different because you have been given a second chance. Your life is different because your old life was killing you. Your life is different because by rights it should be over by now.' We were joined by Geoff and his new girlfriend and Larry handed them burgers on paper plates. We watched them walk away, the young woman who had just started living and the older man who had lived twice, his hand around her waist as he tried not to spill his cheeseburger. 'It's all good,' Larry smiled.

I wanted to believe him. I could feel my scar pulsing, as it always did on these hot summer days, and I wanted to believe that things were just the same as they ever were. But a new heart had not restored my life and family and my future, the way it had for Larry, and the way it had for the rest of the group who met above the florist's shop. My new heart had blown it all apart.

I didn't want to be the old George. Or – more than that – I couldn't be. I didn't know who he was.

I smiled at Larry, and nodded at the dozen patties of prime beef he was grilling, their colours ranging from rare baby-pink to well-done charred to a cinder.

'What you trying to do?' I said. 'Give me a heart attack?'

'Enjoy every sandwich, George,' he repeated, dead serious. 'Who knows how long we have left?'

'But that's true of everyone alive, isn't it?'

He nodded. Then his big moon-like face split with a grin. 'But the rest of the world just doesn't know it yet.'

We were surrounded by gardens and all around us I could hear the sounds of an English summer. Lawns being mowed, music coming from open windows, the laughter of Larry's children in their square swimming pool. The boy, Jack, and the girl, Susie, were playing this game where one of them stayed under water for as long as they could while the other one counted: 'One-elephant, two-elephant, three-elephant . . .'

Larry's wife, Molly, sat with her feet in the pool, her jeans rolled up around her knees, her legs white and skinny, trying to keep the hot dog in her hand dry.

Larry flipped a couple of burgers one last time, pressed them against the grill, smiled when he saw the juice, and then expertly slid them into a pair of buns. 'Medium well,' he said, handing one to me. I smothered it in barbecue sauce, my mouth watering at the illicit treat. We strolled over to the pool with our beers and our burgers.

Larry's daughter was counting. 'Twenty-eight-elephant, twenty-nine-elephant . . .'

The boy burst gasping out of the water.

'You going to be a policeman again?' he shouted at me.

I shrugged and took a bite of my burger. I almost swooned. Larry was a great cook. 'I'm considering my options,' I said to the kid. 'Taking some time out.'

When the law has finally finished with him, a discarded copper tends to affect an air of studied nonchalance, if not outright indifference. Or was that just me?

'But it must have been fascinating,' said Molly. They were all fans of *The Bill*. They watched it together. That's the kind of family they were.

I smiled politely and knelt by the pool, staring at the water. The level was a little low.

'You should always add an inch or two of water every time you have your pool serviced,' I said. 'If you leave it too long, and it gets down to more than a few inches short, then it will take hours to fill, and you'll have to turn on the water supply and then remember to turn it off later.'

I stood up, and took a pull of my beer. There was more debris than I would have liked on the water surface.

'And I would check the skimmer basket,' I said. I thought for a moment, just staring at the blue water rippling in the summer heat. 'It looks slightly over-chlorinated to me. There's no need to overdo that stuff.'

Larry and Molly looked at each other and laughed. 'Wow,' he said. 'Thanks, George.'

'But it's a good little pool,' I said, straightening up. Their garden wasn't really big enough for a pool. It was more of a plunge pool than anything. They even did the maintenance themselves.

'It's big enough for us,' Molly said, and she grinned up at her husband, and so did the children.

Larry's family had a way of looking at him, holding their gaze on his big face for one second more than necessary, as if they were checking that he was really there, cooking barbecue on a summer's day, as if he might disappear if they didn't watch him for every possible moment. They checked him the way a parent checks on a newborn baby. They observed him as though his presence was too good to believe.

And Larry grinned back at his family, a beer in one hand and a burger in the other, bashful with love, the sun on his big bald head, and his face like a full moon seen in the middle of the day.

'You're a good dancer,' shouted the blonde girl.

'A very good dancer,' shouted her blonde mother, and I felt the sweat pouring, and my feet flying, and the night fever, night fever down deep in my bones. I didn't know the tune.

177

It felt like it might be new. One or two years old. Or ten or fifteen years old. 'Do you think you'd be better off alone?' asked the singer, and there was the death of something in there.

'Thanks,' I shouted. 'My wife taught me.'

'What?' said the mother, cupping her ear, and I shouted it again.

'My wife taught me.'

They looked at each other, and I saw something happen to their smiles, a sort of freezing, or souring, just as I turned to catch the eye of the DJ. He was only a kid, not much older than Rufus, but he knew his Stax and his Motown and his Atlantic, he could tell his classic disco from his old school R&B. He watched me draw an S in the air, and then an O, and then another S. He nodded and held up some 12-inch vinyl.

'Married?' mouthed the mother, as they looked at each other. A cascade of synthesised strings poured out of the speakers. The crowd let out a cheer. A woman with the greatest voice I had ever heard, apart from Aretha Franklin, started to sing.

The floor began to move as one heaving mass of dancing old people.

I tapped my wedding ring. 'Nearly twenty years,' I shouted proudly. 'Do you know the SOS Band?'

The mother and daughter looked around, distracted, as if they had only just noticed that there was music in the air.

'The SOS Band are the biggest secret in the history of music,' I shouted, moving more slowly now, doing this thing with my shoulders, this sort of rolling movement. You had to see it. It actually looked a lot better when you saw it. 'Why doesn't everyone know the SOS Band?' I shouted.

The daughter shrugged, and made this *beats me* gesture with her hands and mouth.

'Never heard of them,' mouthed the mother, with a conspiratorial smirk at her daughter, and that made me realise that she didn't really care about dancing to the SOS Band. And I remembered dancing with Lara.

Dancing with a dancer, a professional dancer, is funny. Exhilarating but strange. Inhibiting. Yet ultimately liberating. At first I couldn't do it. And then I realised that, if I was going to keep up with this fabulous woman, I had no choice. I had to dance. And then, some night at the Africa Centre when Soul II Soul were really cooking, I started to love it. And her. And I could not tell them apart, the dancer and the dance.

There was a fluidity about the way Lara moved. It went beyond dance being something that she did for a living, or something she was good at. There was something about the way her body responded to what she told it to do – it was more than grace, more than ease. It was as if, when she danced, she was doing what she was born to do.

And it was that dazzling fluidity that I always noticed. For every move I made, Lara made seven or eight, and they were all sort of joined together. It was seven or eight movements, but it was all one. It flowed. And she made it easy for me. That's what a real dancer does. Lara wasn't remotely snobbish about dancing, she didn't look down on civilians. She loved it, and she thought that everyone should do it, because dancing was as natural to human beings as breathing. But I don't really know if that's what it's like dancing with a dancer, or if that's just what it was like dancing with Lara.

'So – Fred Astaire,' shouted the mother, and she grinned at her daughter, who had a good chuckle at that. 'Where's the wife tonight?'

179

The SOS Band segued into Cameo, 'The Single Life'. I would have preferred 'Word Up' but it was clear that the DJ had hit a theme with all these tunes about being unattached, and how it was the best way to be. The mother and daughter were looking at their watches.

'She was in *Les Misérables*,' I said, looking at the lights. 'And *The King and I*. And *Miss Saigon*. And *Sherlock!* You ever see that show? It closed after ten days.'

But they were gone. And that was fine. I wasn't looking for someone to take home. I already had a girl.

The child came into the supermarket as I was reading tomorrow's papers. A chunky little fellow, about five, with cropped red hair and ketchup down the front of his replica football shirt. Up way past his bedtime.

He came over to where I was standing and began rifling through the bottom rack of magazines. I felt somebody standing by my side and looked up at the security guard. A tall, lugubrious, very thin boy. You wouldn't want to mess with him. But so many people did.

'Hello, Asif.'

''Lo, George.'

Together we watched the small boy pull out a *Doctor Who* magazine, flick through it and then toss it to one side when he came to a picture of the Cybermen.

'Scary monsters,' he muttered, and sauntered over to the fruit and vegetables. His filthy little hands lunged for some black grapes on a middle shelf but he was too short to reach them. He selected an apple from the lowest shelf, took a bite and then kicked the rest of it down the aisle.

'Goal!' he said, chasing after it with his arms aloft.

Rufus came out of the back, pushing aside the big plastic

flaps and straightening his tie. He wore a suit to work now, after his promotion, but I still hadn't got used to it. He looked as though he had stolen the clothes of some adult.

'You can take your tea break now, Asif,' he said.

Asif looked worried. 'There's some kid,' he said, and the boy jogged back down the aisle, booting the remains of the apple before him, and took the hand of a woman who had just collected a trolley.

She was a tired looking redhead who must have been extraordinarily pretty once. She wasn't very old now – early twenties, tops – but the prettiness looked as though it had been worn out a few years and a few men ago. A cheap floral dress, heels. The boys unloading the lorry outside turned to look at her. She looked sexy but exhausted.

'I'll keep an eye on them,' Rufus said. 'Looks like we got a grazer.'

'A grazer?' I said.

Rufus had his eyes on the woman. 'They don't come here to shop. They come here to have a munch on whatever takes their fancy. And it's gone into their greedy mouths before they ever reach the check-out.'

I laughed. 'The profits these places make, they can afford to hand out the odd apple.'

Rufus shot me a look. 'It's still stealing, Dad,' he said.

Asif went off for his teabreak. The woman and the child began their shopping, bickering with each other as the child tore things off the shelf and threw them in the trolley before the woman snatched them up and threw them back. Rufus and I fell into step a discreet distance behind them. Her buttocks rolled and rubbed and rolled against the cotton of her cheap summer dress.

'I'm made of bloody money, I am,' the woman told the child, hurling a family pack of Jaffa Cakes back on the shelf. 'Shall I go and pick some money from the money tree outside, Alfie?'

'Good idea,' said the child.

The woman raised her hand to give him a slap around his shaven little carrot head. But she didn't and the pair of them laughed. They turned a corner.

'How's your mum?' I asked Rufus.

'You're invited round for dinner,' Rufus said, raising a hand to stop me. He peered round the corner of the aisle. The red-haired woman and her scary child had stopped at the bakery department. My son glanced quickly at me. 'She asked me to tell you.'

I immediately forgot about the woman and her child. My thoughts were consumed by Lara's unexpected invitation. What should I wear? What should I bring? Was sex a possibility? Should I try kissing her? How far would she let me go? It felt like a first date.

I realised I was alone. Rufus had turned the corner. The woman and the boy were some way ahead. The child was sitting in the trolley now, his fat little legs facing his mother although he was too big to be in there. He had an almond croissant in his hand and was stuffing it into his greedy little cakehole. Asif was waiting at the far end of the aisle. Rufus was walking faster now. I caught up with him just as he reached the woman, and the last of the almond croissant disappeared into the child's mouth.

'Madam?' he said, and she turned and glared at him. I looked at the child and there were golden crumbs all over his rat-like little face. I looked at their trolley. It was completely empty.

'You got to pay for that, darling,' Asif said, nodding towards the boy.

Her green eyes flashed. 'I'm not your bloody darling,' she said.

'We got CCTV,' Asif said, with a touch of pride. 'You can't come in here to have your dinner.'

'I haven't done anything wrong,' the woman said, and it was so familiar to me, that furious outrage, those hurt feelings. I felt as though I had witnessed it ten thousand times. 'This is a diabolical liberty,' she said.

'Your little boy,' Rufus said quietly. 'He had a gourmet almond croissant.'

'No he didn't,' the woman said, and we all turned to look at the boy as he belched contentedly.

'We got it on camera,' Asif said, placing his long brown fingers on the trolley. He looked at Rufus. 'Shall I get the law, boss?'

'All right, all right,' the woman said quickly, pulling a purse out of her bag. 'I'll pay you for the cake.'

Rufus smiled pleasantly. 'Yes, that would work,' he said, and we all waited as she searched her purse, and then her bag. She hung her head. 'I haven't got anything on me,' she said. 'I left it at home.'

'I'm getting the law,' Asif said, moving off.

'Wait, wait,' the woman said. 'I could bring it in. I would. I mean it. I promise.' All this to Rufus. She took a step closer to him, lowering her voice. 'It's just a cake.' She placed a hand on her son's viciously cropped head. 'He's just a kid. A hungry little kid.'

Rufus stared at her for a while. Then he reached into his pocket and pulled out the money for an almond croissant.

'I'll take care of it for now,' Rufus told Asif, and I could have sworn I saw him throw his life away.

The red-haired woman smiled happily at my kind-hearted son. When the child piped up with some high-pitched whine about going home now, the woman silenced him with a glance.

My dad came into the darkened kitchen holding a cricket bat.

'I could hear someone making a sandwich,' he said. 'I thought it was burglars.'

'What – peckish burglars?' I said.

'Yeah, smart arse. Peckish burglars.' He furrowed his brow at me, tugging at the belt of his dressing gown. I could see the flash of striped pyjamas around his neck. He put down his cricket bat.

I was sitting at the kitchen table with a triple-decker sandwich in my hands. It was a bit too big for my mouth and I had to sort of tilt my head sideways to take a bite. I was ravenous. Through a mouthful of ham, cheese and Branston pickle I said, 'Sorry if I woke you up.'

My dad said nothing as he padded across to the fridge, the belt of his dressing gown trailing like a tail. He opened the fridge door and stood there in its golden glow.

'You didn't wake me up,' he said. 'Old men don't sleep much. And I often get up and have a bit of a wander.' He nodded towards his back garden. It was completely black out there. They always turned off the lights in the swimming pool when they went up to bed. 'Keep my eyes open for them. You know. These bloody kids who use my pool.'

I looked towards the darkness. Was it really true? Did yobs sneak into my dad's back garden in the middle of the night to have a splash and a frolic? Or was that all in his head? Did the Google earth gatecrashers really exist or were they an urban myth? Was there really such a thing as a dipping crew?

'And I sometimes fancy a bit of ice cream,' my dad said. 'Your mother doesn't like me noshing in the middle of the night. Thinks it's bad for me.'

'Maybe she's right.'

'Maybe she is.'

'Do you ever wonder what you are here for?'

He laughed. 'I'm just glad to be here at all, mate.' He turned to look at me, and the light of the fridge threw a halo around his head. My dad at seventy. 'Beats the alternative.' He turned back to the fridge and scratched his head, the ice cream slipping his mind. 'Now where was I?'

I didn't say anything because I knew he would not want me to. But there was no mistaking what was troubling my dad as he peered into the fridge at three in the morning. I knew he was wondering what he was there for.

'Not all memory loss is a sign of dementia, you know,' my dad told me. 'Fancy some ice cream?'

'Cold feet?' he said. 'We get a lot of those in here.'

He had pushed a slim manila folder across his desk but I had not reached for it. I looked up at him. A leering red face, a broken nose, steel-grey hair cropped close enough to show the scars on his scalp. He was meant to be ex-Scotland Yard and maybe that was true.

I looked back at the folder and I could feel my scar pulsing. On a day like today when my blood was up and my nerves were all raw ends, it was as if it had a separate existence of its own, with its own furtive grievances, secrets and fears that it did not need to share. I touched it through my shirt

– that long red livid thing, the wound that would always be with me – but not too hard. As if it was a beast that I did not want to wake.

'That's your man,' he said. 'Plenty of form. A criminal record longer than a bendy bus.' He leaned back in his chair. 'Not often a character like that displays such – what's the word I'm looking for?'

'Altruism,' I said. 'A concern for the welfare of others, no matter the cost to yourself. A philosophy of selflessness and generosity.'

'Altruism,' he said, rolling it around his mouth like some strange new cheese that he wasn't sure if he liked or not. 'Good word,' he decided.

'Good philosophy,' I said.

He nodded at the folder. I think he had some kind of concern about payment. 'You going to pick it up or what?'

We eyeballed each other across the desk, two big men alone in a shabby office. He was badly out of shape but it was easy to believe that he was a former policeman who had left the Met under some sort of cloud. A copper from the old school. He reminded me a bit of Keith but even more of my dad. He had that cop thing about him. The feeling that, even when they are all smiles, they could turn in an instant.

Commercial, Private and Matrimonial Investigations, it said on the dusty glass of his one-room office. Tracing specialists. No find, no fee.

I had found him up a flight of stairs in a West End backstreet and had half-expected a world-weary redhead on the front desk, like the receptionist in a Raymond Chandler story. But there was just him. Member of the Institute of Professional Investigators, it said on a framed certificate behind him, and it sounded ludicrously grand for this man in this place. But he had done the job that I had asked him to do.

'Your man came from a big family,' he said. 'Although it's not quite as big as it used to be.'

The scar pulsed with a steady rhythm, as if trying to avoid drawing attention to itself. I still had not touched the file in front of me. I wasn't sure I wanted to. Perhaps coming here had been a mistake.

'Get a move on,' he said, the bonhomie fading like a broken bulb.

'You'll get your money,' I said, pulling out my wallet.

'I should give you a discount,' he said, perking up a bit. 'Anybody can find a dead guy.'

sixteen

I went to kiss Lara on the cheek and she sort of ducked, as if afraid I might try to do something stupid, like stick my tongue in her ear, or down her throat, and I ended up kissing her once on top of the head. She stayed down, waiting to see if it was over, and I kissed her again on the top of her head.

Then she straightened up and took the wine I was holding.

'You didn't have to,' she said. 'But I love wine from . . .' She squinted at the label, and then held it at arm's length. 'Lithuania,' she said.

'Very underrated, Lithuanian wine,' I said, and I followed her inside, a guest in my own home. My mouth watered at the smell of roast beef. 'Something smells good,' I said. 'And it's not me.'

'I'll round up the tribe,' she said.

'I'll help,' I said.

'You don't have to do that,' she said, and the formality between us made me want to cry. I didn't want to make

188

small talk with her, I wanted to make wild, mad love beneath the tropical palms. 'Just go and make yourself . . .'

I waited. At home? A drink? Comfortable?

Then she shrugged. 'Come on then,' she said, and I followed her upstairs, her little dancer's body so close that I could have reached out and touched it. But that would have really put a crimp in the evening.

Ruby had a DO NOT DISTURB sign on the handle of her bedroom door, a souvenir of a school skiing trip to Austria when she was eleven. The sign had been placed there as a joke, but somewhere over the last five years it had lost every molecule of irony.

Lara knocked softly on her door. I could hear Ruby talking on the phone with one of her friends. No reply. Lara knocked again.

'*What?*'

Where did all that anger come from? Was that my fault? Because I wasn't under this roof? Lara knocked again and this time opened the door, ignoring the non-ironic DO NOT DISTURB sign.

'I'll call you back,' Ruby said into the phone and flipped it shut. 'Hello, Daddy,' she said, and slipped the phone under her pillow.

'Hello, angel,' I said.

'Dinner,' Lara said, and it occurred to me that my wife and my daughter had started to communicate in sentences of one word or less. But then Ruby managed a two-word sentence.

'Not hungry,' she sighed, and stretched on her single bed, her arms behind her head. Her phone vibrated and she pulled it out from under the pillow, her smile lighting up as she read a text message. As if this was her real life, not the two people standing uninvited in her bedroom doorway.

'I didn't ask you if you were hungry,' Lara said, and Ruby's smile fell away. 'Did I ask you that? I don't think so. I didn't ask you anything. I just told you – very politely – that dinner was ready.'

'What's this then?' Ruby said. 'Tough love?'

'Downstairs,' Lara said. 'Five minutes.'

We left without closing the door.

'Every time I see her,' I said to Lara, 'she gets bigger.'

'Really?' Lara said. 'Because to me she's always the same little cow.'

She went into Rufus' room without knocking. I hovered in the doorway. There was a musty man-smell in the room and the curtains were drawn. I could hear him snoring, but it was a different kind of snoring from what I remembered. There was real grown-up exhaustion in the sound. It was the snoring of a working man who was knackered. Lara pulled back the curtains. It was just starting to get dark outside.

'Rufus? Time to get up. You've got work. And I've got some dinner for you. And your dad's here. He's brought some lovely Lithuanian wine.'

Rufus groaned, sat up in bed and collapsed again. His chest was alarmingly hairy. Why was I always so freaked out by the sight of my son's hair? He was a man now. He groped for the cheap alarm clock by his bed and sighed. Seven o'clock, it said.

'I was going to say hello to Dad and get something to eat on the way to work,' he said half-heartedly, knowing full well that his mother would veto this plan.

'No,' Lara said. 'Let's all have dinner together.'

She closed his door behind us and looked at me grimly.

'Everybody loves roast beef and Yorkshire pudding,' she said. 'Don't they?'

I took her hand at the top of the stairs. 'Lara,' I said, shaking my head. 'It's so good to see you.'

She patted my hand. And then her face fell. 'My sprouts are burning,' she said, and dashed downstairs.

So we stood by our old familiar places at the dining-room table. Lara at one end, me at the other, Rufus and Ruby facing each other across the middle. Ruby flopped down, staring at the screen of her phone, her thumb flashing across the keyboard. After my offers of help were declined, I took my place at what I once ludicrously thought of as the head of the table. Lara and Rufus went off to the kitchen.

'Hey,' I said, and Ruby looked up at me. I once loved that face more than anything in the world. And I still did. I leaned forward. 'Be nice to your mum,' I said. 'Please.'

Ruby raised her plucked eyebrows, the injured party, sorely misunderstood. 'Daddy, I would be, if she just – you know.'

'What?'

She pouted. 'Let me do what I want. Instead of always expecting me to do what *she* wants. How can that possibly be fair?' Then she got up and came over and embraced me. 'I didn't give you a hug, did I?' she laughed, and I felt my heart fill and then overflow with love. She could always do that to me, from the day she was born. My daughter would glance my way for a moment and it would make everything all right. Then she went back to her seat, looking at her phone. 'You should keep your hair like that,' she said as an afterthought. 'Don't cut it.'

I pushed my fringe out of my eyes and tucked a few tangled strands behind my ear. 'Do you think so?' I said.

'Definitely,' she said, not looking up.

Lara and Rufus came back with dinner. A joint of roast beef, steaming bowls of vegetables, a plate of giant Yorkshire puddings. Rufus picked up a carving knife the size of a samurai sword.

'Let your dad do it,' Lara said, and she smiled at me as she went to put on some music. I carved the roast beef. Rufus dealt out the vegetables. The music began to play.

I recognised it immediately. The CD was *City to City* by Gerry Rafferty. The track was, 'Baker Street'. Lara joined us at the table as Ruby looked up from her mobile with theatrical shock.

'Oh great,' she said. 'My favourite. Dad rock.'

'Do you like it?' Lara said, sawing a carrot in half. The carrots were a bit hard and the Brussels sprouts were a bit on the soft side. Lara had been distracted from cooking by rounding up our family. Or what was left of it.

'Oh *yes*,' Ruby said. '*Love* it, Mum. It's just my sort of thing.'

'That's good,' Lara said.

We were all silent for a bit. The only sound was the chewing and cutting, Gerry Rafferty and the bip-bip-bip of the text message Ruby was writing. I looked at Rufus. He looked at me. Then we both looked at our dinners. Rufus tore into his food. I couldn't tell if he was famished or anxious to get away from us all.

Lara nodded at Ruby. 'Can you put your phone away, please,' she said. Then she glared at me, just this fleeting look of suppressed rage, and I thought – What the hell have I done? Nothing. And as Lara turned back to our girl, I saw that maybe that was the problem. But I couldn't be the glowering big man at the head of the table. That wasn't me any more. And so my family swirled around me, cut from their moorings.

Ruby had not looked up. In front of her the plate was untouched. Roast beef and Yorkshire pud. The vivid orange and green of the veggies. My daughter was thin and pale. It looked exactly what she needed. But her eyes were on her phone.

'Just let me finish . . .'

Lara's cutlery slammed against her plate. '*Now.*'

Ruby glared at her. 'Aren't you going to call me *young lady?*' she said. 'I love it when you call me that.'

'Not if I can possibly restrain myself,' Lara said.

She stared at Ruby until she placed her phone on the table with an elaborate sigh.

'Ah, it's really great, Mum,' Rufus said.

'It is,' I quickly agreed, thinking I should have spoken up sooner. 'Really great.'

Rufus had cleared his plate and reached across the table to get some more of everything. Then he went off to the kitchen to forage for more Yorkshire puddings. Ruby was frowning at her untouched meal as if she had only just realised that she had been presented with fried stoat.

'Sorry?' she said, all innocent enquiry. 'But what is this exactly?'

'Roast beef,' Lara said. 'Didn't I tell you that we were having roast beef?'

'Possibly,' Ruby said. 'But I think I may have been *attempting* to have a conversation with *my friend.*'

Rufus returned from the kitchen. 'No more Yorkshire puddings,' he said, as though it was the news the world was waiting for, bless him.

'Didn't you know?' Ruby said, giving her plate a little shove. She picked up her phone but didn't flip it open. 'I thought you knew.'

Lara shook her head. 'Know what?'

Ruby gave a nod. 'I'm a veggie.'

Lara smiled. 'Since when? When did you become a vegetarian, Ruby?'

Ruby shook her head, as if the event was so far back in history that the exact date was lost in the mists of time. 'Tuesday,' she said.

'Then eat your vegetables,' Lara said. 'Eat your Yorkshire pudding.'

'It's great, Rube,' said her brother, and my heart went out to him. Rufus was the one who should have done the carving. He was the one attempting to hold it all together, to soothe the troubled waters between mother and daughter, while I just sat there in embarrassed silence sipping my Lithuanian wine.

But Ruby looked as though she had been asked to levitate.

'What?' she said. 'Eat vegetables and so-called Yorkshire *pudding* when I am staring at a slaughtered animal?' She looked at her plate and quickly looked away, holding her stomach. 'What am I meant to do with the *meat*, Mother? Meat is murder.'

Lara nodded. 'And so is living with you.'

Then Rufus was on his feet, his empty plate in his hands. 'Can't you two please stop bitching at each other for five seconds? Can't you stop while Dad's here?'

'Apparently not,' Lara said, miserably spearing a Brussels sprout.

'Haven't you got some shelves to stack?' Ruby asked her brother. He stared at her, his face burning, and I thought for a moment that he might start crying. But he slammed out of the room and I could hear him in the kitchen, rinsing his plate before he put it in the dishwasher.

'What's eating Gilbert Grape?' Ruby laughed, and she gasped and so did I as Lara reached across the table, picked up Ruby's plate and hurled it across the room. Sprouts flying like shrapnel. Carrots like arrows. The Yorkshire pudding bouncing off the music centre, and giving Gerry Rafferty a jolt. And the beef and gravy making a hell of a mess on the curtains.

'Whooh!' said Ruby, raising her hands in surrender as she stood up. 'Not completely mental or anything. Not remotely mental at all.'

Then Lara and I were alone.

She stared at her plate.

'I thought that went rather well,' I said.

She laughed briefly. 'Sorry,' she said.

I shook my head. 'Not your fault,' I said.

'Ah,' she said. 'I don't know about that. But it's not just me, is it? You used to be able to control her with a look. Remember that?'

I remembered. But it felt like some other life.

'I don't want her to be scared of me,' I said. 'I don't want to control her with a look.'

'But she's not your friend. She's your daughter. And if there's no control, then you end up with Yorkshire pudding on the curtains. Do you prefer that?'

She wearily got up from the table, her right hand absent-mindedly massaging the unhealed spot behind her right knee, and then drifting up to that nameless area between the top of her hip and the bottom of her rib cage, those endlessly painful places where she felt her old dancing injuries the most.

'I'll tell you something,' she said. 'She's not going out with that bloody guy tonight.'

That guy? That bloody guy? What bloody guy?

I followed Lara upstairs. Ruby's door was open. We watched her touching up her make-up – when did the make-up start? We watched her consulting her phone – what bloody guy? We watched her getting ready to leave.

'Excuse me, folks,' she said, heading towards us.

'You're not going anywhere,' Lara told her.

'Watch me,' Ruby said.

Lara grabbed her arm as she tried to brush past us. I could see it in her eyes – Lara had never come this close to hitting her. But I knew that she wouldn't. Because she couldn't. Not if Ruby set fire to the curtains, not in a hundred years. Lara could never hit her and Ruby would always have that over her. But Lara would not let go of her arm. And I just stood there, not really a father at all, just my daughter's useless friend.

'Ouch,' Ruby said, squirming dramatically in her mother's hand. '*Ouch!*'

'What's wrong with you?' Lara said, getting right down to it.

'What's wrong with me?' Ruby said. 'I'll tell you what's wrong with me, Mummy dearest.' The tears came to her eyes. 'It's too late to start playing happy families.'

Lara let her go. And seconds later I could hear her feet on the stairs, moving fast, desperate to get away before anyone had the chance to grab her again.

'I'll talk to her,' I said.

'You can't talk to her,' Lara said. 'Not any more.'

I went down the stairs after her. The front door was open. I didn't want her to go out. I called her name and somehow I thought that would be enough.

'Ruby.'

'Oh, leave me *alone*.'

Then she was out on the street and I saw a car parked outside with a man inside, a man I didn't recognise, and it took a long, clogged-up moment for me to realise that he was waiting for Ruby. He was big and he had a few days' worth of stubble on his face, but you couldn't tell if it was because of fashion or sloth.

He reached across, pulled a handle and kicked open the passenger door. He was a man and not a boy and my daughter was sixteen years old. And I didn't know where they were going, and I didn't know who he was, this bloody guy, and it felt like there was so much that I didn't know. In fact I felt as though I knew nothing of the world, apart from the fact that my daughter found it unbearable to be in the house that she grew up in.

'Please, Ruby,' I said, 'stay home.'

I was begging now, happy to beg, no pride left, ready to try anything. But she ignored me, or she didn't care, and the stubbly man gave me this smug leer as Ruby slid in beside him.

The door slammed shut and the car pulled quickly away, and I stood there for a long time, even after the brake lights had blinked once and the car turned a corner and they were gone.

Rufus was standing in the doorway. He was dressed in his suit and tie, ready for a night in the supermarket. I put my hand on his shoulder, and his long, gangly limbs seemed reassuringly familiar.

'Let me have a word with your mum,' I said. 'And I'll get the bus with you.'

He looked sheepish. 'But, Dad,' he said, 'I've already got a ride.'

And then I noticed the other car. A baby-blue Mini with dents all over it. The car of a driver who was both careless and unlucky. The shoplifting redhead was sitting at the wheel, scrutinising her blowsy features in the mirror on the back of the sun shade. There was a child seat in the back, but there was no ginger-nut little thug sitting in it. He was probably out mugging old ladies. It was still quite early.

Lara came to the door and we watched them drive away. 'Did you notice?' Lara said. 'He didn't even put on his seat belt.'

'Try to make a U-turn . . . try to make a U-turn . . .'

There's something wrong with this sat nav, I thought.

The unfamiliar streets of the Elephant and Castle drifted by my window, jumbled and drab, and the posh lady on the sat nav kept trying to get me to turn around and go in another direction. But I was sure I was heading the right way. I was sure that this was the place.

'If possible, try to make a U-turn.'

My father's Ford Capri felt heavy and unfamiliar and sheered from time. The sat nav gave the old banger a veneer of modernity but there was no power steering and hardly any brakes. It was possible that I had missed my destination, distracted by the sheer effort of driving this knackered old motor.

And then I saw her. Right in front of me. The girl. I slammed my right foot down hard on the faint-hearted brakes, and the Capri came to a screaming halt inches from the girl.

She turned to look at me, her face so pale and pinched it looked as though it had never seen sunlight. She stuck up two fingers.

'*You have arrived,*' sighed the lady of the sat nav, washing her hands of me.

The address I was looking for was at the top of a low-rise block of council flats. It was a still day, but the wind seemed to whistle down the long walkways. Four blocks of flats faced a common square that was crowded with children, cars, overflowing recycling bins. The block was only five stories high and there was no lift. I took a breath and started climbing.

Everywhere there was music and television and voices. Laughing, threatening, pleading. The smell of food and urine and pets. The sense of lives lived piled on top of each other. I passed an old lady on the stairs and we politely said good morning to each other. At the top floor I stopped and wondered what I was doing. And then I went to the last flat at the end of the walkway and rang the doorbell.

Nobody answered.

I felt relieved, and exhaled a long sigh of nerves and looked out at the city stretching off below me. I turned away just as three young men stepped on to the walkway, one white, one black, one brown. They looked like a Benetton commercial of petty criminals. They were walking next to each other and I had to press myself against the wall to let them pass.

And then I saw him.

And he saw me.

The boy from the back seat of Keith's car.

And before I knew what was happening, he had slammed me up against some poor bugger's window and he had the blade of a carpet cutter resting on my right eyelid. His face was so close that I could smell the lager and Lynx body spray.

'What do you want?' he said.

'I just want to talk about your brother,' I said.

He took the blade from my eye.

'My brother?' he said.

Then there were shouts from below and his friends were off and running. But there was nowhere to run to, and they scuttled from one end of the walkway and then back the other way, straight into the waiting arms of a dozen or so coppers in uniform. They were up against the wall when the red-haired lad in a suit and tie appeared, an inspector, smiling as if he was among old friends. He nodded at me.

'You can sling your hook,' he said, but I just stood there, unsure what was happening. He looked affronted when I did not move. 'Go back to your life while you have the chance,' he said, green eyes blazing. 'God has thrown another log on your fire.'

I just stared at him, not breathing. He got in my face.

'Move!' he said.

I moved.

seventeen

By now the big houses were all empty.

The rest of London remained, sweating it out on the underground and the steaming streets, but from The Bishops Avenue to Prince Albert Road, and out west to Holland Park and Richmond, most of the houses with swimming pools had been abandoned for the summer. Even the help was gone, packed off to the old country or attending to their employers in some sunny corner of the globe. It was the best time, a peaceful time. With a gaoler's bunch of carefully labelled keys, I let myself into the garden of the big house in Highgate and you would not believe that a city could be so still.

My body was tanned and hard. I felt lighter, stronger than I ever remembered, as I pulled off my shirt and set up my service tools and chemicals. I knelt by the pool, watching the flow of the water for a few minutes. And then I went to work.

Winston trusted me to do even the bigger jobs alone now, and I moved easily through my tasks. Cleaning the skimmer basket. Checking the water temperature with a floating thermometer. Rigging up the vacuum hose and sliding it into the pool. I was skimming the surface with the leaf rake, listening to the silent hum of summer in all those abandoned gardens, when Winston came through the back gate, holding a propane gas cylinder like it was a baby. He came over to the pool and set it down.

'Treat this stuff with respect,' he said, nodding at the propane. 'It's heavier than air. So if it flood a burner tray without being ignited, then it just sit on the bottom of the heater. You can't smell it because it just sit there. It don't float out, see? So if you put your face by the opening, trying to work out what wrong, and then it ignite – *boom*.' He smiled happily. 'It blow your head off.'

'I'll be careful,' I promised.

Winston nodded, satisfied that he would not be fishing my head out of a swimming pool, and picked up the gas cylinder. Then he stared thoughtfully at the untouched perfection of the water.

'Everybody be coming home soon,' he said.

He made it sound like a bad thing.

And then there was a man.

I should have seen that coming. How could I have missed that? With our marriage in limbo, it had never crossed my mind that Lara was going to meet a man.

I watched her as she stood in the doorway of the school hall, and one by one the girls filed out in their tutus and their trainers to where the grown-ups were waiting.

I stood with them, the mums and the au pairs and baby-sitters and a surprising number of dads, until the last of the girls had been collected, and then I slipped into the hall. There was a young woman covering the piano and I waited until she had gone before I went across to Lara. She was sitting on the steps to the stage, massaging her right side, and I gave her the shoebox I had brought with me. 'You're right,' she said. 'I've been thinking. And you are right.'

I looked at the shoebox in her arms. But she didn't open it.

'I don't want to swim with dolphins or argue with philosophers or understand the secret of the universe,' she said. 'But I do want to go back to work. I want another chance.'

I looked around the school hall. 'You're already working,' I said, wishing she would open that box.

'I mean *dance*,' she said. 'On stage. Professionally. Do what I was trained to do.' We could hear the cries of the little girls getting changed. 'I love my kids. But I mean . . .' She smiled at me, her eyes shining with excitement. 'Getting another go . . .'

'Open the box,' I said.

And she did. It looked like a random collection of photographs. Holiday snaps, school pictures, photo-booth mucking about. But it was more than that. It was the story of Lara and me; it was the history of our family. She held up a picture of Ruby, aged eight, smiling a gap-toothed smile. Red school jumper, grey dress, white shirt. The smile splitting her face in two with gummy delight. We laughed together, remembering her at that age, dumbfounded that the little girl in the picture had once existed. Then Lara put the picture back in the box, and I felt my spirits slide. This wasn't what I had hoped for.

'Martin said –'

'Who's Martin?'

She shot me a look. 'Just a friend.'

'A friend? A friend? What – a man friend? A friend with a penis, is he?'

I grabbed her left hand and she let me. It was still there, her wedding ring, the reflection of the ring I wore on the third finger of my own left hand. But for the first time I saw that the ring could remain there even as the marriage was fading.

Lara sighed. 'He's just a friend. The father of one of my girls. A single dad. He may have a penis. I don't know. I suppose it's possible.'

'A single dad? What kind of man becomes a single dad?'

'I don't know,' Lara said. 'A good one?'

'A good one? You don't know the wife's story. Let's hear the wife's side before we start deciding that this guy is Nelson bloody Mandela.'

Lara shook her head.

'I haven't had sex with him or anything,' she said, and I shrugged as if that wasn't the issue, while inwardly exhaling a sigh of infinite and eternal relief. If she had not had sex with him, then we still had a chance.

'Can't you think about anything else?' Lara said, as if she could read my dirty little mind, and I happily chomped on the bait.

'Yes, one minute you're just good friends and the next minute he's sending you saucy text messages and giving you Al Green compilations. One minute you're just good friends and the next he's got you bent over the dishwasher and he's taking you roughly from behind. I know exactly how the friendship thing works.'

Lara stood up. 'You are completely out of line,' she said. 'Just because you're too immature to be friends with anyone who doesn't look like bloody Keith, that doesn't mean every other man is the same.'

I stood up with her, the desperation rising. 'Don't you like the photographs?' I said.

'Lovely,' she said.

'Keep them,' I said.

'Thanks.' But she was mad at me. I knew that I should shut my cakehole. Then I opened it again.

'Is he better than me?' I said. 'Just tell me that and I'll shut up about it.'

She put her hands on her hips. 'What's that mean, George? Better than you? A better human being? Better in bed? Why don't you ask him?'

And there he was, right on cue, looking through the glass window of the door, grinning bashfully as he raised a hand in salute to Lara.

She strode over and let him in and a bundle of pink nylon and blonde curls burst into the hall ahead of him. A girl, about five, wearing her tutu and trainers with flashing lights in the soles.

And then he came in – a big man in a business suit. Cresting forty, I guessed, just like Lara. He looked as though he had played some sport in his youth. He looked as though he still did.

Lara brought him across to meet me. 'Martin, this is George, my husband,' she said.

'Hi,' I said, shaking his hand. 'I'm George. Her husband. We're married. What is it, Lara – twenty years now?'

But it didn't even make him blink. Why should it? They were just friends.

And as I watched him – one eye always on his little girl even as we were shaking hands, making sure his daughter did not stray too close to the edge of the stage, someone clearly put on this earth to protect and provide – I could see the appeal.

I knew nothing of the man.

But I could see he was no spring chicken.

The new security guy watched me as I hovered by the wine rack, visibly tensing every time I picked up a bottle to look at the label. He was a Middle Eastern kid who looked as though he had been in the job for a week, and it had been a hard week. Perhaps there was a gang of hardened Chardonnay thieves operating in the area.

A man in a crumpled suit and tie came quickly down the aisle and it took me a long moment to realise that it was my son.

'I'll be ten minutes, Dad,' he said, and he touched fists with the store detective. 'You had your break yet, Jamal? Go for your break when you get a quiet minute.'

It wasn't just the clothes. Rufus had put on some weight. The extreme thinness of youth had gone. And there was something about his hair. There seemed to be much less of it. Was it just his junior management short back and sides? He couldn't be going bald, could he? He had only just started shaving.

A couple of black teenagers came into the supermarket and Jamal immediately went off to tail them. Rufus was out on the street where a lorry the size of the *Titanic* was making a delivery. I was holding a nice bottle of Estonian white when Rufus came back up the aisle.

'Nancy prefers red,' he said. 'I'll be out the back. Come through if you like.'

I obediently put the bottle back. Mustn't upset the great dictator, I thought. I found a decent bottle of Latvian red and when I had paid for it I went through the long thick plastic strips that separated the supermarket from the storage area. It was much colder back here, but Rufus had taken off his suit jacket and rolled up his sleeves. And he had done this fussy little old man thing with his tie, tucking it inside his shirt to protect it.

He stood in front of a huge pile of food – fruit, vegetables, bread, muffins, croissants, pancakes, cakes – holding what looked like some sort of aerosol spray. He aimed the aerosol at a loaf of sliced white bread and squirted blue ink all over it.

'Did you get red?' he asked me, not turning round.

And I laughed. I saw it, but I didn't quite believe it.

'What are you doing?'

He carefully squirted blue ink over a stack of bagels. 'All this stuff is past its sell-by date,' he said, as if that was any kind of explanation. 'But we can't just throw away food.' Squirt, squirt. A few almond croissants went to meet their maker. 'People might take it out of the bins.'

I shook my head in disgust. 'What? You mean hungry people? Poor people? Homeless people? People like that?'

'Any kind of people. People who are not actually paying for the stuff.'

'Yeah, that would be awful, wouldn't it?'

'I don't make the rules.' He gave a helpless shrug. 'I know, Dad. It's a complete waste. But what can I do? It's company policy.'

'You're just obeying orders, right?'

He looked at me and sighed. There was blue paint on his hands.

'Can't you sell it at a knock-down price?' I asked. 'To customers? Or staff? Or just give it away?'

'Who should we give it to, Dad?'

'I don't know. Some poor bugger who is starving in the

Third World. Some poor bugger who is hungry in Crouch End.'

'Too complicated,' he said, squirting blue ink on some chocolate muffins. 'And probably a violation of health and safety rules. We'd get sued.'

'It's not complicated at all,' I said. I picked up a bagel that he had missed and took a bite out of it. Tasted fine.

'If you can't sell this food, then let's work out how we can get it to people who are hungry. I mean it, Rufus. This is madness.'

He wearily ran a hand across his forehead. 'Just doing my job, Dad. What else can I do?'

'Refuse to do it,' I said. 'Make a stand.'

'I can't,' he said. 'I'm too busy making a living.' He handed his spray can to a small girl in a Muslim headdress. 'Finish this off for me, will you, Sophia?'

I watched him unrolling his shirt sleeves, putting on his jacket, taking his tie back out. I didn't want to fight with him. I wanted anything but that. Still I needed him to tell me that he understood. This was all wrong.

'A mad world, isn't it?' I said, as we went back out through the plastic flaps. 'Half the planet going hungry, and the other half squirting raisin pancakes with blue ink.'

He didn't look at me. 'I just work here,' he said.

Nancy and her son lived in a two-bedroom flat in Finsbury Park, one of those crumbling Victorian buildings where the welcome mat is hidden under takeaway menus, junk mail and letters for tenants long gone. Music seemed to be coming from a dozen places at once. The smell of yesterday's kebab hung in the air. A tube train rattled from somewhere deep below the building. Lara had told me that Rufus was spending more and more time here. It was as though he had already moved out.

As soon as Rufus let us into the first-floor flat it was clear that there was a problem with Nancy. She didn't want to be kissed by Rufus and mumbled a reluctant hello to me, although she claimed my bottle of wine quick enough. She said she had been expecting us earlier and the takeaway pizza she'd had delivered was already cold. As she moved away with little Alfie buzzing around her bare legs, demanding pizza and attention, Rufus placed an apologetic kiss on the back of her head and I saw the swell of her belly.

Alfie was laughing with joy. And I could not take my eyes from my son, who was grinning at me, as pleased with himself as the cat who brings home a half-dead sparrow. I wanted to grab him and escape from Finsbury Park, run down the stairs and jump on the back of the first bus to anywhere, and reclaim his life, and spare him from the next fifty years.

But I didn't.

I just looked at my boy and I wanted to weep.

Again my eyes drifted to his hair. He really seemed to be losing it, that thick yellow hair that had been shorn in the interests of company policy. His hairline was already receding faster than his dreams. Or perhaps he had different dreams now.

But it wasn't possible. I was seeing things. I had to be. My son losing his hair, his older girlfriend getting pregnant. This couldn't happen yet. It was all too soon. I was seeing into the future. This was how things would be, if I failed to act. Then a chicken nugget hit me right between the eyes. And I wondered why I hadn't seen that coming.

Nancy, the homemaker, was in the coffin-sized kitchen, sawing up the takeaway pizza as her brat whined under her feet. Beyond the prettiness, she was such an ordinary thing, such a graceless, short-tempered lump, and so totally unworthy of my smart, beautiful, funny, stupid boy.

'You could have any woman you want,' I said.

He was laying the cutlery on a miserable little table.

'Don't try to live your life through me,' he said. 'Just because you've messed up your own.'

'Why not? Isn't that what every parent does? Oh, Rufus – you could have had anyone . . .'

He looked up at me, a Disneyland knife and fork in his hand.

'I want her,' he said. 'I want Nancy. Can't you be happy for me?'

I glanced towards the kitchen.

'Don't think so,' I said.

I took my place at the dining-room table, and it was like sinking into a shallow grave. Alfie joined us, his filthy fingers falling on the pizza like vultures on roadkill. More chicken nuggets flew through the air, as thick as arrows at Agincourt.

'Oh, don't you bloody start,' Nancy told him.

It was her wisest advice. Don't start. She staggered around the rickety table, glumly parcelling out the Texas BBQ pizza, the slices of pepperoni curled with time, and she glared at the child as if she was already weighed down by the next one. 'Don't start!' she cried.

Too late, I thought.

The first thing you noticed about the prison were the women and children. Hordes of them. Teenage mums with babes in arms and middle-aged mums with teenagers hauled from school to pay a visit to their father. And then there were the mums in the middle, neither young nor old, but already trailing children who were almost fully grown and ready to have children of their own. In their arms they carried packets of cigarettes and biscuits. The guards lumbered around them, as patient as shepherds.

I had been to prisons. Lots of them. But I had never had to join the queue before. I had never been processed. I had always been let inside with the wave of a card and a smile. I had never passed through all the checks, and felt the doors closing behind me, and time drag, and the walls closing in. By the time I made it to the visiting room, he was waiting for me, ready to talk, knowing long before me that we would only be doing this once.

'We didn't know our mum,' he said. 'She went. She walked. Too much for her. Never any money because our old man liked the horses. Another man, maybe. I don't know. But our dad, he looked after us. All of us. Four boys and six girls with just our dad looking after us. That was unusual back then. Still is, I suppose. And then he died. Our dad. At thirty-nine. Heart attack. Just conked out in a betting shop, collecting his winnings. I used to think that was quite old. Not a bad innings. But as I get older, I see that it was no age at all.' Then he laughed. 'But you want to talk about Frank.'

He handed me a photograph. A good-looking young man giving the thumbs up. He looked like he was at a party, a bit drunk, but happy.

His brother grinned at me. Frank grinned at me.

We meet at last, I thought.

'We were too young to look after ourselves. Frank was the oldest and he was only thirteen. And so we went into care. And I know you hear a lot of stories about care, and

I reckon most of them are true, but it wasn't like that for us. Because we had each other. And we had my brother.'

'Your brother,' I said, 'Frank – he did this incredible thing. He saved so many lives.' I held up the photograph. 'Can I keep this?'

'No,' he said, taking it back. I watched him slip it inside his shirt and waited. He looked around the visiting room and sighed.

'Our dad was a smoker,' he said. 'And a drinker. And I reckon his diet tended towards the unhealthy end of British cuisine, know what I mean? And his heart was not so good. But – here's the thing – they reckon he would have made it if there had been a donor. I don't know. Maybe it's true. That's what my brother always said. But that's why he had the card – the little blue card with the red heart.'

I wanted to know about Frank's family. I thought perhaps I could help them in some way. Or at least tell them that I would always be grateful. And the brother told me there was a woman and a baby somewhere, but he wasn't interested in that, or he didn't care.

Yet he wanted me to understand.

'My brother – he was a rogue. A thief. Frank was a very bad boy indeed. But he took care of us. And that would have been enough for me. But then he did this one good thing for other people, people he would never know, and it made up for all the bad stuff. He found it in himself – because of our old man, because of this father he had to honour – to do this one good thing for other people. My brother – he was a kid from care. People looked down on him all his life. We got free meals at school – any idea what that's like?' His hard eyes glittered at the memory of free school meals, and all the rest. 'But he did this one

212

good thing – and that makes him a better man than you'll ever be.'

I nodded, and smiled, and stood up. It was time to join the queue of women and children waiting to be let out. It was time to go home.

'A better man than both of us,' I said.

eighteen

I was waiting for him when he came out of work.

I was loitering by the front doors of the supermarket, ignoring the dirty looks of the store detective, as a lorry-load of cheap beer was being unloaded. Bloody cheek, I thought. I don't want your gnats'-piss lager. I want my son back.

'Dad,' Rufus said, and I looked at his shabby suit and his thinning hair and I felt like crying. He looked older than me.

'Here,' I said, stuffing the envelope in his hand. 'Just take it and go.' I gave him a gentle shove. 'Go tonight. Go now.'

He looked at the envelope in his hand. It said Flight Centre on the front, and there was a drawing of a jumbo taking off into the wild blue yonder. We stepped aside to let a pallet of poor boy's brew pass by.

'What is it?' he said.

'A present,' I said. 'A ticket to Bangkok.'

He looked at me. 'What's in Bangkok?'

'Everything,' I said. 'Travel. Adventure. Escape.'

'Why would I want to escape?'

I looked at him to see if he was serious. When I saw that he was, I took him gently by the arm. We began walking to the tube station.

'The flight is in three hours,' I said, glancing at my watch. 'You get the tube to Paddington and then the airport express to Heathrow.'

He stopped, that slow smile spreading across his face. I recognised that unhurried, measured grin. I had been looking at it all his life. He was still my boy. That's why I couldn't let him do it. That's why I couldn't let him throw it all away. I still recognised him as the child I had loved.

'I'm not going to Bangkok,' he said, not moving. 'There's nothing in Bangkok for me.'

He held out the Flight Centre envelope. I didn't take it.

'There's life in Bangkok,' I said. 'You don't have to stay in the city. Get a plane to one of the islands. Go up north.' I began rummaging in my pockets for the remains of my money. 'I don't have much,' I said.

'I don't want your money,' he said, not smiling now. 'And I don't want to go to Bangkok or anywhere else. My life is here.'

He pressed the envelope against my chest. I could feel the scar throbbing angrily against it. I took the envelope.

'What's wrong with you people?' I said. 'I mean – really? What is wrong with you?'

'Who are you talking about, Dad?'

'Your mother. Your sister. You. It's like you're all – I don't know – asleep or something.'

He was looking back at the lorry parked outside the supermarket. They were taking in the last of the gnats'-piss on wooden pallets. Gin alley was stocked for another twenty-four hours. A diesel engine thundered into life.

'You think I'm asleep, Dad?' he said.

I shook my head. 'Not you,' I said. 'I think you're in a coma.'

He looked at me with the sting in his eyes. He was so easy to hurt, that boy. I didn't know how he was going to last for thirty minutes in the life he was creating for himself, and it broke me up.

'Just leave me alone,' he said, his voice breaking. 'I mean it. Stay away from me.'

Then he was gone, and I called his name a couple of times but he didn't look back. So I took a few quick paces and I threw the ticket to Bangkok at the back of his shabby suit with all my might. It fluttered unwanted into the grey North London gutter. Then I laughed out loud. I had offered him the chance to be in Bangkok tomorrow night with a cold Singha beer in his hand. And what had he chosen instead?

So stupid, I thought.

So stupid, the lot of you.

It was more like a cathedral than a swimming pool.

We stood at what would once have been the shallow end and stared down at the empty pool. The six lanes fell away gently and then suddenly steeply, like an ocean bed, until they would have been higher than a man at the deep end. There was a niche with a small bronze fountain at the shallow end, and on its tiles an engraving of a mermaid cavorting with a couple of dolphins. Winston crouched down and ran a loving hand along the edge of the mermaid's face.

'Look at that,' he said. 'White Sicilian marble, that is.' He stood up and nodded at the walls. 'Them, too. Those Victorians knew what they were doing.'

The walls curved up to a ceiling full of skylights, and as the sun blazed through the glass and struck the white marble it made the old public baths look like a railway station in heaven. At the deep end, there was some kind of crest on the wall, and a lion and a unicorn held each other as if fighting, or dancing.

'They built this place in the good old days,' Winston said. 'When someone thought the working man should have nice things too.'

A few men in hard hats brushed past us, carrying tools and speaking Polish. We watched them jump into the pool. One of them swung a sledgehammer, and struck the tile, as if testing it. It smashed with a sound like breaking glass. We could hear the rumble of demolition outside, voices raised above the drone of machines.

'What are they doing with it?' I said.

Winston laughed. 'Luxury residential development,' he said. 'And without you and me, their cappuccino machines will be underwater by Christmas.' He slapped me on the back. 'Know how to find the plumbing ports for the main drain, do you?'

I nodded. 'You showed me.'

Winston looked pleased. 'Watch one, do one, teach one,' he said. 'Just like doctors.'

He climbed down the ladder into the pool and approached the men with their sledgehammers. The smashed tiles around their boots looked like broken teeth. Winston held up his hands and they stared at him.

'Not until I say so, friend,' he said, raising his voice as if it might help with translation.

I went to look for the plumbing ports to the main drain as the place began to fill. Men in suits. Women from the council with clipboards. More builders. They all wore hard hats, apart from us.

Suddenly there was a sound like gunfire and I looked up to see a large crack appear in the far wall. The crack split the crest with the lion and the unicorn down the middle, and they seemed to fall apart, the long dance over as the crack became wider, and then the wall abruptly caved in, kicking up a cloud of ancient dust and making everyone in the room take a step back, covering their faces against the grey cloud. Beyond the broken wall you could see a bulldozer, and daylight, and the men in their hard hats.

And we all stopped what we were doing and just stood watching as the marble wall came down and the new world came crashing in, and I could taste the grit in the back of my throat, and I could feel it in my eyes.

The woman who opened the door was clearly Larry's mother.

Tall, on the heavy side, with a face that radiated concern and kindness. She stood in the doorway staring at me with my flowers in one hand and my bottle of wine in the other. The thoughtful guest who did not know that dinner had been cancelled. The kids looked over their grandmother's shoulder, red-eyed from crying.

'Someone should have called you,' the old lady said.

Geoff and Paul were standing outside the ward.

We hugged each other awkwardly, the embrace of men who had nothing much in common apart from the man who was inside, lying in a hospital bed.

'What happened?' I said.

'They think it's chronic rejection,' Geoff said. 'They don't know yet.'

'How long has it been for him?'

'Five years,' Paul said.

'So,' said Geoff. 'It's time.'

I went inside. In the dull light, I could see that Larry was sleeping. So was his wife. Molly was sitting by the bed, holding his hand. There was a plaster on his neck where they had inserted a catheter tube for his latest biopsy. He'd probably had dozens by now, all these procedures to remove another tiny piece of his heart. And now his body, and his borrowed heart, had just had enough.

Molly stirred and looked at me.

'I'll sit with him,' I told her. 'Go home to your kids for a while.'

And so I sat with my friend. Geoff and Paul joined me, but after an hour or so they drifted off. There is only so much bad tea you can drink, only so much hospital time you can kill. It was right that they went. I was the only one with nobody waiting for me.

Five years, I thought. Then it was time. The coronary arteries carrying blood around the new heart had been thickening and narrowing for years. Larry would have had regular angiography, X-ray examinations of the blood vessels, and he probably even had a good idea that this was about to happen. And Larry was a success story.

He had avoided the skin and lymph gland cancers that come as a side order with many transplants – the onion rings of heart-replacement surgery. He had lived with the drugs. He had even helped others. He had helped me.

What was happening to him now was just something

that was very possible after years of living with a borrowed heart. All the things that can go wrong, I thought. You can't even think about all the things that can go wrong, else you would go nuts. And yet I couldn't stop thinking about them.

I must have slept because I was suddenly jolted upright by the sound of his voice.

'Ah,' he said. 'I've had my time.'

'Do you want me to give you a slap?'

He laughed. 'Ever make one of those lists, George? One of those bucket lists?'

'What's a bucket list when it's at home?'

'A list of all the things you want to do,' Larry said, 'before you kick the bucket.'

'Can't say I did.'

'Me neither.' He was quiet for a bit. I suppose it was late now. We could hear those night sounds of a hospital outside his room. 'The reason I never made one is that all the stuff I wanted was right in front of me.' His big face was smiling. 'You know, the ordinary stuff. To watch my kids grow up. To grow old with my wife. To be a family until my children had families of their own.'

'No skydiving?' I said. 'No climbing Everest? You call that a bucket list?'

He laughed.

'Enough for me,' he said, and he arched his back, settled on the bed with a sigh, and I could sense the pain. I asked him if there was anything I could get him.

There was nothing I could get him.

'Lara?' he said. 'The kids?'

'All fine,' I said.

And I saw now that I had let them all down. There were

no excuses. I hadn't been enough of a father, enough of a husband, enough of a man. My wife. My son. My daughter. I had lost them all because I deserved to lose them. I had gone my own way. First as George the cop. And then as George the man in search of life. And it had left me alone. How could I deny that they were all better off without me?

'Promise me you'll enjoy every sandwich,' he said, his eyes closed now.

'As long as it doesn't include hospital food,' I said.

He smiled, and then after a while his breathing changed, and I knew he was sleeping. Not proper sleep. Medicated sleep. Hospital sleep. And I slept too, sitting in the chair by the side of his bed. Another poor imitation of sleep. Junk sleep. But it must have lasted for a few hours, because the next time I bolted awake it was almost morning, with the birds going barmy and light creeping into the room.

I looked at my friend's face and it seemed set. I swallowed hard, stood up and looked more closely. His face had settled into an expression that I had never seen before, that I had never seen in life.

I reached for the metal box with the button to call the nurse and then suddenly he stirred, moaning from somewhere deep inside his medicated sleep, and I put down the metal box.

There was a dead man in that room. There was a man overwhelmed by the way his life had got away from him. There was a man so marinated in despair that it choked him.

But it wasn't Larry.

I walked to the far end of the platform and stood with my back pressed against the wall. The first train would be here soon.

It was empty at that end apart from a middle-aged couple. The type of people who walk to the far end of the underground platform to escape the craziness of the city. And who can blame them? Certainly not me, I thought, as I pressed harder against the wall. They watched me out of the corner of their eye for a while and then, as unobtrusively as they could, began to move slowly back down the platform, away from me, and closer to the normal people, and closer to the yellow lights that picked out the destination of the next train.

BAKER STREET – ONE MINUTE, it said.

I took three easy steps and suddenly there I was, right at the edge of the platform, looking down at the furious movement among the black tracks. Rats, I thought, just as the rush of wind and noise came pouring out of the tunnel.

I looked into the darkness but I could see nothing. Yet the noise was getting louder, the wind stronger. My scar began to throb. I swallowed and lifted my gaze from the tracks to the advertising on the far side. *The Best a Man Can Get*, it said, and I realised I never knew what was actually being advertised these days.

The noise in my head got louder. The wind grew stronger. I sensed the awful movement down on the tracks.

And then the phone in my jeans began to vibrate. That was strange. That was impossible. I should have been beyond all signals down here.

And less than an hour later I was at the wheel of the Ford Capri. Trying to get the hang of the manual gearbox as I negotiated the traffic in Hackney.

My mum spotted him. 'There he is,' she said, the relief all clogged up with something else, and she began to call his name. And there he was. My father, still in his pyjamas and dressing gown and slippers, standing outside a Victorian terrace where curious dark faces watched him from a crumbling bay window. I pulled the Capri up behind an overflowing skip and walked up to him.

'Bertie's in there,' he said. 'I want to see Bertie.'

It was the old house. He got that bit right. I remembered coming here as a kid. Until I was about five, and my grandmother died, and the council took it back.

This was the old neighbourhood, although I could not believe that the old neighbourhood really existed any more. But my dad thought differently. To him, this was still the old neighbourhood. But Bertie was the older brother who had died on a Normandy beach more than sixty years ago, and the faces at the window were laughing at my dad. They were only kids. They didn't know any better. I would have laughed myself at that age.

My mum put her arm around my dad's shoulders and gently tried to lead him away. But he didn't want to go. He wanted to see his brother. My mum gave him a kiss on his unshaven cheek. I think she may have laughed.

And I took my father's hand.

nineteen

It was not a good place to be buried. Is there such a thing as a good place to be buried? I think there is – but this wasn't one of them.

The flyover swept over one corner of the graveyard and any chance of peaceful contemplation of eternity was shattered by the roar of lorries rushing their heavy loads to the M25. And it went on forever, this gigantic field of headstones in fifty shades of white, like the cemetery of some forgotten war.

I thought it would take me a while to find his grave. Because it wasn't a new grave, with freshly dug topsoil, waiting conveniently at the end of a line. It is easy to find new graves. But he had been here a while now, his last resting place surrounded by headstones that were as alike as snowflakes.

Except Frank Twist's grave was different from the rest. I saw it instantly.

It was the one with all the flowers.

I made my way towards it, and as I got closer I saw that

the flowers were fresh and they were dying and they were everywhere in between. The flowers on his grave looked like something from a natural history programme, where the camera fast-forwards through the mortal span of some living thing. Before my eyes, they bloomed and faded and withered and died and fell to dust. Flowers from service stations and flowers from high-end florists and wild flowers too. I cleared away some of the oldest bouquets and placed my small tribute against his headstone.

Frank Twist
1988–2007
Our beloved brother

I felt like I should do something more. Say a prayer. Stay a while. Or at least feel something more than the numb self-consciousness that I felt standing at his grave.

But here's the thing – I wasn't the only one. As I stood at the graveside I could feel them coming from every corner of the cemetery. There were so many who were in his debt, and some of them were coming now, to lay their grateful flowers.

Not a Frankenstein, but an angel.

And so I gave my own silent thanks to this man I would never know, and I went back to my life, and the air was full of diesel fumes and flowers.

There was a white picket fence running around the pool with a wooden gate that flapped in the summer breeze. Winston poked it with the toe of his boot.

'Look at that,' he said, and I had never heard him sound so disgusted. He knelt down by the gate and when he stood up he was holding a rusty, broken lock in his hand. Behind us we could hear laughter coming out of the open windows, and the sound of corks popping. 'House worth millions and they can't spend a couple of quid on a decent lock,' Winston said.

A man came quickly across the lawn, trying not to spill his drink. People were coming home now, coming home from all over the world. The man was tanned and well fed. My age, but from a different kind of life. He wanted to get rid of us before his party began. The pool guys. He didn't realise that we weren't pool guys. We were water technicians.

'Are you going to be much longer?' he asked Winston. And then, as if remembering his manners, he quickly added: 'The pool looks bloody great, mate.'

And it did look good. Like a sheet of turquoise glass shot with gold. Not a leaf in sight, I thought proudly.

Guests were spilling out of the house. Thin hard women and their larger, softer menfolk. Above their chatter I could hear a baby crying.

'You have children in the house?' Winston said.

'Only Tarquin,' the man said, looking back at the house.

'Can the boy swim?' Winston said.

'He's only one,' the man said, wondering what any of this had to do with his party. More guests were coming out of the house and the help was moving among them. Filipinas in black dresses carrying trays of drinks and canapés, East European nannies trying to herd the children that frolicked around them.

Winston handed the man the broken lock and he took it with the hand that wasn't holding his drink. 'Then we get this sorted out before we go,' Winston said. He turned to me. 'In the back of the van there's a box of Chubb locks. Bring me one, will you?'

The man attempted a smile. I could tell he wanted to get shot of us. 'I don't want to put you to any trouble,' he said.

'No trouble, man,' Winston said.

He made one last try to get us off the premises before his winging began.

'Really,' he said. 'It's not your job.'

Winston shot him a look.

'Believe me,' he said. 'It's our job.'

I answered the phone on the third ring, suddenly awake, and there she was, unchanged, as she had been long ago.

'Daddy?' she said, and the voice was so small and frightened that I remembered a four-year-old child at the dentist, a little shining-eyed girl who had refused to drink anything but apple juice when she was a toddler, and now had cavities in her two back teeth. When you have loved them from day one, somewhere in your heart they never grow up.

'Can you come and get me?' Ruby said.

'Yes,' I said, sitting up in bed, groping for the clock. It was past three in the morning, and I felt my stomach fall away. 'What's wrong?'

She didn't reply. I could hear a rushing sound. This constant noise and then a big rush. And I realised that she was running taps, and flushing a toilet, and trying not to be heard by anyone but me.

'Can you just come and get me?'

'Of course, angel.' Fully awake now, tucking the phone between my shoulder and ear as I pulled my jeans on. She said something but her voice had dropped to a whisper.

'Speak up a bit, Ruby.'

'I have to keep my voice down.'

I could feel the panic flying. 'What's going on? Where are you? What's wrong?'

'Have you got a pen, Daddy?'

'Just tell me where you are. I don't need a pen.'

She told me. And then there was a banging on her locked door. And a man's voice.

Then the line went dead.

My father was shuffling out of the bathroom as I came down the hall.

'Didn't wake you up, did I?' he said.

'You didn't wake me, Dad.'

'I was just having a pee. Unfortunately that seems to take about fifty minutes these days. Sometimes I have a little rest in the middle. Have a cup of tea and a biscuit. Like half-time.'

He followed me downstairs and into the kitchen. He sat down at the table, as if settling for a chat.

'I have to go out,' I said, snatching up my keys. 'I can't talk now.'

He looked me up and down as if twigging that I was fully dressed. 'Which one is it?' he said.

I turned and looked at him. 'Ruby,' I said. 'She's – I don't know. There's some sort of trouble. I'm going to get her.'

'I'll come with you,' he said.

'Not necessary,' I said. 'But thanks.'

'Drive you there,' he said. 'In the Capri. Or were you going to get your bike out and pedal?'

And so he came with me.

He went up to his bedroom and I could hear him talking to my mum, and when he came back down he had a

228

tracksuit pulled over his pyjamas. A swatch of old-fashioned striped jims-jams stuck out of his sleeve as he drove us from the suburbs to the city and across the river, peering out of his windscreen as if looking through thick fog, though the night was as clear as glass. I was happy there was no traffic.

We were silent, apart from when I gave him the address and he slowly punched it into his sat nav. The woman's robot voice directed us to a square in New Cross. The lights were on in a first-floor flat. The windows were open and music was coming out. Hateful music. Pimp this and bitch that and look at the size of my Mercedes Benz.

'What a bloody racket,' said my dad.

'That's Fifty Pence,' I said.

'About what it's worth,' my dad said. 'With inflation. How we getting in there?'

'I thought we might knock. Ring the bell. What was your plan? Kick the door down?'

'It wouldn't be the first time.'

We both got out of the Capri. I saw there was no point in trying to stop him coming in with me. And the truth was, I felt relieved to have him by my side. Even if he was an old man who clearly had his stripy pyjamas on under his tracksuit. Because my dad was scared of nothing.

I pressed the buzzer for Flat 2 and the front door opened without protest. There were drifts of junk mail shoved up against the wall. The place had the flaking, neglected look of rented property. We went up a ramshackle flight of stairs and knocked. Nothing happened. I knocked harder. And then I kept on knocking until the door was opened by an unshaven, blurry-looking man in his twenties. The guy from the car. He looked bigger standing up.

'I'm here to collect my daughter,' I said, and that struck him as funny.

He led the way into the flat. My dad followed me and I could hear him coughing behind me. The air was thick with the sickly sweet fug of cigarettes and spliff.

Into another room. Three other men. I was expecting boys. But these were men. One of them was rolling a joint and the other two were playing a video game on a big flat-screen TV. Cities on fire. Robot soldiers moving through the flames, blasting everything that moved. And where was Ruby?

'He's here for his daughter,' the man announced, and they all got a good laugh out of that. They thought that was hilarious. The one rolling the spliff, a fat skinhead, looked up at me.

'Which one is she, mate?' he said.

'He's not your fucking mate,' my father said, and they all laughed again.

But not so loud.

My dad brushed past me and took the spliff out of the fat skin's hand. He looked at it for a moment and then crushed it in an overflowing ashtray.

'Stunt your growth,' he said.

He knew how to do it – how to control a room. How to walk into somewhere and get a bunch of strangers to pay attention. He could still do it. But he was old now, and getting sick. And we were outnumbered.

'Dad's army,' said the one who had let us in.

'Yeah,' said the fat skinhead, staring at my dad. I could see that he was going to be the one. You can always tell who is going to be the one. He was not smiling now. They all stood up. 'Upstairs,' he said. How big was this place? The skinhead nodded at a spiral staircase.

'After you, fat man,' said my dad.

They all looked at my dad for a while. And then the four of them started up the winding stairs. We followed them.

Ruby and another girl were sitting close together on a sofa. Ruby looked at me and her grandfather and then at the carpet. The other girl was quietly crying.

'Let's go,' I said.

Nothing happened.

The fat skinhead perched on the end of the sofa, and draped a bare, beefy arm across the back. He was one of those guys who do a lot of weights at the gym and feel they have to wear a sleeveless shirt. And I saw the fear in Ruby's eyes.

'You all right, angel?' I said, and she nodded quickly. She made no attempt to move.

'She's all right,' said the fat skinhead.

'He didn't ask you, fat man,' my dad said.

The fat skinhead stood up. 'Granddad,' he said, 'you're really starting to wind me up. You know you're trespassing, don't you? The law would call you a burglar.'

'I am the law,' said my dad, and I might have smiled if I hadn't been so scared.

'No one's keeping them here,' said the one who had answered the door, the stubble-chops from the car. And I saw that, despite his size, he was one of nature's vicious weeds, the type that always attaches itself to the local bully. He was dangerous because he would go along with anything. But he wouldn't make the first move. I looked into the eyes of the fat skinhead.

'Let's go now,' I said, not taking my eyes off him, not looking at the girls.

And still nothing happened.

'They can go whenever they want,' he said, the voice of reason. He frowned at them. 'Do you want to go?' he demanded.

I stared at Ruby. She was looking at the ground.

'I don't know,' she said.

'She doesn't know,' one of the men chortled.

I went across to the sofa and took my daughter's hand. And I also took the hand of the other girl, who I recognised from the school, and playdates when they were both very young.

'We're leaving right now,' I said, and made for the staircase. My dad stood to one side to let us pass. The men exchanged looks. But then we were going down the stairs, the girls ahead of me, and my dad close behind. I could hear voices, and then men talking among themselves, and then they all piled down the stairs, and I knew that this was it.

'Naughty, naughty,' said the fat skinhead, and I turned to look at him as he came towards me.

'We were just having a party,' one of the men said.

I stopped, and stood there not moving, just waiting. My dad and the girls kept going. I heard the flat door opening, quick footsteps on the stairs. I didn't take my eyes from the fat skinhead standing in front of me.

'Party's over,' I said, and when he lunged forward I took the handgun out of my jacket pocket and shoved it into his fat ugly face.

'Relax,' he said. 'Everybody relax.'

'That's my daughter,' I said, and my voice was shaking, everything was shaking, and I could not stop it now. 'And if you ever go anywhere near her again I will kill you dead and they can lock me up and I will still be glad I did it. Do we understand each other?'

He nodded politely, his hands in the air. 'No problem,' he said. 'That's all cool.'

I turned to go. And I should have just gone. But then I couldn't stop myself from turning back, and raising my weapon. They all curled up in terror, crouching on the floor with their hands in the air. I pushed the barrel of the gun into the fat skinhead's ear. The room was silent apart from their whimpers and the sound of the fat skinhead urinating on the carpet. Then I pulled the trigger. I pulled the trigger of Rainbow Ron's gun. There was a metallic click, but it wasn't like the sound of a firing pin striking the chamber of a real weapon. It was the sound of a toy.

'Bang, bang,' I said. 'You're dead.'

Then I was off, slipping the fake gun back into my pocket. I could hear the fat skinhead's friends laughing at him. But he didn't find it funny. He caught me at the top of the stairs, the wet stain still spreading on his trousers.

'Hey, pops,' he said, 'let me tell you all about your little girl.'

But that was all he got out, because I dug my big toes into the ancient carpet and dropped my shoulder as I brought a right uppercut into his abdomen, then threw a left hook to his jaw which broke with a surprisingly loud crack. As he was dropping, I drove a right cross into his face with all my weight behind it, and even though he was falling away from me I felt the teeth as they shattered against my knuckles. He went down the stairs like an overweight stuntman, coming to a halt where my father and the girls were waiting.

'When did you learn to box?' my father asked me.

'I don't know,' I said, my heart pounding.

It was still dark when we got her home.

Lara was waiting at the window, every light in the house on, and the door was already open as we came up the path. Lara reached out for Ruby, but she walked straight past her.

The three of us watched her slowly climb the stairs, and I had that old feeling from around ten years ago, the feeling I had when she dashed into a road without looking, or danced on a coffee table covered with glasses, or reached out for a lit candle, or dangled upside down from a climbing frame until her face turned scarlet – that parental feeling you get when your kid just about gets away with some act of childish madness, a trembling rage mixed with a relief that is so overwhelming you don't know whether to cry or scream.

'She's okay,' I said to Lara. 'Just leave her for a bit.'

She looked at me and my dad and shook her head. My hair was all over the place. I was holding my hand where the skin had torn on my knuckles. My father patted her shoulder and chuckled, as if to say, *Kids, eh?*

'You're bleeding,' she said.

'I'm fine,' I said.

She started to babble a bit. 'But where was she? What happened? Should you call the station, get someone to come out?'

I looked at my old man and smiled. *I am the law.*

'I mean real policemen,' Lara said, deflating us a bit, 'not you two.'

'She's all right,' I said. 'She was frightened for a while, but she's all right now. I promise you.'

Lara looked upstairs and we could hear Ruby clumping around in her room. And I saw it all well up in her – the relief and the strain, the stress of being the only parent in the house. Every line in her face seemed to tighten with it all.

'That little . . .'

I touched her arm, and she looked at me.

'She's just young,' I said. 'I think it's just that, Lara.'

We went into the kitchen and Lara made tea. After a bit, we left my dad and went upstairs. The door to Ruby's bedroom was closed. The DO NOT DISTURB sign still hung from the doorknob. Lara knocked softly and went inside without waiting. I stood in the doorway, watching her.

The curtains were drawn and Ruby was buried deep inside her bed, the duvet pulled up so high that only a tuft of brown hair was sticking out. For the first time I noticed she had blonde highlights. Lara touched the tuft of hair, and then she gently kissed it, and then she sat there for a while as if not quite knowing what to do. Ruby did not move, but I don't think she was sleeping.

So we went downstairs and made more tea, and some toast. Ruby's favourite. Thick sliced white bread, lavishly buttered, and strong tea with one heaped spoonful of brown sugar and just a dash of semi-skimmed milk. That's the way we all drank it in our family. Builder's tea, Lara called it.

Lara put it all on a pink tray, a relic from our daughter's childhood, and I followed her as she carried it upstairs. She didn't knock this time, just quietly opened the door, put the tray on the floor and left. She looked like a warden feeding her prisoner, and for some reason that made me choke up. Perhaps it was just exhaustion. I watched Lara gently close the door behind her. I thought that perhaps Ruby was sleeping now.

But later, when it was starting to get light and it was time for my dad and me to go, I went upstairs and the pink tray was sitting outside Ruby's bedroom door. The DO NOT DISTURB sign was still in place, but the tea and the toast had gone.

twenty

As Jazzie B sang about the Africa Centre being the centre of the world, I sipped champagne from a paper cup and felt my body start to sway to Soul II Soul. I made a vow to not get drunk. Not tonight. Not on Lara's fortieth birthday. Then the DJ put on some early Duran Duran, and my body stopped moving. So I couldn't have been that drunk.

They had let her have the school hall where she taught dance. I would have thought it was way too big, this great assembly hall in an inner-city comprehensive, but the place was full. Because they all came. All the friends that she had drifted away from, or who had drifted away from her, as the years and partners and children got in the way. But they were here tonight, and as they filled the floor to the sounds of the eighties, I remembered many of them from way back at the start, all these dancers in their twenties who would go from *Les Misérables* to the Africa Centre and keep on dancing. They were middle-aged women now, but there was still something about the way they moved to Blondie, Wham!, Madonna, Michael Jackson and the Thompson Twins – a strange and inexplicable passion of Lara's, the Thompson Twins – you could see that they still had it in their blood. Their husbands, knocking on a bit now, struggled to keep up, the way I had struggled to keep up. Lara was in the middle of them, dancing with her daughter, and shouting something up at the DJ on the stage.

'"Girls Just Want to Have Fun"!' she shouted, and he nodded. He got it. A request. The Style Council somehow segued into the exultant opening of the Cyndi Lauper classic. I went to check on my parents.

They were on the far side of the throng, watching the action. My mum was smiling and tapping her foot to 'Girls Just Want to Have Fun'. My dad was thoughtful, an unopened can of Red Stripe in his hand, flinching a bit at the volume. Nan was with them, sipping a sherry that she had already made last for two hours, and nodding her head as if she had always considered this to be Cyndi Lauper's finest moment. The three of them sat on their rickety school chairs, forming a little ghetto of old people, and I asked them if I could get them a drink. But they were all fine. 'Don't worry,' my mum said. 'You go and enjoy yourself, love.'

And I thought that maybe she was right. I could have a few more drinks without the risk of running amok. Maybe I could even go and have a dance. Perhaps I should wait for a bit of danceable music to come on – New Order, Yazoo, Divine, I wasn't fussy – and get out there. Throw some shapes, as my daughter would say. I watched her laughing with her mother, the pair of them shining with sweat and punching the air to some prehistoric Kylie.

On my way to the bar – a wooden table more used to serving tea and biscuits at PTA meetings – I came across

Rufus, Alfie in his arms, jogging up and down on the spot, the carrot-haired kid laughing hysterically. Nancy stood next to them, but lost in another world, watching the dancing. Her little black dress was like a second skin, and she gnawed at her bottom lip and clutched her handbag in both hands, as if uncertain whether she should have a dance or go home. I could see the gentle swell of her belly clearly now. Keith walked by, glanced longingly at Nancy's rear, and kept walking, his eyebrows raised. He found me at the bar, putting on my dancing shoes with Red Bull and vodka.

'Got some ID, sonny?' he said, slapping me on the back. He got a beer and turned to face the dance floor, but his eyes drifted back to Nancy's rear end.

'The kid's probably having the best sex of his life,' he said philosophically.

'That's what I'm afraid of,' I said.

Keith sighed and raised his beer can. We clinked drinks. 'The eighties,' he said. 'The decade that taste forgot. Or was that the seventies? Or the sixties?'

I shook my head. I couldn't remember. But as 'Material Girl' gave way to 'How Soon Is Now?' I thought, But it's always good, isn't it? When you're young. How could it be anything but good?

Then Martin turned up. All self-effacing and handsome, hovering in the doorway, dressed in a striped shirt and black jeans, like a banker on the first day of the weekend. Lara spotted him and came through the dancing mob to get him, her face all wet and happy. And she did this thing to him – this little peck on the lips, a kiss that seemed more about reassurance than passion. She took his hand. I looked away, sinking my drink, choking it all down. The loss. The jealousy.

The thought of her with another man. It was a sickening lump of gristle that I had to fight to hold down. It was as real as that.

'She looks great,' Keith said.

'Yeah,' I said, wondering how long before I could decently go home.

At first Martin played it beautifully. He was taken to the centre of the throng to meet Lara's oldest and dearest friends – all those girls who'd played peasants and prostitutes in *Les Mis* twenty years ago – but it was difficult to talk out there, or even to hear someone's name. So Lara dragged Martin to the bar – they were holding hands all this time – with a few happy forty-something women in tow. Martin looked at me and smiled. I nodded, and twisted my mouth into this stiff rictus grin, and moved away as slowly as I could without breaking into a trot. And I saw how far from the shore we had let our marriage drift.

Lara's friends screamed when the Human League's 'Don't You Want Me?' came on, and they bopped back to the centre of the dance floor where their husbands – mostly city guys who had been real studs two decades back – were gasping for breath and holding their tickers. But Lara led Martin around the fringes of the party to meet the old folks. Nan was all smiles, nodding happily as Lara made the introductions, then over the heads of the dancers I saw the utter confusion on the faces of my mum and dad as Martin stooped his large frame to shake their hands. But they were decent people, and easily won over with a bit of prefabricated charm, and soon they were smiling along with Martin and Lara, the happy couple.

I turned to go. I was determined that I wasn't going to look back. But Soul II Soul's 'Back to Life' came on as I got to the door – Caron Wheeler with the voice of a lovesick angel – and I couldn't stop myself. And as I turned I saw Lara trying to lead Martin to the dance floor. And I saw him refusing. I mean, really refusing. Shaking his head and lifting a protesting hand, and all the while this embarrassed smile. The man meant it. He wasn't going to dance. Lara danced with her nan instead. She slowly led the old lady to the floor where they gently swayed from side to side to something by Spandau Ballet, holding hands all the while, and Martin stood on the sidelines with his petrified grin.

And so I knew he had no chance.

Time was away and somewhere else as I busied myself in the kitchen, making myself a nice cup of builder's tea. Strong. One sugar. A dash of semi-skimmed – just a dash. And drink it while it's hot. Builder's tea. The way we all drink it in my family.

It was very late now, so late that very soon it would be early, and as I moved around the darkened kitchen of the old house, I could feel more than hear that it was almost empty.

Rufus had gone home with Nancy and her boy. Ruby had gone home with her grandparents. There was only Lara and Martin in the house, asleep in what I could remember an estate agent once calling the master bedroom.

And me, of course. Down in the kitchen with my builder's tea. Watching the windows for the first sign of the new day, and seeing nothing. The nights were getting longer now.

Then they must have heard me. I heard footsteps on their floor – my ceiling. Whispered, urgent voices. One of them – Martin – going into Rufus' room and rummaging for a weapon. A baseball bat banged on the floor like a wooden leg. Then Lara's soft footsteps coming downstairs. She was wearing a simple silk kimono over pyjamas. I can't tell you how relieved that made me feel. I was afraid she might be in some kind of sex wear. Dressed like a – but I don't even want to think about it. She stopped breathing when she saw me.

'I want to come home,' I whispered.

She was standing in the doorway. 'Maybe you should call first,' she said quietly, shaking her head. 'This is a bit on the creepy side.'

'Sorry,' I said. 'I was trying to keep the noise down.' I lifted my mug of builder's tea in salute and apology.

'Martin has called the police,' she said, folding her arms across her chest. She still hadn't come into the kitchen. She nodded at my tea. 'If you drink quickly, you might just have time to finish it before they get here.' She had been speaking in a stage whisper, but now the volume was rising. 'You bloody maniac,' she said. 'Breaking and entering in the middle of the night.'

'I had to tell you. About the coming home thing.'

'Right now? Right this very minute?'

'Because soon it will be too late. If you let this guy get between us. Great party, by the way. Happy birthday.'

She came slowly into the kitchen and sat down at the table. 'It's not my birthday any more,' she said, running a hand across her face. 'Forty. How did that happen?' I sat down at the far end of the table. Our old places. I smiled at her and she shook her head again. 'Can't you see how weird this is?'

'But the thing is – you chose me. And I chose you.'

'A long time ago.'

'Nothing has changed,' I said. 'You're still my North Star.

You're the light that I follow. It doesn't make sense without you. None of it.'

She looked up, as if something had suddenly occurred to her. 'Are you on drugs?'

'I just had to tell you, Lara. Not that man. Please – if you're going to dump me, dump me for a guy who will dance.'

Martin came into the kitchen in his pants. He had a great body, actually. If I had a body like that, I would probably walk about in my pants. With my sophisticated radar for violence, I immediately noticed that he wasn't carrying a baseball bat. Just his BlackBerry. You could take someone's eye out with one of those things. I suspected that he had been sitting on the stairs listening to us. In his pants. It's a difficult look to pull off.

'The police are on their way,' he said, and just at that moment I heard the siren. I wondered if it was for us. Impressive response time, I thought. 'Kick him out,' Martin demanded. 'Kick him out or I'll do it myself.'

Lara looked at the table.

'Just . . . leave him alone, will you?' she said.

Martin's jaw dropped. His good teeth glinted in the fading moonlight. 'You're not listening to his bullshit, are you?' he said. 'Because I'm not listening to it.' And then he looked at me for the first time. 'You've been making her life a misery for years. With your cigarettes and your selfishness and your scrotum-hugging jeans.'

I looked at Lara accusingly. She looked away.

'Oh yes, I've heard all about you,' Martin continued triumphantly. 'And I know exactly what you need.'

He went back upstairs to get his baseball bat.

We watched him walk from the kitchen.

'You have to go,' she said. 'The police will arrest you. And he will hurt you. And – and I want you to go.'

'Do you?'

'Yes, I do,' she said, as if this was her final decision. She placed her hands on the kitchen table. 'We all have to move on, George. We all have to start over.'

'But I can't,' I said. 'And I don't want to. Because it is you. And it is you if we are together or if we're apart.'

'A bit awkward, that,' Lara said, her voice a little softer than before. 'A bit awkward about it being me, if we are together or apart.'

'You can see the problem,' I said.

'Absolutely,' she said.

'I know you're not the best-looking woman in the world,' I said.

'And you were doing so well,' she said.

'But there's no face on the planet that I would rather look at,' I said.

'You haven't seen them all.'

'Enough to know,' I said. 'Enough to know the face that I will be thinking of when I take my last breath.'

Martin came back into the kitchen. I had expected him to be holding a baseball bat above his head, but he was unarmed. Maybe he thought that he would be the one to get nicked if he hit my head for a home run. He was probably right. Then he looked about, and snatched up a frying pan.

'Get out,' he said, more confident now he was armed with a cooking implement. 'Get out or I'll mess you up so bad you'll never be the same again.'

I stood up but made no move for the door. He edged towards me, the frying pan twitching above his head. He stole a quick glance at Lara.

'How did he get in here anyway?' he said. 'The long-haired freak.'

And I could hear our siren now. It was just a few streets away. An eight-, nine-minute response time. Not bad. They were coming for me.

But Lara was smiling. Now she was standing too.

'He has the key,' she said. 'He's always had the key.'

I took it out of my pocket and placed it on the table. 'You can have it back, if you like,' I said. 'But I love you, Lara.' I held up a hand. 'You don't have to say it back.'

And then he hit me with the frying pan.

I saw it coming from a mile away. He made the classic mistake of bringing his arm way back before he swung. He practically sent me an email. He wasn't used to hitting people. I caught the blow on my forearm and I would have happily given him a bunch of fives in the cakehole if Lara's voice had not stopped me.

'Please, just go,' she said.

I looked at him and he looked at me. He was still holding the frying pan. I couldn't tell if he was planning to hit me again or rustle up some breakfast. Neither of us moved. Outside, a bird began to sing. We looked at Lara.

'Both of you,' she said.

There was a time, not so very long ago, when I could sleep through the day. It was lovely. My mum would sing and do her work and my dad would grumble over his chores and the sun would shine beyond my blackout curtains and none of it would disturb those long happy hours of oblivion.

But now I lay in my single bed, turning over my pillow a hundred times, emptying my washing-machine mind of all thought, and still sleep would not come. I felt the bone-deep weariness of my body, and craved rest, almost wept for the lost land of nod, yet still I remained bobbing above the surface of consciousness. Where does it go? This glorious ability to sleep your life away?

I saw that we can only do it when we think we have all the time in the world. But now I saw time running out on me, time having enough of me, and I knew I would never sleep like that again. It was lost to me, the blissful oblivion of youth, and I would never get it back.

So I rose from my bed and began pulling on yesterday's clothes, and in the room next door I heard the slow, unsteady footsteps of my father.

There were kids playing football in the park.

Mostly boys, but there was a girl in an England shirt on one team. Skinny, tall, brown hair tied back. She was nobody's kid sister, and just as good as the lads, stiff-arming a tackler away as she turned from facing her own goal and hoofed the ball upfield.

I watched them for a bit, amazed as always that among that riot of replica shirts, they still knew which side they were on. Then there was an overstruck cross and suddenly the ball was coming out of the sun, flying towards me.

I fixed my eyes on it, steadying myself, and when I swung my right foot, the ball connecting sweetly with my instep, I felt a pop of sudden pain in my knee. The ball flew back to them but the pain stayed behind, hissing beneath my kneecap, and I hopped with alarm, afraid to put my right foot back on the ground.

They stood watching me. Their game had stopped. The girl in the England shirt was holding the ball.

'You all right, mister?' she said.

I nodded and smiled and gave them a cheery thumbs up. They went back to their game, their shouts and cries following me as I hobbled from the park, trying to walk it off.

At first I thought it was a dipping crew.

I heard footsteps on the grass and then in the gravel that bordered the pool, footsteps treading softly, trying not to wake the house. I lay in my bed not breathing, staring at the ceiling and waiting for the splash of bodies slipping quietly into the water.

Instead something hit my bedroom window.

It was small and hard, like the first hailstone of a summer storm. Then it happened again, and I leapt from my bed and moved quickly to the window.

I pulled back the blackout curtains just in time to see Lara throw another stone at my window. This one missed. She had a handful of gravel, scooped up from the side of the pool, and she stood on tiptoes every time she lobbed another one. I lifted my window and a small stone immediately hit me in the eye.

'Fuck,' I said, staggering backwards, my palm slapped against my wounded eye. A few more tiny rocks landed in my bedroom as I grovelled on the carpet. Then they stopped. When I went back to the window she was looking up at me. My eye was already getting better. I could almost see out of it. Lara put a finger to her lips, and glanced at the window next to mine, where my parents were sleeping.

'What time is it?' I said, a hoarse stage whisper.

'Time to come home,' she said. A more natural voice than my own, but very quiet, and meant just for me. Then she smiled, and let the gravel slip through her fingers. 'Our kid is going to have a kid,' she said, and laughed, as though it was a miracle. And it was – one of those everyday kind of miracles that are the most impossible of all.

'Does that mean we're getting old?' I said.

'It means we're alive,' she said. 'Don't you know the secret of life yet? With all your books and your thinking and your staring at the stars? Don't you know the secret of life yet?'

I looked up at the sky. The stars were not out. There was just the orange glow that hung over the city at night like a dome. Then I looked back at Lara and waited.

'The secret of life,' she said, 'is more life. Are you coming or what?'

'What about that guy? Did you have sex with that guy?'

What I was hoping for was the news that my unexpected visit had interrupted the bastard's coitus. What I was hoping for was the breaking news that no man had touched her. But she did not have the time for any post-match analysis of the past. And, if you want to know what I think, I don't believe they did anything. She was here, wasn't she? She wasn't with him. She was in the garden.

'I'm lonely,' she said. 'I miss you. Come home.'

'I'll get my things.'

She bridled with the first flash of irritation, and I saw that you can love someone, truly love them, and they can still get on your nerves. And I saw it cut both ways. The petty chores of daily life were still out there. I hadn't escaped them. They hadn't gone away. If I went back, the broken boiler would be waiting in ambush for me, somewhere down the road.

'Don't worry about your bloody things,' Lara said impatiently. 'Don't you know how late it is?'

Then I thought I saw something stir in the shadows behind her. Was this the dipping crew at last? Lara looked over her shoulder and stared into the trees at the end of the garden.

'What is it?' she said.

I watched the dancing shadows. But I couldn't see anything. It was probably just the wind, and my imagination, and my torn retina.

'Nothing,' I said. 'Don't move.'

I quickly pulled on some clothes and headed for the door, and then stopped and looked back at my bedroom. The scattered clothes. The CDs left out of their jewel boxes, abandoned like yesterday's toys. The books with their passages dramatically underlined. The curling remains of my take-away pizza. A half-drunk bottle of cider.

And the weird thing is, I don't even like cider.

Then I turned my back on all these things and I ran to my wife.

part three

the dipping crew

twenty-one

'There are your default dreams and then there are your other dreams,' she said, just as I was sleeping. 'The default dreams are what everyone wants – your children to be with someone who will make them happy. Your parents to stay healthy. The money worries to go away.'

I struggled above the surface of sleep, more conscious of her physical presence than her words. It was strange and right to share a bed with Lara again. There was a dislocated normality about being by her side – like the way you feel when you awake from a bad dream, or when you get out of hospital. It's as though your life can begin again, and something that was lost has been restored.

I was more than ready for my sleep. That happy exhaustion was upon me, the kind you only get after sex with someone who you have loved for a lifetime. But she kept talking, and I could tell that it was one of the things I was going to have to get used to now I no longer slept alone. I had forgotten Lara did that – liked to talk after sex, liked to talk when I was aching for my kip. But it wasn't like before, and it wasn't as I thought it would be. She didn't want to talk about proper jobs and pension plans. All that had slipped her mind. Her head was somewhere else now.

'You don't have to think about the default dreams,' she said. 'They take care of themselves. Or they don't. But you have to think about the other ones. The dreams beyond the default dreams.' Then she paused. 'Can you hear that?'

In the city silence of our room we could hear the boiler wheezing and spluttering in the bathroom next door.

'It's going to blow,' I said, and I thought – plumbers. Money. The hell of Yellow Pages.

'No,' she said. 'It will wait until it gets a lot colder before it goes. That's what it does.'

We listened to it gasping and clicking for a while. And we laughed in the darkness. The decrepit boiler would not be amusing on the bleak winter day it decided to pack up. But it was funny now.

'I am never going back,' I said. 'To my old job.'

'I guessed that,' she said, and I saw her smile. 'We'll be fine. We can sell the house. Downsize. Now there's only three of us.'

'I never wanted us to have to sell the house,' I said.

'There are more important things,' she said.

We lay there for a while, listening to the boiler.

'It's called a bucket list,' I said. 'The things you want to do before – you know.'

'Before you fall off your perch,' Lara said.

'Before you kick the bucket,' I said. 'It's called your bucket list.'

'Drive through Paris in an open-top sports car,' Lara said. 'Dance again on a West End stage and get paid for it.

Go to the slums of Buenos Aires and see where the tango began.'

I thought that maybe you could drive through Paris in an open-top sports car and just get stuck in the traffic on the Champs Élysées. Or you could be in a musical on Shaftesbury Avenue and the people wouldn't come and the critics would be cruel. But I knew she would go to Buenos Aires one day. Lara had been dreaming of that for twenty years, long before either of us had ever heard of a bucket list, or ever thought we might need one.

I could hear it when she slept.

It was there in a catch of her breath, a shift in her body weight, a sigh that came from somewhere deep in her sleep. The sound of the pain.

It had been there for almost as long as I had known her, as inseparable from Lara as the colour of her eyes. The old injuries, the aches and pains that she carried with her like a birthmark, the wounds that had been left after the wounds were healed. Those souvenirs of her dancing days.

Some of the pain was as specific as a page torn from an ancient diary – the cruciate ligament repaired at the Wellington Hospital, the torn cartilages that accounted for the bumps of scar tissue she carried on both her knees – but some of it was wrapped in mystery, and put down to wear and tear, and never even thought about.

She didn't complain. She wasn't the type. And I had grown accustomed to the sight of her massaging herself, her fingers digging into the area behind her knee, or the spot where her rib cage met her hip, as she drank her morning coffee or watched TV or got undressed for bed. In a marriage you learn to look straight at things – and never see them.

It was different at night, as she slept by my side, and I felt her shift or stir with some nameless hurt. The pain never seemed to wake her. But it woke me, and on that first night home I lay next to my wife for hours, my eyes wide open in the darkness, the way we only do with our newly born and beloved.

Just listening to the sound of her breathing.

There is only one house in the world where you can walk in and go straight to the fridge, and that is the place you grew up in.

We didn't ask Rufus what was wrong. Suddenly he was there in the hallway, grunting a sheepish greeting, and we followed him into the kitchen. He took a carton of full-fat out of the fridge and chugged it down, standing there with the door open, his tie dangling around his neck like a wonky hangman's noose. Lara stood on tiptoe and kissed his cheek, livid with shaving rash, and she gently closed the fridge door. I hugged him and it was still like embracing a bag of bones, despite the business suit from Next.

'So how are you?' he said, and I laughed, because I always found it funny when my children attempted to make small talk.

'I'm fine,' I said. 'How you doing?'

'I'm all right,' he said, scowling. 'Why wouldn't I be?'

'No reason,' I said mildly, not rising to the bait. I worked it out in my head. There was less than a month till his wedding. His mother offered to make him something, grabbing his belt and shaking it, indicating that he was too thin. He laughed and moved away from her, clutching his carton of full-fat, telling her he wasn't hungry. He was an assistant manager now, and almost a married man, and he wasn't used to having someone grab his belt and shake it. I felt like doing something to him too – maybe ruffling his hair, or slapping him on the back, or lightly punching his arm. Anything for some physical contact with my son. But he was an assistant manager now, and almost a married man, and there were black rings under his eyes. So I didn't touch him. I didn't want to violate the terms of our awkward hugging convention.

The three of us went into the living room. The TV was on. We fell into our historic armchairs and corners of the sofa and Rufus reached for the remote, flicking through the channels until he saw Gene Kelly and Donald O'Connor tap-dancing and playing the violin at the same time.

'*Singin' in the Rain*,' Lara said, touching Rufus on the arm. 'Don't turn it off.'

He reluctantly put down the remote and leaned back, staring at the ceiling with a slow exhalation of breath. It was like hearing someone let go of their youth. Lara looked at me without expression and then she turned back to the film.

Debbie Reynolds was jumping out of a cake at a Hollywood party. She looked shocked when she saw Gene Kelly. She had told him she worked in the theatre, and here she was jumping out of a cake in her underwear, the little liar. Lara laughed and Rufus looked at the screen and I saw a flicker of recognition on his face. 'How many times have we seen this?'

His mother didn't look at him. 'You can never see *Singin' in the Rain* too many times,' she said. I tried to work out what was so different about him. His hair was cut so short. He looked as though he was in the army or something. We did not say anything for a while. When Donald O'Connor

257

was doing, 'Make 'Em Laugh' – dancing on his knees, defying gravity, walking into walls – I looked at my boy's face. He was almost smiling. That scene used to make him fall off the sofa. I suppose he was a lot younger then.

'How do you even know if you are with the right person?' he said, not looking at us. I thought about it. You just knew, didn't you? If you had doubts, then you were not with the right person. But I did not want to tell him that.

'It's like believing in anything else,' Lara said. 'It's an act of faith.'

'But do you think people can stay together these days?' he said, still watching the screen as Gene Kelly tried to win back Debbie Reynolds. 'Not just – you know. Go their own way after a few years. Do you think that two people can stay together forever these days?'

'I think it gets harder,' Lara said. 'But I still believe.'

We watched the film for a while. There were footsteps on the stairs and Ruby came into the room and said, 'Hey you,' to her brother. She sat on the arm of the sofa next to him. I went off to make four mugs of builder's tea and when I came back Gene Kelly and Debbie Reynolds were singing, with Gene dressed as a thirties tennis player and Debbie standing on an inexplicable ladder.

Ruby laughed shortly. 'Is your ladder really necessary?' she said. But she flopped down next to her brother and he put his arm around her.

And Gene Kelly fell in love with Debbie Reynolds. Kelly sang and danced in the rain. In a dream he met Cyd Charisse, a gangster's moll in a green dress who in the end leaves him for a silver dollar, and nobody ever danced like that before or since.

'Cyd Charisse,' Ruby said. 'Your favourite.'

'That's right,' Lara said. 'My all-time favourite.'

'I might stay overnight, Mum,' Rufus said. 'Is that all right?'

I thought, Stay for the next ten years if you like. Stay forever. But I knew he wouldn't – I knew that he couldn't – not with a baby on the way. Our son wasn't that type, the type who stays away when there is a baby, and that was one of the reasons I loved him.

'Stay as long as you like,' Lara said.

He didn't even stay for the night.

Autumn had blown in now and many pools were being closed down for the winter months. I had thought that September would mean less work for Winston and me, but our workload actually increased as the days got shorter.

'You can't just cover them up,' he told me, as we pulled into the crunchy gravel driveway of a big house in Richmond. There had been a BMW X5 parked outside for weeks. 'The end of summer is the hardest time of all.'

Winston produced his huge gaoler's bunch of keys, and let us into the garden by the side gate. There was a scattering of leaves over the pool. It still looked impossibly blue, even in the tired sunlight. From a house nearby I could hear a Beach Boys' song, but it seemed all wrong, like a Christmas tree on New Year's Day.

Winston fished the leaves out as I super-chlorinated the water – Winston favoured a triple dose – because any dirt or debris would leave stains and be much harder to remove when spring came around. We coated the metal ladders with petroleum jelly to stop corrosion and covered the diving board. I watched Winston use the garden hose to squirt a little water into a dozen plastic milk bottles.

He tossed them on to the surface of the water. I hadn't seen that before.

'That way if the water freezes the ice will crush the milk cartons,' he said, 'and not the walls of the pool.' A gap-toothed smile. 'You want to cover the pool?'

I nodded and walked across to the small shed in the corner of the garden. Inside were the gas-fuelled heater and the pool's control panel.

I hit the button for the cover and stepped outside to watch it slowly unfurl from the deep end. The Pacific Ocean blue began to disappear under a white metallic cover etched with rust. In less than a minute the water was gone, and it was as if it had never been there at all.

As we were leaving, the family arrived home in a black cab, a man and a woman and a teenage boy, and we helped them get their suitcases out of the cab and into the house. Up in his room, the kid put on some music and the silence of the house was broken. The man wanted to give us money but Winston wouldn't take it, and the woman wanted to give us tea but there was no milk in the house.

So we said goodbye and left them, tanned and shivering in their summer clothes, dressed all wrong for London at this time of year, but happy to be home.

The queue started at the stage door and ran a hundred metres down Shaftesbury Avenue. Tourists and office workers gawped at the long line of men and women, most of them very young, some of them alarmingly attractive, but the dancers did not seem to notice.

I realised with a jolt that this was probably the exact spot where we had met, and I was smiling and just about to mention it to Lara when word came down the line.

'They're looking for six and six,' said the young woman in front of us, and Lara told me that meant they were going to hire six male dancers and six female dancers. 'Six boys and six girls,' Lara said. There were no men and women in the chorus line. Only boys and girls.

'What are they looking for?' said the boy behind us, and he really was a boy, a few years younger than Rufus. Lara said, 'Six and six,' and he excitedly passed it on.

Lara clutched my arm and smiled. 'It all comes back to me now,' she said, and we turned and looked at the queue, which was growing by the minute: that long line of lean, aching, pain-racked bodies now stretched halfway down Shaftesbury Avenue. Her eyes were shining with it all.

The anticipation of a job, the raw excitement of standing in the street with a hundred other dancers, but also the hedging of bets, the preparation for rejection, the expectation of failure – just to draw some of its sting. The girl in front of us began stretching.

'What is it anyway?' she sniffed. 'Yet another Sherlock Holmes musical. Not the one that closed after a few months. The other one. The one that closed after a week. The one with the exclamation mark.'

'That's right,' Lara said. 'I was in it.'

The girl looked blank. Then she looked at Lara more closely and perhaps believed her. What's twenty years when you're still a teenager? A lifetime.

When we were inside I hung at the back of the auditorium. The place seemed to be made of worn red velvet. There was one man sitting alone at the front of the stalls. He was a well-preserved old gentleman in dark glasses, like a rock star at sixty. When Lara came on to the stage with fifty other dancers I felt a shiver of fear and pride. A woman was on

261

stage with them. Thin as a whippet, bossy as a prison guard. Clapping her hands, getting them into line, giving them impatient instructions. The music started.

They danced. The woman kept barking at them. She didn't stop. They followed her drill. Fluid movement to mechanical orders. Everybody looked incredible to me. They seemed to obey the choreographer without having to think about it. And then they all stood there, soaked in sweat, shoulders heaving with diaphragm-filling breaths, as the woman went down into the stalls to talk to the man who sat all alone in that red velvet auditorium. I saw the fingers of Lara's right hand flutter to the pain in her right hip, and then fall to her side. When the woman came back on stage she moved through the lines, touching shoulders and saying, 'Thank you.'

Those she touched left the stage quickly and without a word.

But Lara was still standing there.

Larry had lost weight.

A face-changing, shape-shifting amount of weight. His clothes hung on him like a collapsed circus tent, his favourite green Lacoste shirt sagging to reveal a pencil-length of scar on his chest. His wife was going to have to make him get a new wardrobe.

But he looked good – better than I had ever seen him. He was going to die one day, but that was something that he shared with everyone else on the planet, so I couldn't let that get me down.

I looked at him and smiled. Sometimes you look at an old friend and just the fact that they are still here can stab you with happiness. That was how I felt about Larry.

We were in the hall above the florist's shop. My eyes

drifted to the rain pitter-pattering on the window. One floor below there was nobody at the tables and chairs of the cafés on Hampstead High Street, and I realised that somehow the season had changed when I wasn't looking.

A new guy was on his feet, his hands rolling around each other, as if he was washing them. He wasn't that old – somewhere in his thirties, I guessed – but he looked dangerously overweight.

'I put on all this weight after the operation,' he said, hands wringing. Larry – the changed Larry – was smiling encouragement. 'They told me that the steroids would pile on the pounds, but I don't understand why all the exercise I'm doing isn't having any effect. My wife is worried that I am . . .'

His voice trailed away. We knew what his wife was worried about.

'That's normal,' said Geoff, his arms folded across his chest. 'Your new heart is without a nerve supply for the first year, so it responds much more slowly than you would expect to exercise.'

The new guy looked at Geoff. 'I didn't know that,' he said.

Geoff smiled encouragement. 'Don't worry too much about it,' he said. 'It gets better.'

Larry crossed the room and embraced the new guy, and thanked him for sharing.

Then it was time for our prayer. I stood and reached out my hands, and they were taken by Paul on one side and Geoff on the other. We closed our eyes and bowed our heads. It was a real prayer, you see.

'We are grateful to our families for their support,' said Larry. 'We are grateful for the gift of life. We are grateful for the skill of our doctors. And we are grateful to the donors who made it possible.'

God knows I was grateful for all those things. But, still, I thought that maybe I would skip next week's meeting. It was different now that I was back at home.

I wouldn't feel guilty about not turning up. Our meetings were well attended now, with as many regulars as Narcotics Anonymous and Belly Dancing for Beginners put together. And I had never really taken to the whole hug-a-stranger thing.

It had taken me long enough to learn how to put my arms around my own family.

I thought it was going to be the two of us. My son and I. But it was never going to be just the two of us ever again.

The black cab pulled up outside the main entrance to Selfridge's and I saw that Nancy and Alfie were with him in the back. And I thought, Couldn't they get the bus? Does my son work so hard just so she can ride in cabs?

Alfie got out first, and I said, 'Hello, Alfie,' and he stared at me blankly. Then his mother emerged, an emphatically pregnant thing easing herself on to the pavement, giving me a brittle little smile even as she gave instructions to Rufus. He was still in the back seat, slipping some notes through the glass to the driver, and I instinctively reached for the money in my back pocket. But he'd already taken care of it.

I stood with Nancy and Alfie as she chastised her son for his latest infraction. And as the great mass of humanity on Oxford Street flowed around us, I thought to myself, Who are these people? Rufus joined us. We didn't hug – Nancy was between us. We went inside.

'Don't start,' Nancy told Alfie, but unfortunately he did

start, and he didn't stop. He clearly did not wish to be in Selfridge's. There was a toy hammer sticking out of the back pocket of his jeans and a plastic spanner sellotaped behind his ear.

'I've got lots of jobs for you to do in my house,' I said cheerfully, and he frowned at me with suspicion.

Nancy had a list. The thing that Rufus and I had planned to buy was not on her list, and I was hoping that she might give my son an hour off for good behaviour. But no. We tagged meekly along as Nancy unsmilingly made her way through the clothes for expectant mothers, the children's department and ladies' shoes. Nancy was attempting to squeeze one of her feet into a Jimmy Choo sandal – like an ugly sister taking her shot at the glass slipper – when we realised that Alfie was missing.

I felt it in the pit of my stomach. That sick panic when a child is missing. There is no fear quite like it in this world. And I had every sympathy for Nancy as she began to call her son's name, again and again and again, louder and louder, ever more desperate. She stared around, frantic with fear, one foot in a Jimmy Choo sandal and the other one bare.

I gently touched her arm. 'You really have to keep a close eye on them in a place like this,' I said, and I didn't mean *you*, I meant *all of us*, but still she turned on me with such fury in her eyes that I realised she hated me.

And then Rufus was suddenly coming towards us with Alfie in his arms, the boy twisting his head to look back, waving his rubber hammer, and I could see the workmen on the far side of the store who had attracted the boy's attention. They were tearing down something old and erecting something new.

Nancy grabbed her son and shook him. He dropped the

toy hammer in his fist and began to whimper. And Rufus had such a sweet, open-hearted grin on his face that I put my arm around him and patted his bony shoulder twice, and I didn't care if it was allowed or not.

Then we went off to do what we had planned to do all along, and we chose the suit that my son would be married in.

twenty-two

I sat with my fingernails digging into the worn leatherette of the Ford Capri's passenger seat, my right foot involuntarily slamming down on brakes that were not there, slick with sweat despite the winter chill.

My mum leaned forward from the back seat and I could hear her sharp intake of breath as my dad paused at a deserted roundabout, waited for a while, looked around uncertainly, waited a bit more, muttered a few words to himself that may or may not have had anything to do with driving, and then slowly lurched off just as a lorry with the right of way came hurtling towards us. We caught a glimpse of the driver's face, contorted with shock and rage as he swerved past us, leaning on what sounded like a ship's horn.

'Keep your hair on, mate,' commented my dad, 'nobody wants to find it.'

He veered off the roundabout without indicating, crossing two lines of traffic and narrowly missing a silver-haired old lady in a Nissan, who stuck two fingers up at him and mouthed, 'Wanker.'

My dad had been a fast, competent driver for as long as I could remember. He had an old-fashioned attitude to driving – to him, a man wearing a seat belt was only slightly better than a man wearing a dress – and when admonished by my mum for regarding the speed limit as purely optional, he always cited his clean licence. When I thought of him in my childhood, I pictured him behind the wheel of a car. At home, at work. He was one of those men who derive real joy from driving, and he did it very well, or at least with a kind of belligerent proficiency. I could not imagine a time when he would not drive. And now that time was here.

We were moving the last of my stuff back home. There wasn't much – a few cardboard boxes in the boot of the Capri, crammed with clothes and CDs and books that had seemed important once. But the ten-mile run from suburb to city confirmed what my mum had been telling me for a while. My dad's driving days were done.

'He's all right when he's going straight,' she told me as my dad unloaded the boot. 'It's the bendy bits that throw him.' She looked back at my dad hefting a box of paperbacks. 'You talk to him.'

So I asked him to help me make the tea, and watched him slowly shuffle about the kitchen, not forgetting anything, but making the organisation of boiling water and fetching milk and dunking tea bags and spooning sugar and collecting cups seem as complicated as conducting a symphony orchestra.

'Dad,' I said, 'thanks for the lift.'

He nodded curtly. My dad had never got used to the glib Americanism of, 'You're welcome,' and I don't suppose he ever would now.

'You know, that Capri's getting really old.'

His face brightened. 'Like me!' He measured out the sugar, as careful as a nuclear physicist dishing out the plutonium.

'It's been a great car, but I really think it's getting past its best.'

I had steeled myself for furious denial, or some resentful argument at the very least. But he just reached for the milk, and looked thoughtful.

'Not really roadworthy any more,' he agreed. He looked up at my mum as she came into the kitchen, expecting to have to pull us apart. She looked at us warily and started opening cupboards, seeking biscuits.

'I was just talking to Dad about the car,' I said.

He grimaced at her. 'Just about got through its MOT last time, didn't it?' he said.

Mum nodded. She shook some Jaffa Cakes on to a plate. 'But it's been a lovely little car,' she said.

My dad picked up a Jaffa Cake and looked at it as if he had never seen one before. 'Too much rust, see?' he said. 'Even if the engine is still running, the rust gets them in the end. Take care of the engine and it will run forever. But you can't do much about the rust.'

My mum took his hand. 'Never mind, eh?'

She really loved him. And whatever happened, she was not going to stop loving him.

'It's had its day,' said my dad, with a total lack of sentiment or self-pity. There was no talk of a new car.

'Yes,' said my mum. 'And what a lovely day it was.'

The following weekend we took the car to a dealer, but he told us the list price wouldn't be worth the storage space. It took me a moment to realise that he was telling us the Capri was worthless. The dealer tried to be kind – he suggested advertising for a collector. Perhaps someone in the specialist market would be interested, he said, although to be honest he doubted it. These collectors wanted something in pristine condition. The Capri had too much rust. He gave us an address on the other side of the river.

So my parents sat in the back seat holding hands and I drove the Ford Capri to what was called a salvage yard, although it seemed to be exactly the opposite. It was a killing field and a graveyard, and across those Kent flatlands you could see it from miles away. From a distance it looked like a mountain range of finished cars. Up close, as I drove through the gates, guard dogs showing their teeth, cars rose above our heads, they stretched into the distance, they seemed to go on forever. Ridges and hills of mangled metal, destroyed by accident or time.

I didn't have to rush the paperwork, because there was a queue for disposal. Lined up and ready for systematic wrecking were corroded buckets with foreign plates, accident write-offs that still had blood smeared on their broken windscreens, the untaxed and the uninsured and the unloved. And some that had just had their time.

We were allowed to watch from a safe distance. A removal lorry gently lifted the Capri off the ground and moved it to where a giant forklift truck was waiting. The forklift carefully transported the Capri to a wrecking crane. As the forklift retreated, the crane swung round and dangled five massive steel claws above the roof of the car. The claws opened. They came down with a prehistoric scream of metal. They sunk into the Capri, picked it up off the ground and slammed it back down. The wheels all came off. There was an element of cruel theatre about it all. It reminded me of the kind of wrestling where men wear masks and Lycra. Meticulously choreographed violence that was no less real for being premeditated.

The metal claws kept their grip on the Capri. They lifted it higher, and swung it around to where a machine like a giant's sandwich maker sat below a steep hill of mangled steel. The crane manoeuvred the Capri into the giant's sandwich maker. When it slammed closed, the windows dramatically exploded in a storm of broken glass.

The giant's sandwich maker kept opening and closing until the Capri was no longer a car. The crane came back, lifted it out of the sandwich maker and started tearing it to pieces, like a vulture devouring roadkill. My mum looked away. Then it was lifted and dumped at the top of the hill of mangled steel.

My mother slipped her arm in my father's arm, a gesture that had started when they were teenagers and had never ended. She laid her head on his shoulder. There were tears in her eyes, but my dad was almost jaunty.

When the noise subsided, he gave me a wink and nudged me in the ribs. He nodded at the mountain of dead cars and grinned as if he thought he was getting away with something.

'I'm not complaining,' he said. 'I reckon I had my money's worth.'

He was looking up at what had once been his car, but he was thinking about something else.

I lurked at the rear of the red velvet auditorium, leaning on the back of the last row of the stalls, and nobody bothered me.

There were not many people about at that time of day. One of the director's assistants gave me a strange look when she went off to get coffee, but she didn't say anything when she came back. I think it's because I dress almost exactly like a caretaker.

I watched the thin, bossy woman – the choreographer, Lara had told me – move across the stage, among a dozen of the men – the boys, they called them, and although most of them were in their twenties, there were a few on the far side of thirty who were not boys by even the most generous definition of the word.

And as the choreographer selected and discarded, she identified the chosen ones with a name or a colour or an item of clothing. She knew some of the names. A lot of the names. But she couldn't know everyone. There were new people coming through all the time. And old boys and girls dropping out. But even if she only identified someone by the colour of their kit, somehow they all knew who she was talking about. What they didn't know at the moment they were singled out, was if they were being chosen or rejected, if they were wanted or not.

If they were *right*.

'Diego – the boy in the sweatband – combat trousers – Johnny – Penguin T-shirt and the red top.'

I watched their faces as they went from the awful moment when they didn't know if they were being asked to stay or told to go, to the next moment, when they knew that they had been accepted or rejected.

'Stage left,' said the choreographer. 'The rest – thank you very much.' She clapped her hands twice, instantly subduing the murmurs of joy and despair. 'Next group.'

I saw Lara waiting in the wings.

272

At this stage the boys and girls danced apart, as separate as kids at a high school prom, and those who were not dancing stood on the edge of the stage, learning the steps, moving to the music, evaluating the competition, massaging away the aches and pains and wear and tear.

Lara was kneading the back of her right leg. I knew from her sleeping that the pain was almost constant now. In both her hamstrings. In her right hip. And most of all in her tendons, where the muscle holds the bone, and a dancer feels the miles on the clock. She filed on stage with her group of girls.

'Pick it up from, '*Who's the private dick?*' the choreographer commanded, and the tape started up, and it sounded like music hall grafted on to the last days of disco. It was Watson's big number at the top of *Sherlock!* They would be dancing behind him, a motley collection of Edwardian gentlefolk, flower girls and Peelers in top hats.

> *Who's the private dick with the gruff sidekick?*
> *It's elementary, it's elementary.*

'Give it to me stronger,' she said, and they moved like a flock of birds, a school of fish. By now they knew the moves and were reaching for that moment when they could do them without thinking. I watched Lara. I was aware of the other girls, but I watched only her.

> *A single hair or a bloody stain,*
> *And he's straight in there with his giant brain.*
> *Yes, he does some coke but they don't complain,*
> *Because it's elementary.*

'Step, push, step, step, touch, kick – strong arms!' the choreographer barked. She was circling them like a teacher in an exam room, clapping her hands, squinting at them, keeping them on the beat. 'Seven, eight – the hounds of HELL – step, pivot, step, touch . . . that's it, that's it.'

> *From Baker Street to the hounds of hell,*
> *Who's the master sleuth? The brutal truth*
> *Is that it's elementary.*

When it ended, Lara stood there with her hands on her aching hips, filling her lungs, holding the breath for a count of four, then letting it go as slowly as she could. She blinked, the salt of the sweat stinging her eyes, as the whippet-thin choreographer moved among them, her eyes on the director like an auctioneer whose gaze was fixed on the richest man in the room. Making the cut.

'Okay, okay. The girl in red – Megan – the girl in white – pink shorts – Debbie – Coco . . . stage left. The rest of you – thank you very much.'

Lara was the girl in white. And the girl in white was still there.

I don't think she could see me lurking at the back of the stalls, but as she left the stage she smiled and gave a quick thumbs up to all those empty seats, all that worn red velvet, and the darkness beyond.

'Maybe it will be all right,' Lara said, holding the wide brim of her wedding hat so that the autumn wind couldn't take it. 'Maybe it will.'

She was trying to cheer me up. We were on the steps of the registry office, and we were waiting for a wedding to exit before we could go inside. A laughing middle-aged man and woman were coming out, and their friends and relatives were pelting them with confetti. Lara and Ruby and Nan and I took a step back, but the wind blew stray confetti in our faces, and we entered the registry office covered in small scraps of pastel-coloured paper. Lara gave my arm an encouraging squeeze and I nodded, showing her I appreciated the effort. But how was I meant to feel? We were covered in confetti before our son's wedding had even begun. That didn't seem right. Nothing seemed right.

'*Registry of birth, marriage and death,*' Ruby said, reading the gilded sign above the door. 'Which one do we want?'

All three, I thought.

'Be nice,' Lara said.

A few familiar faces were already inside. My parents – my dad in an old suit, my mum in a hat so new that it broke my heart. She had had her hair done – one of those frozen Margaret Thatcher hair-dos that resemble a medieval helmet.

Keith was there – Uncle Keith, Ruby still called him, but Rufus had dropped the uncle bit, which somehow made him seem even younger. Faces from Rufus' work. The security guys. The little Muslim girl. But the friends from school had drifted away, and the friends from stand-up had not been made. Rufus had invested his life in this one unremarkable woman. And it was like watching someone you love flush their life down the toilet.

Nancy's side was better represented. Lots of earrings. Especially on the men. They looked as though they were on their way to Ascot. For a bit of light mugging. Tough guys in tight suits with short hair or no hair. Tarty-looking women with boob jobs and gold ankle chains. And that was just her grandmothers.

Lara dragged me over into the heart of the mob and attempted to make some introductions. But Nancy's mother – a fierce blonde of fifty with great legs and a West Ham United tattoo – and Nancy's father – who you wouldn't want to meet even up a very well-lit alley – were both with new partners now, so just meeting the parents was four people right there. I smiled weakly. But it was all too complicated for me. It was all too much.

And then they were there. The groom and the bride and the bride's souvenir from a previous relationship, dressed in a suit and bow tie that somehow made him resemble a performing monkey. If his mother hadn't been gripping him tightly by the wrist, I swear he might have done a bit of juggling. We filed into the office where the deed would be done.

'Stop sighing,' my wife hissed at me.

But we were gathered there beyond the sight of God. No bride in white, no biggest day of your life, no unsullied future. Just my son pledging his troth to an older woman with a bun in the oven and somebody else's brat by her side, a child in a bow tie who mined his nose and then speculatively examined his findings. I wanted it to be over. I wanted to go home.

The registrar droned on. A smiley fat geezer, he was, and you could almost believe that we were not the tenth on his list today. The usual Hallmark card clichés, with all hope that heaven might be watching dropped from the programme. But then the bride spoke. A traditional Irish vow; the registrar beamed. I had not realised her family were Irish.

'As light to the eye, as bread to the hungry, as joy to the heart, may thy presence be to me,' she said. 'Here is my hand to hold with you – to bind us for life and grow old with you.'

And I noticed for the first time that she was wearing a pale yellow dress that seemed appropriate for a second wedding.

She was clearly pregnant, but what I saw – now that I looked – was that her face seemed to have softened. It was as though the day had drained all the hardness and bitterness out of her.

And somehow it made the cynicism seep out of me, like a wound being cleaned of poison.

And when Rufus turned to look at her, nobody could doubt that he loved her, and that this was the happiest day of his life, and that whatever the coming years might bring, he was exactly where he was meant to be today.

And who was I to deny them? Who was I to claim that my son was throwing his life away? Perhaps my dark fears would all come to pass, but it was impossible not to give them the benefit of the doubt today, especially when I saw what the boy – Alfie, his name was Alfie – had in the hand that wasn't spring-cleaning his nose. In that tiny fist he clutched the rings, and now he held them out to the registrar, as his mother and my son smiled down at his little shaven carrot-topped bonce.

Yes, I thought. Maybe it will be all right.

Lara knew she could do it now.

By the last day of auditions, the pain was excruciating. In her tendons and in her right side, where the hip met the lowest rib. But she knew she could do it, and when she talked about it, her eyes shone with that truth. Technically, she was a better dancer than all of them, the dance-school graduates and the drama-school alumni.

The music started. They danced. It was the one about the private dick with the gruff sidekick.

And when the music stopped, the whippet-like woman glanced at the old man in the stalls, and then after a moment she said, 'The girl in white – thank you very much.'

Lara stood there, letting the failure grow and take shape, and the choreographer quickly crossed the stage and touched her arm. A rare act of compassion, or just getting it over with? Getting the girl in white to understand, and leave the stage.

I could not hear her – nobody could – but you could read her lips.

'Sorry, darling,' she said. 'Too old.'

Lara sat on the edge of our bed, massaging her side, and I wanted to tell her that their rejection meant nothing, that she was the best of the bunch, that I was proud of her, and all the rest of it.

But I couldn't tell her any of these things because by now the pain was too much to ignore. I could no longer put it down to the demands she had put on her body. I could no longer look past the pain. It coloured everything.

'You really have to see someone,' I said. 'You know that, don't you? This is not right.'

She sat up and looked at me. Everything ached. She did not have to tell me that. I could see it.

'Yes,' she said wearily. 'I will.'

I waited. She took off her clothes for bed. Down to her

pants and a T-shirt, and I was still waiting. She smiled at me. 'I promise, okay?'

Still I just stood there. 'When? When will you see someone? This can't wait, Lara. You've got to go now.'

'Can I do one thing before I go?' she said, the smile growing. 'Is that allowed?'

But I wasn't smiling. I was angry and afraid. 'Why can't you go now?' I said.

And she laughed at me. 'Oh, George,' she said, shaking her head. 'You're such a bloody grown-up.'

She slept well that night.

I can't explain it.

But there were none of the catches in her breath that signalled the pain and discomfort invading her dreams. None of that. It was a cold night – they were all cold nights now – but the touch of our bodies made the bed warm, and at some point, without waking, she abruptly threw back the sheet.

Lying on her belly, her bare back angled towards me, that skin I knew better than my own.

And I could not sleep. I slept badly that night, or perhaps not at all. I thought perhaps that if sleep did not come then I would at least manage to pray. But prayer was as distant as sleep.

So I stared at my wife's back as she was sleeping, and among the familiar birthmarks and beauty spots and freckles, I traced a constellation of stars.

twenty-three

There were a couple of Red Bull cans floating in my parents' pool, bobbing on the water like spent shells.

I reached for them with my leaf net as my dad came and stood by my side.

'It's the new thing, Dad,' I said. 'They call themselves the dipping crews.'

'Dipping crews?' said my father, and I saw a flicker of fear on his face. I knew that sometimes he wondered if he was being told something for the first time, or if he had heard it before and just forgotten.

'You know,' I said gently. 'They look online for houses with swimming pools. On Google Earth. On the Internet, remember?'

'The computer,' my dad said.

'That's right. Then the little bastards go round when people are sleeping or away and they take a dip. They have a party in your pool.'

'They have a good time,' my dad said.

My mum came across the lawn and slipped her arm around

my father's waist. We all looked at the water. Not quite as lovely in the pale autumn sun.

'We might have to get rid of this thing,' my mum said, nodding at the pool. 'Getting more trouble than it's worth.'

I knew she thought it was getting dangerous now that my dad was not very well. She shook her head as she watched me dump the cans on the grass.

'Bloody kids,' she said.

'The dipping crew,' my dad said mildly, as though it were perfectly reasonable for strangers to invade his home while he was sleeping, and then get us to clear up their trash.

The dipping crew.

My dad wasn't angry about them. But that was all right. Because I was angry enough for both of us.

I had bought a .22 air rifle on the Internet and it stayed in the boot of Lara's car until my parents had gone to bed.

Then I brought it into the house and I sat in the kitchen with the lights off, the gun resting between my legs, my chair pulled up against the sink, the window above it slightly ajar so that I could slip out the rifle when the time came. In the garden the swimming pool shone like black glass in the moonlight.

I knew that Keith would have laughed at my air rifle. But it could give someone a mark that they would carry with them to the grave. It could take someone's eye out. Keith would have laughed, but I knew that it could make someone change their mind in an instant.

'George,' Lara said, and I felt her hand on my shoulder.

I didn't look at her. 'I'm just going to talk to them,' I said.

She shook her head and sighed. Upstairs I could hear my mum helping my dad in the bathroom. The gentle encouragement on one side, the half-hearted resistance and complaints on the other. They did not sound like a married couple. They sounded exactly like a parent and a child, and it tore me up.

'He had a good day,' Lara said, very softly, but as if I had just alleged the very opposite.

'But they get less,' I said. 'The good days get less.'

I squinted and leaned forward at some movement in the back garden. A young fox emerged from the rose bushes, sniffed at the ground and moved on.

'It's still him,' Lara said. 'It's still your dad.'

'Mostly it's still him,' I said, and I thought of that old Zen sword. *If you change the blade, and then you change the handle – is it still the same sword?* 'But then one day there will be a point where it is not him any more. Not the boy she fell in love with, not the man she married. Not her husband. Not my dad. Somebody else.'

'No,' Lara said, her voice little more than a whisper in the darkness. 'It will still be him.'

I hung my head, pressing the barrel of the .22 against my face. I looked up at her and smiled.

'Yes,' I said. 'Of course.'

She put her arms around my shoulders. I could feel her breath on my face. Her voice in my ear.

'Please don't be so angry,' she said. 'Please don't be so angry about everything.'

I turned my head and looked at her. 'Are you going to go?' I said. 'Are you going to see that bloody doctor?'

She stared at me for a long moment and then she nodded. 'I'm going tomorrow,' she said.

Then we heard the voices. And I was on my feet, lifting the .22 to my shoulder. Lara put a hand on my arm, but I took a step away from her. I wanted to hurt someone. I wanted to hurt these people who came to this garden in the night.

They came out of the same spot as the fox. A dipping crew of two. They looked up at the house, and they must have seen only darkness. I took them for two girls at first, because of the length of their hair. But it was a man and a woman. I leaned across the sink, silently edging the barrel of the gun out of the open window.

I saw them shuck off their jeans and T-shirts and slip without sound into the swimming pool. I pressed the butt of the gun tight against my shoulder, felt my finger on the trigger, and held my breath. They disappeared under the water and seconds later silently broke the surface. My finger tightened on the trigger, squeezing it back. Then I saw their heads come together. I watched them kiss. And I felt my wife next to me. I knew she saw it too.

I pulled the gun from the window and held it by my side. And Lara took my hand and we watched them. Not that there was much to see. Their heads drifting without sound across the water. Coming together for a few moments and then coming apart. Black shadows against more blackness, the light of the night and the city seeping into the garden, catching the beads of water on their heads and making them shine like jewels.

Lara said at one point that this was how David Attenborough must feel out in the wild, and we both laughed, very quietly, and apart from that we said nothing. There was nothing to say. She knew that I could see it too.

They were beautiful.

And at some point I put down my gun and pulled Lara on to my lap and I held her as she held me and the boy and girl in the pool got lost in their night-swimming.

It was an hour before dawn when they finally emerged from the pool, shivering in the chill of the morning mist, sleek as a pair of seals, and burnished by what remained of the starlight.

twenty-four

You could tell by her shoes.

Everyone at the *milonga* could tell by her shoes. They were high-heeled and strappy, with thin leather soles. Jet black. Shiny as a mirror. Her shoes said that she was there to dance.

You heard it all the time in Buenos Aires. If you are not there to dance, then go in trainers or sandals. If you are not there to dance, then dress like a wallflower, dress like a tourist. Lara's shoes marked her out as a dancer.

The *milonga*, which was a kind of shifting dance hall, was in a sports centre in a quiet *barrio* in Barracas, in the south of the city. The venue was a surprise. I knew by now that the tango had little to do with the elegant couples you saw at the *tangueria* dinner shows that brought the tourists in by the busload. I had been expecting a smoky bar, with perhaps a few ladies of the night and loitering sailors on shore leave, reflecting the working-class roots of the dance. But this *milonga* was in a sports hall with basketball hoops on the wall. And here was the real thing.

Lara and I stood on the edge of the dance floor and watched

the dance flow before us. The couples all moved in an anti-clockwise direction, as if trying to make time run backwards, and they were of every age imaginable. Boys just out of their teens danced with women old enough to be their mothers. Pensioners gripped each other like young lovers. A man in his sixties wearing a blue suit partnered a young woman whose cropped T-shirt revealed a stomach as flat and hard as a washboard. Age did not matter at the *milonga*. What counted was how you did the dance.

Lara smiled at me and took my hand and pulled me on to the dance floor. It was like joining a school of fish. There was no room and yet somehow we found room. I felt the pinch of my brand-new shoes, selected for the thinness of their leather soles, and I could feel the fear in the pit of my stomach. We assumed the position, smiling self-consciously, and then we counted. The lessons we had been taking in the salon at Confitería Ideal in Suipacha had taught us tango etiquette as well as steps, and after six days we knew enough to count eight *compases*, bars of music, before joining the dance.

And now, on the seventh day, we danced.

It was fine. I mean, I didn't step on her toes and make a complete idiot of myself. I didn't fall over. And she was beautiful, of course – just a joy to hold and behold and dance with as she followed my clumsy lead with almost imperceptible shifts of weight, her feet inside her high heels never seeming to leave the ground and yet never still, never resting, full of grace. Fluid and fast – that was what I noticed when I danced with Lara, and what I had always noticed when I danced with her. How she seemed to make ten movements for every one that I made. And so we danced, moving always and forever against the clock.

We danced until five melodies had come and gone – until the end of a set. And then she smiled at me and took my hand and led me from the dance floor. Then I saw the man watching us.

He was perhaps fifty, dark and lean, with a full head of hair that he was clearly proud of, the black streaked with silver. If anything made him look his age it was the combination of jacket and jeans. He came over to us. Or rather, he came over to Lara.

The man had eyes that were such a dark shade of brown they were almost black. His teeth were bone-white in his lined, handsome face. Up close he looked his age but was somehow more impressive. Some people say that the Porteños of Buenos Aires are the best-looking people in the world. This guy would definitely have agreed with them.

'*Permiso,*' he said. '*¿Como andas?*'

'*No entiendo.*' Lara laughed. '*¿Usted habla ingles?*'

'No,' he said, and then he nodded – just a small, subtle dipping of his chin. Blink and you would have missed it. She looked at him for a moment and then made the same gesture. He held out his hand. She took it. And then Lara danced with him. Not the way she had danced with me. They really danced.

They had told us at Confitería Ideal that the tango is 'an emotion that is danced'. It would have sounded like a line for the tourists if it did not chime so completely with what Lara always said about the musicals she had fallen in love with as a child. When the heart is full, you don't talk – you sing. And when the heart overflows, you don't sing – you dance. I stood and watched them dance. And I wasn't the only one.

As couples reached the end of a set they would drift to

the edge of the dance floor and watch them. And as the space cleared on the floor, Lara and the man grew into it, becoming more expansive in their movements. It was real tango, the way it had been danced one hundred years ago in the brothels and the bars. It had nothing to do with tuxedos and evening gowns and five-course meals and busloads of tourists in swanky nightclubs. This was some thing of rough beauty born in the worst slums of Africa and Europe and Latin America. It was like making love remade as ballet. And all you could do was watch them.

When their set was finished Lara dipped her head and thanked the man, as tradition demanded. He nodded in return and asked her something – you didn't need any *Castellano*, as the Porteños called their Spanish, and you did not need to know anything about tango etiquette to know that he was asking if he could dance with her again later in the evening.

Her face was shining with sweat and happiness. She was ramrod straight, as though she was unbreakable. I had never loved her more. And she shook her head – no. The man watched her as she came over to join me. Every man and woman at the *milonga* watched her.

'I'm ready to go home now,' she said.

twenty-five

I could feel the wet grass of my parents' lawn on my bare feet as I walked out to the swimming pool, the boy padding by my side, holding the leaf net above his head like a flag.

When we approached the water I touched his shoulder and he stopped, looking up at me, waiting. I smiled down at him, thinking that I was going to have to get a fence put up around the pool.

We looked up at the sound of laughter coming from the house. At the garden table, my dad and my daughter were sitting across from each other with a chessboard between them. Over the last year Ruby had decided that the game was good for the old man, and now she leaned back grinning, her hands across her belly while my father stroked his face and pondered his next move.

The boy and I approached the pool, our bare feet leaving puddles on the concrete that skirted it. Alfie stared solemnly at the thin film of leaves that covered the water. Winter was coming on hard now, and I knew that there would be a month of Sundays like today. That gave me a good feeling, and I knew that the boy felt it too. Of all the things he helped me with, skimming leaves was his favourite job.

We set to work, the boy holding the net out across the water while I stood by his side, adjusting his grip and posture, like an instructor helping a golfer with his swing, sometimes murmuring instructions and encouragement, sometimes getting him to take a step back from the water, but mostly saying nothing, and just letting him get on with it.

He had the hang of it now.

Alfie edged around the pool, carefully depositing small mounds of wet leaves behind him on the concrete. When he had completed one circuit we gathered the leaves in our arms and carried them to the end of the garden. There was a pile of dead wood and fallen leaves back there and I told the boy we would burn it all later, when it was dry. He nodded as if he understood, but I knew he wished we were doing it now. I touched his hair and laughed, and we turned to rejoin the others.

My son was coming out of the house, with his own son in his arms. The baby was crying. He had his first teeth coming through and his parents had been up all night with him. As we got closer, the crying subsided from an unbroken howl to a few breathless sobs, and my mother and Nancy came out of the kitchen, carrying trays. Ruby carefully picked up the chessboard, trying not to disturb the pieces, and moved it to one side. My father was smiling to himself. She hadn't beaten him yet.

They were laying the table. Something smelled good.

'Look,' said the boy. In the grass he had found a long thin stick, charred black at one end. He handed it to me.

'You know what that is, Alfie?' I said, examining the piece of wood. He shook his head. 'That's from a rocket,' I said.

His eyes were wide.

'A real one?' he said. 'Not a real one?'

I nodded, giving him back his stick. 'A real rocket,' I told him.

I looked up and Lara was there, standing in the doorway, a scarf tied around her head. She looked vaguely South American. But apart from that, she was unchanged.

I glanced down at the child, making sure he wasn't going to do anything dangerous with the stick, like poke his eye out or something, and when I looked back up she was still there.

Smiling at me. Waiting for me.

'Ready, steady,' I said, and Alfie laughed and threw aside his stick from the firework and we began to race each other across the lawn.

As we reached the rest of our family, settling themselves at the table, they all looked up at us. The baby had stopped crying.

'Look, Dad,' my son said to me. 'I made him smile.'

Inside:

Q & A with Tony Parsons

Extract from Tony's previous bestseller
My Favourite Wife

Don't miss: Tony's other books

Inspired by George?
Escape with our competition

Q & A with Tony Parsons

Starting Over **feels a lot more like your earlier books, especially since your last novel,** *My Favourite Wife,* **was set in Shanghai. Was this a conscious decision?**

TP: I wanted to write a book in my room. Some books you have to wander the world before you can write them. And some books you can write in your room. *My Favourite Wife* took three years to write because I spent so long on research, in Shanghai. I loved writing *My Favourite Wife,* but I didn't want to spend another three years on a book and I wanted a book that would allow me to walk my daughter to school. So, yes, I wanted to return to basics. I wanted to write a book set in neighbourhoods that I knew and I wanted to write about themes that I had already explored, modern men and women trying to make it work, modern dilemmas – what it feels like living your life caught between your parents and your children. *Man and Boy* was a book that was written in my room. I had to get out a bit to live the experiences that filled the book, but once I had them you could have locked me in a basement for a year and I would have come out at the end of it with a manuscript.

Then what's different about *Starting Over?*

TP: The protagonist is older, his children are teenagers – with all the complications and horrors that implies. He has been married for nearly twenty years – and that's interesting, being in a relationship that defines your adult life. And he has health issues – which is really the basis of the book. George has a heart attack and he is given the heart of a 19-year-old kid. And it makes him a boy – for good and ill. He becomes a sex bomb again to his wife, a friend to his children, a worry and a burden to his parents – and in the end drives everybody nuts. Including himself! So he has to grow up again. I like it because it feels like familiar territory – I think it's recognisably the writer of *Man and Boy* and *Man and Wife* – but with a new twist.

It reads like a search for enlightenment.

TP: Well that was the idea, how do we live our lives? How much should we care about the planet and society in relation to how much we care about our loved ones? Do we want to be friends to our children or parents? At what point do we stop expecting our parents to take care of us, so that we can take care of them? And at what age does a man look stupid in jeans? It is about the search for wisdom, but hopefully done in a comic, moving, accessible way. I mean, *Siddhartha* (by Herman Hesse) is a search for enlightenment. But then so is 'Groundhog Day'. And I like the element of the fantastic – George getting his new heart, and being changed by it. There's this condition called cellular memory syndrome, where recipients of organs allegedly take on the characteristics of the donor. It doesn't really matter if it's true or not, I just loved the idea of it – like an adult fairytale. It's a bit like Peter Parker getting bitten by a spider and becoming Spiderman, or Bill Murray waking up in 'Groundhog Day' and discovering that today is exactly the same as yesterday. What do you do? Live your life for the people you love, try to make the world a better place, fight crime? Or stuff yourself with cream cakes? It seems to me the great human dilemma – should I fight crime or stuff myself with cream cakes?

How did you research _Starting Over_? You can't make it up or look it up on the Internet?

TP: During the writing process you realize that there are gaps in your knowledge that you can't bridge with either your imagination or research. So you go and talk to people, you have to get out a bit. I spoke to cops, doctors and dancers – if you speak to cops, doctors and dancers, the book almost writes itself. They all have interesting stories to tell. I met a policeman when someone tried to steal my car, and I was struck by the way he carried himself. A big guy, clearly on the side of the angels, nice and polite but you wouldn't want to mess with him. I used that for the way George carries himself. And then there's people like my doctor, who is always endlessly helpful when I am writing about medical issues and inspirational people like my friend Su-man Hsu. Su-man was a dancer – still is, among other things – and I used some of her experiences for Lara's background as a dancer in West End musicals. Su-man was in 'The King and I' and Lara was in 'Les Miserables' and 'Sherlock!'. As a writer, you are interested in the mechanics of this other life. What's it like at an audition? Where do you go after the show? Dancers live completely in the physical world and that always interests writers, who are stuck in their heads. It's why so many writers are interested in boxing. And Su-man gave me Lara's dream – the dream of one day dancing the tango in Buenos Aires. I think it's a wonderful dream. I would never have come up with that if I had stayed in my room.

You once said that writers have just three tools in their tool box

TP: Yes – experience, research and imagination. It's as true of Dan Brown as it is of Dickens. I really believe it. Novels are made of three things; life as you have lived it, life as others have lived it and life as you can imagine it. Experience, research and imagination. You live it, you find out about it, you make it up. And you use those three things in different combinations on every book, and on every day of your writing life. I have been doing this for quite a while now, and one of the good things about being a writer who is getting older is that you know what you need and what you have to do to get it. *Starting Over* was meant to be pure imagination, but it takes a long time to write a book, and you realize as you go along how it can be improved and deepened by using your own life, or the lives of others. And in the end, when it works, you can't really see the joins between what was made up and what really happened.

Can you give us a little teaser about what you might tackle in your next novel?

TP: It will be a sequel to *Man and Boy* and will be the third book in the trilogy that began with *Man and Boy*, continued with *Man and Wife* and concludes with *Men from the Boys*. *Man and Boy* came out in hardback in 1999 so Harry will be turning forty now. Little Pat is no longer the cute little four-year-old he was back then. They all have ten years of hard road behind them and I have some ideas about how to make it relevant to what's happening in our country and the world today. Harry at 40 is very different to Harry at 30.

Is that why you want to write it now, because it is ten years since *Man and Boy*?

TP: Well, I like the idea of that gap – not least because John Updike always left ten years between his Rabbit novels. The real inspiration for *Men from the Boys* came from the death of an old army buddy of my father's, who died last year at the age of 86. He was in the Royal Naval Commandos with my dad during World War Two and I saw quite a bit of him over the years, because these Commandos were closer than brothers and they didn't lose touch with my family even after my dad died. There are so few of them left now, when this friend of my father's died – and I like to think he was my friend too – it was like losing the final bond with my dad. So I want to write about Harry and what is happening with his son and his wife and his stepdaughter and his ex-wife. But I also want to honour that generation – the generation who fought World War Two, the generation who raised me. I think I have worked out a way to do it that will be surprising and unexpected. My favourite review of *Man and Boy* described it as, 'A love letter from a father to his son, and from a son to his father.' And to me that was exactly right – *Man and Boy*, *Man and Wife* and *Men from the Boys* are about the love that exists between the generations, and the way the love gets passed down from grandparent to parent, parent to child. My parents have been gone for a long time now – my dad died in 1987, and my mum in 1999 – but I think I came close to expressing my feelings about them in *Man and Boy*. *Men from the Boys* will be a chance to express that one last time, because soon that generation will be totally lost. So there is all that – plus I cared about those characters in *Man and Boy* and I want to find out what happened to them.

Exclusive extract from
My Favourite Wife
– out now in paperback

The elevated freeway of Chengdu Lu runs right above St Peter's, the Catholic church in Chongqing Nanlu. As the bride and groom stepped out into the sunshine the cheers of the congregation mixed with the buzzsaw of the traffic flowing high above the church spire.

Holly was in Becca's arms, throwing confetti with her eyes screwed up, as if she was the one being bombarded. Most of it went over Bill. He looked at his wife. She looked beautiful today. And he wasn't the only one who noticed. When they had entered the church, it seemed to Bill that men on both sides of the aisle, the neat little Filippinos and the big affable Australians, all looked at his wife with a certain hunger. And now it seemed to Bill that, despite the two thousand or so nights they had spent together, he looked at her in exactly the same way.

Yet he knew that only he saw the fragility there, only he saw how the woman he loved was struggling to hold it together and put on a good front. They all look at her, he thought. But I'm the only one who really sees her.

He watched Becca smile at the sight of Shane and Rosalita, and it made him smile too. The happy couple were a study in opposites. The groom as big and blond as his bride was tiny and dark. Shane grinning like an idiot, bashful in the glare of all this attention, Rosalita laughing and waving to her friends in the crowd, centre stage at last, happy to be top of the bill.

'He gets youth and beauty, and she gets affluence and

security,' Mrs Devlin said, suddenly appearing at Bill's side. She lazily threw a fistful of confetti. 'At least that's the plan, I suppose.' She sighed wearily, as if she had seen it all many times before. 'What could possibly go wrong?'

The three Devlin boys were running wild, dodging in and out of legs, assaulting each other with confetti mixed with gravel that they had scooped up from the ground. The smallest one got caught in the eyes by one of his brothers and began crying.

Holly eyed them warily and Bill picked her up. She didn't much care for boys. She took Bill by his ears. It was her new way of getting his attention. He felt her sweet breath on his face.

'We're going back for a while,' she whispered. 'But you're staying in your home.'

He felt the panic fly up in him. 'My home is with you,' Bill whispered. 'Always. Wherever you are, that's my home. Okay?'

She thought about it, staring at her father with the solemn blue eyes of her mother.

'Okay, Daddy,' she quietly agreed, and they held each other as they stood there in their wedding clothes, and the chatter went on around them.

'We must do something with our children,' Mrs Devlin was telling Becca. Bill thought she meant some kind of military discipline, but apparently it was a play date with their daughter that she had in mind. 'Does Holly like pandas?' Tess said, baring her teeth at Holly. 'Do you like pandas, dear?'

'I like cows,' Holly said.

'We found this place near Renmin Square with a giant panda,' Mrs Devlin said, straightening up, ignoring Holly's affection for cows. 'A sort of Chinese circus. Well, their version of a circus. And the panda – he drives a car!'

Devlin grimaced. 'They do have a taste for the grotesque,' he murmured.

One of his sons crashed against his legs.

Becca smiled apologetically, and said nothing.

'They're going back for a while,' Bill said, and Mr and Mrs Devlin took it in and quickly looked away with frozen smiles, as if embarrassed to intrude upon a marriage more fragile than their own.

On the first floor of the Portman Ritz-Carlton, Becca and Holly joined the queue to congratulate the bride and groom.

Bill drifted off in search of a rest room and then he saw them coming – a group of casually dressed Chinese men and young women making their way down a spiral staircase.

The girls all had the look, that Shanghai look.

The look that summer was a tall slim girl in heels and tight white trousers. Straight shoulder-length hair, worn its natural jet black. In the chic, self-confident Shanghai of the new century there was a lot less of the highlighting and lightening than you saw among women in other parts of Asia. And the Shanghai look was no make-up, except maybe a little lipstick, and a short-sleeved or capped top to show off long, slender arms.

Everything about the look accentuated height and length and a willowy beauty that was specifically Chinese. The Shanghai look could make a young woman of quite average height appear over six feet tall.

It took him a moment to see that one of the young women with the look was JinJin Li.

He stood transfixed as the group walked past him as if he wasn't there.

If she saw him, she gave no sign.

And he knew that she saw him.

And he wondered, how did it work? Her unknowable life. Her unimaginable nights. How was it played? Bill saw that the man was about forty, big and fit but balding, the high school jock running to seed, too old for her by far.

How did the arrangement work? Did she get a certain amount of money paid directly into her bank every month? It had to be. Was the apartment in his or her name? How many times a week did they meet? Did he fuck her every time? Did his wife suspect a thing?

And did he love her?

Bill felt a ridiculous anger towards her, and towards the man. But what did he expect? What would he prefer? That she would stay as a teacher in Number 251 Middle School and meet some nice boy who would want to marry her? Yes, that was exactly what he wanted, that was exactly what he would have preferred.

There was a live band at the reception and after they had played their opening number Rosalita climbed on stage to sing 'Right Here Waiting for You', a beautiful power ballad about longing and loyalty that she supplemented with much slow grinding and wicked grinning.

'Ah, the unblushing bride,' Mrs Devlin said. 'In her element at last.'

Becca and Holly hit the dance floor and Bill made his way to the end of the queue for the buffet, his head swimming with the lights and the candles and the smell of orchids, and the hole in his future as he wondered what his life here would be like without them.

He steeled himself when Devlin approached him with a sympathetic smile, but his boss said nothing, just patted him twice on the back and let his hand linger for a moment on Bill's shoulder.

Then Devlin was gone, moving off into the chatter of the guests and the muffled battery of champagne corks, and Bill stared after him with gratitude.

Bill could see what Becca would never see – the good that was in this city, and the kindness and generosity of these people.

His wife was immune to something that increasingly had Bill in its grip – the glory of this place and time, the magic of what was happening here.

Everyone's life would be better, eventually. He could be a part of that, contribute something, and make a difference.

And his life would get better too. He would not be held back the way he would be held back in London, where in the end they always wanted to know what school you went to and what your father did and what your real accent was like. All that sad old bullshit that had been going on for centuries in England. They didn't really care how well you did your job back in England.

The thing that Alice Greene complained about – the educated elite lording it over the huge pool of cheap labour, driving the economy on and on – most of the people in this room saw that as a good thing. Of course it wasn't fair. But when had China ever been fair? Tell me when, he thought.

As he moved away from the buffet table he found he had loaded his plate with jam doughnuts and foie gras. Nothing else. Just two jam doughnuts and a sliver of foie gras. A ridiculous meal, he thought, smiling with embarrassment at his choices.

He hesitated for a moment and then he thought – but why not? Really – why not?

Why shouldn't you have whatever you want?

Don't miss: Tony's other books ➜

My Favourite Wife

Into the booming, gold-rush city of Shanghai fly Bill and Becca Holden with their small daughter Holly – a young family seeking their fortune far from their north London home.

When tragedy forces Becca to return to London with Holly, the friendship between a lonely family man, working night and day, and a neglected second wife grows into something more – something that threatens to destroy all their lives. And when Becca and Holly come back, it is time for all of them to learn something about the meaning of love and the bonds of family.

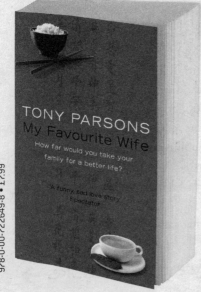

'His stories show all too well how we muddle along in search of love and fulfilment, and when we fluff it... sometimes that's just because it's easier'
Observer

978-0-00-722649-8 • £7.99

TONY PARSONS
My Favourite Wife
How far would you take your family for a better life?

'A funny, sad love story'
Spectator

Man and Boy

Harry Silver has it all: a beautiful wife, a wonderful son, a great job in the media – but in one night he throws it all away. Then Harry must start to learn what life and love are really all about.

'One of the finest books published this year... Hilarious and tear-jerking in turns' *Express*

'Parsons has written a sharp, witty and wise book straight from his heart. His characters are all nitty-gritty, bounce-off-the-page, real people; his dialogue is brilliant' *Daily Mail*

TONY PARSONS
Man and Boy

'I cried five times and laughed out loud four'
James Brown, Observer

978-0-00-651213-4 • £7.99

'Packs an enormous emotional wallop' *Time Out*

One For My Baby

Alfie Budd found the perfect woman with whom to spend the rest of his life – then lost her. He doesn't believe you get a second chance at love.

Returning to the England he left behind during his marriage, Alfie finds the rest of the world collapsing around him. He takes comfort in a string of pointless, transient affairs, and he tries to learn Tai Chi from an old Chinese man, George Chang.

Will Alfie ever find a family as strong as the Changs'?

And can he give up meaningless sex for a meaningful relationship?

'Another brilliant novel that combines laughter and tears, love and sex – and real human emotions'
Evening Standard

978-0-00-651481-7 • £7.99

Man and Wife

Harry Silver is learning to juggle his
many commitments – to his wife and
his ex-wife, to his son, his stepdaughter
and his mother, to his own work and his
wife's career.

And then someone walks into his
life who is going to make it even
more complicated...

A sequel to the international bestseller *Man and Boy*, *Man and Wife* also
stands on its own as a brilliant novel about relationships in the new
century – about why we fall in love and why we marry – about why we
stay and why we go.

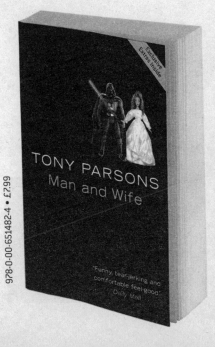

978-0-00-651482-4 • £7.99

TONY PARSONS
Man and Wife

*'Funny, tear-jerking and
comfortable feel-good'*
Daily Mail

'Funny, serious, tender
and honest... Tony
Parsons is writing about
the genuine dilemmas
of modern life'
Sunday Express

The Family Way

It should be the most natural
thing in the world.

Paulo loves Jessica. He thinks that they are
complete — a family of two. But Jessica can't be
happy until she has a baby, and the baby
stubbornly refuses to come.

Megan doesn't love her boyfriend anymore. After a one-night stand, she
finds that even a trainee doctor can slip up on family planning. Should
you bring a child into the world if you don't love its father?

Cat loves her life. After bringing up her two youngest sisters, all she
craves is freedom. But can a modern woman really find true happiness
without ever being in the family way?

'His best since the
very fine Man and Boy'.
Robert Yates, GQ

Exclusive Extra Inside

TONY PARSONS
The Family Way

978-0-00-715124-0 • £7.99

'Elegant and packed
with emotion ...
smart, stylish and
packs a weighty
punch'
GQ

Stories We Could Tell

Sometimes you can grow up in just one night

On a hot summer night in 1977, London rages around three young men who are about to learn the true meaning of friendship.

Hip young gunslinger Terry is basking in his scoop on rock star Dag Wood. But Dag has set his sights on a photographer called Misty — Terry's girlfriend. Who gets the girl?

Ray is about to be sacked from his music paper from crimes against cool and the only thing that can save him is landing an exclusive interview with John Lennon. Can he find his hero in time?

And Leon seeks sanctuary in a disco called the Goldmine as he goes on the run from the meanest gang in town and meets the dancing queen of his dreams. But are her dreams the same?

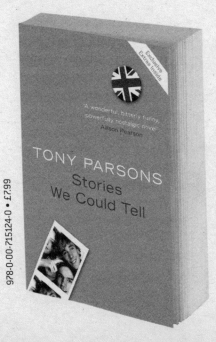

'The trio's rites of passage are handled beautifully and poignantly and Parsons brilliantly captures a bygone era'
Irish Independent

978-0-00-715124-0 • £7.99

ESCAPE THE DAILY GRIND WITH OUR FABULOUS COMPETITION!

see overleaf for details

WIN A LUXURY HOLIDAY FOR TWO
TO THE EXOTIC ISLAND OF MAURITIUS

To celebrate publication of Starting Over, we have teamed up with key2holidays to offer one lucky reader the chance to win a luxury stay at the Paradis Hotel & Golf Club on the exotic island of Mauritius. The winner, plus a guest, will jet off on an Air Mauritius flight and spend 7 nights at this fabulous Beachcomber hotel.

SPECTACULAR IN EVERY SENSE!

On the spectacular site of the Le Morne Peninsula, seven kilometres of beach ring the lush grounds of the hotel. This is the first choice for sports and action or relaxation in the perfect peace of the Spa by Clarins. A par 72 international golf course is tucked between the mountain and the sea and guests may use two other courses close by. Scuba divers will find many interesting sites while fishermen will be thrilled by big marlin catches in the breeding grounds close off-shore. Paradis Hotel & Golf Club – the name says it all.

For your opportunity to win this fantastic prize, simply log on to:
www.harpercollins.co.uk/startingover to enter

key2holidays Let Us Take Care Of You…
a world apart

key2holidays is a specialist Holiday Company offering tailor-made holidays world-wide. Each of our travel consultants are experts in a number of destinations so they can plan a great value holiday for you, whether you are looking for a romantic escape or honeymoon, escorted or private tour, family holiday, boutique beach retreat, all-inclusive resort, or adventurous break; or combining a number of holiday experiences into one multi-centre itinerary. **Visit us at key2holidays.co.uk or call one of our consultants on 020 7963 6600.**